THE JOURNEY

THE JOURNEY

NICHOLAS HILL

The Book Guild Ltd

First published in Great Britain in 2022 by
The Book Guild Ltd
Unit E2 Airfield Business Park,
Harrison Road, Market Harborough,
Leicestershire. LE16 7UL
Tel: 0116 2792299
www.bookguild.co.uk
Email: info@bookguild.co.uk
Twitter: @bookguild

Typeset in 11pt Minion Pro

Printed and bound in the UK by TJ Books LTD, Padstow, Cornwall

ISBN 978 1914471 964

British Library Cataloguing in Publication Data.
A catalogue record for this book is available from the British Library.

To all you beautiful people who can't see what you have got.
Forget the past and live for the present.
The future will look after itself.

INTRODUCTION

TWO WEEKS LATER

After one last look at the Bentley, I turned to cross the cattle grid and head up the hill on foot.

I had woken before the others and at half eight, after leaving a note on the kitchen table, I called Darren to ask him to pick me up on his way to work.

Twenty minutes later, I watched him push open the showroom doors and ease the Bentley out onto the forecourt. At least it could give me some enjoyment before it landed me in prison.

'Don't bother putting anything in its place, Darren. I'll have it back on Monday, as good as new,' I said, as he handed me the keys.

'No problem, Mr Duggan.' He smiled. 'Enjoy your drive.'

I intended to. The day was bright and sunny and I was looking forward to escaping from the nightmare my life had become, even if it was only for a few hours.

I climbed into the car, opening up the roof before pulling out onto the main road. I immediately felt the surge of power from the massive V8 turbo. The vehicle was as heavy as it looked, but the ride was lively and playful once it got moving.

I was soon deep under the River Mersey in the Kingsway Tunnel, emerging into the grey streets of Liverpool a few minutes later.

I cautiously made my way north along "Scottie Road", looking out for speed cameras. Losing my licence on top of everything else that had happened over the past two weeks was all it would take to push me over the edge.

I remembered the shabby rows of smoke-stained Victorian terraced houses from when I was a child. They had once been the homes of Liverpool dockers and other proud, hard-working families; the beating heart of Liverpool. There used to be a pub on every corner. Along with the houses, they had disappeared to make way for road improvements, supermarkets and anonymous, modern estates.

My own family had its roots in this area and I felt nostalgic as I drove on through Bootle, Fazakerly and past the entrance to Aintree Racecourse.

I had been making good progress, but my luck changed when the traffic lights ahead of me turned red.

I pulled up next to a couple of local lads hanging about at the side of the road.

'Nice car. Any chance of a lift?' one of them shouted, trying to impress a small group of girls standing nearby.

'Sorry, guys, but there's a bus stop up the road,' I replied, pointing at a graffiti-covered shelter a hundred yards further on.

The lights changed to green and I heard the girls laughing as I accelerated away.

*

An hour after I had set off, I was on the M58 motorway and at last I could put my foot down.

It wasn't long before I was heading north on the M6, the green fields and dry-stone walls of the Lancashire countryside replacing the dreary and monotonous northern suburbs of Liverpool.

I enjoyed the open road and couldn't help letting the car creep up over the speed limit, but where was I heading?

The last two weeks had been a rollercoaster of emotions and, now the funeral was behind me, I had to start dealing with the future.

Being told I had never been a proper father was bad enough, but I couldn't believe what my best friend, Mike, had said to me as he drifted in and out of a drunken slumber.

That would have to wait until after he had saved me from the money-laundering accusations, but what if they did manage to convict me? I could end up in prison for the next ten years, losing everything I had ever worked for. The only positive thing to have come out of the last ten days was a brief, if dangerous, infatuation, but where was the future in that?

*

After another hour, I finally left the motorway.

The roads were clear and I was soon passing through the outskirts of Bowness, on to Troutbeck Bridge and down to the shores of Windermere.

The Lake District had always been a special place for me. A refuge from whatever was going on elsewhere.

There were boats everywhere: an assortment of expensive-looking yachts, their sails billowing in the breeze, motor cruisers and small hire boats.

The Windermere steamer, the *Tern*, was making its way up the lake. I remembered a photo of my father as a boy, standing on the deck with his father and years later, he took me out on the same boat. I had taken the same photo of the boys and me when I still meant everything to them and I wondered if they would continue the tradition with their children. Would I be close enough to them to know?

I wanted to stop but pressed on through Ambleside towards Rydal, finally parking at the entrance to Upper Loughrigg a couple of miles further on.

*

I was out of breath when I reached the top of the slope, but I carried on along the track until a row of terraced granite cottages came into view. They were swathed in flowers of every type and colour imaginable, and the wisteria that had colonised much of the building gave its thanks with a rich pink and purple bounty.

The track narrowed and I passed through a small copse, where the green leaves of the trees sheltered a thick carpet of bluebells. Seconds later, I emerged to catch my first glimpse of Rydal Water.

The lake's surface seemed alight in the spring sunshine and I quickened my pace down towards the southern shore.

Although the smallest of the sixteen lakes, I had always found it the most beautiful. Teresa and I would often bring the boys here for a picnic when we wanted to escape the crowds.

The last time we had been here, it was pouring with rain and the lake had been dark and gloomy with Nab Scar rising up into low clouds on the opposite shore.

Today, it was bright and calm and the beauty of the scar was reflected in its mirror-like waters.

I sat down and reached to find Teresa's heart-shaped keyring in my trouser pocket. I would have given anything to have turned the clock back to that wet and miserable day, but I smiled when my eyes settled on Heron Island.

The tiny piece of land was covered in trees and I remembered telling the boys it was inhabited by a band of hairy little folk who lived on the fish they caught at night.

'Can we go over and see them?' asked Peter when he was about eight.

'Boats aren't allowed on the lake, I'm afraid, Pete,' I replied.

'We could swim, then,' suggested Matt.

'The thing is, they hate outsiders. The last man who set foot over there was never seen again.'

'Did they kill him?' Matt's eyes had been wide open in amazement.

'Not only that but afterwards, they had a big party where they roasted his body on a fire and ate him. When they'd finished, they left his bones in a neat pile here on the shore so his widow could bury them. They even wrote a note saying that it had made a nice change from fish.'

'How do you know all this?' asked his elder brother, eyeing me suspiciously.

'I read it in the *Liverpool Echo* last year. It was on the front page.'

PART ONE

TWELVE DAYS IN APRIL

ONE

MONDAY MORNING

The sun was already shining through the bathroom window and I was feeling good for a Monday as I went through my daily routine of teeth, shit, shave and shower.

I worked at the garage Monday to Saturday and, with the ritual of the Sunday roast long since abandoned, I had once again spent the previous day in quiet solitude. Not that I minded being alone, but it would have been nice to have had the choice from time to time.

Spring had come early and I spent the morning picking up on the pruning and weeding missed by Ted, our gardener. He wasn't getting any younger and it was difficult to get him to do anything other than race around the garden on the mower.

After a light lunch of smoked salmon, brown bread and a couple of glasses of a nicely chilled Chablis, I tucked myself away in the study to read a book about medieval Europe. I had given up my dream of a life in academia, but history was still my passion, even if Teresa thought it was a form of escapism.

I lost all sense of time until a pang of hunger told me it was time for dinner. The others were still out and I wanted to wait for them, but I eventually gave up and went through to the kitchen to put some leftovers into the microwave. Then, after an unremarkable meal, it was back to the study for the first whisky of the evening.

It had been a Sunday like the others. Although rested and ready for the week ahead, I would have felt better without that last glass of Glenmorangie, dozing in front of the dying embers of the fire. Teresa hadn't even bothered to wake me when she got in and I have no idea what time I made it upstairs to bed.

*

I stood naked in front of the mirror, steaming from the heat of the shower, and I was pleased to see what good shape I was in for a man in his late forties.

Unfortunately, this was wasted on my wife. Fitting out part of the pool house as a gym had been one of my better ideas. Six months later, I had a well-toned body that would have been the envy of many, even if nothing would shift the stubborn layer of fat below my belly button.

I still had a full head of hair that had somehow managed to stay brown and I tried to persuade myself that I could pass for someone ten years younger.

I could remember the row when I had explained my plans for the gym to Teresa.

'You'll use it for a week or two and give up. Why can't you buy me a new Land Rover instead? It's not fair, you with all your fancy cars and me with my old banger.'

'Honestly, Teresa! If it weren't half full of horse feed and you cleaned it now and again, your Discovery would be immaculate.'

She stood there, glaring at me.

'Do you never miss having a car full of noisy children and a big bouncy dog, slobbering all over them?' I asked.

'I do, but you miss Bruno more than having young kids around,' she replied. 'Anyway, I'm not sad he's gone; we couldn't take him anywhere.'

'I know, but when was the last time we went away together?' I asked. 'The boys used to look forward to going off to the Lakes at the weekends, staying up in the hills, miles from civilisation.'

'Or in that big hotel on Windermere if you'd had a good week.' She smiled. 'Yes, I did enjoy our trips to the Lakes. The walks, the sailing, the cosy pubs. What was it that Peter used to ask?'

'Are all these lakes here because it never stops raining? I used to ask my father the same question. Those were good times, Teresa. Every Sunday, we'd go off to bed tired but happy. It seems a long time ago.'

She gently squeezed my hand before turning to leave, but our conversations didn't always end so well.

We had started drifting apart as soon as the boys left school and we no longer shared the task of making sure they were happy and healthy. We should have enjoyed the new freedom this gave us, but it only made us realise how little we had in common.

One morning a few months later, I had got through my first kilometre on the running machine when Teresa barged into the gym and stood in front of me, her hands on her hips.

'You look as if someone's thrown a bucket of water over you. Don't expect me to call an ambulance when you give yourself a heart attack.'

She was struggling to control her emotions and it was a few minutes before she was ready to relaunch her attack.

'Who are you doing it for, anyway? It's not as if you've shown me any attention recently. No, don't tell me! You're trying to impress that Joanna. I told you she was trouble; you should be ashamed of yourself.'

'*Don't be ridiculous. You should see how she hovers around Peter's desk all day. Why would she be interested in an old man like me?*'

She didn't seem convinced.

'*He'd never waste himself on her. It's bad enough he threw away his degree when he came to work for you. No, he'll settle down with someone over in Liverpool. One of his old university friends, I reckon.*'

From the look on her face, she knew who she was talking about, but I didn't pursue it. Peter became very secretive about his private life after he finished his degree. Although I knew nothing about what he did in his spare time, I suspected he was more open with his mother.

'*Well, it's about time he found someone and there's nothing wrong with Joanna,*' I said. '*I bet she learnt a lot more when she went off travelling than a lot of girls who've been to university.*'

'*When she was shagging her way around Europe, you mean? Yes, I bet she could teach us all a thing or two,*' sneered Teresa in reply.

Our discussion was going nowhere and I was fed up to be having yet another argument about nothing.

'*I'm sorry, Teresa, but you've made it very clear for some time that the only living thing you've wanted between your legs is that horse of yours,*' I replied. I knew this would shut her up, at least for the time being.

'*Well, apart from Jackpot, what else is there in my life?*' she asked, bursting into tears before leaving me to get on with my workout.

But these were not the thoughts I needed on a Monday morning and, washed and dressed, I put a smile on my face, straightened my pocket-handkerchief and headed off downstairs.

*

All was calm in the kitchen. At her usual post, Teresa was hovering between the AGA and the fridge, a mug of coffee in one hand and a plastic spatula in the other.

Our youngest son, Matthew, was ploughing his way through a large bowl of cereal, with all the determination he lacked in everything else he did. Peter was next to him, waiting for his mother to finish cooking his bacon and eggs.

His dark hair was immaculate as always. Dressed in a navy suit, he looked fresh for someone who had been out since Saturday evening. As usual, I hadn't heard him sneaking back into the house long after the rest of us were in bed.

'You're looking smart, Pete,' I greeted him. 'How was Liverpool?'

'Good, thanks, and how was your Sunday?'

Teresa glanced over at me.

'Quiet as usual. You should get your friends to come over here one weekend. We've got the space and it will be warm enough for a barbeque in a couple of weeks.'

'Thanks, Dad.' He smiled politely, still looking down at the plate his mother had put in front of him. I knew it would never happen.

We had bought the house at the bottom of the market when the boys were still young. It had been owned by the same family since the 1930s and needed major renovation.

The large kitchen had open views over the River Dee and North Wales and was the first room to be updated.

Unlike our friends, we had chosen traditional, hand-finished oak units to create a warm living space. A large table in the middle of the room had once been the heart of our family life.

'I expect you'd like an omelette?' asked Teresa, rinsing the frying pan.

'That would be great,' I replied, taking a mouthful of tea.

'You're also looking very smart this morning,' she continued, looking me up and down while cracking a couple of eggs into a Pyrex bowl. 'Nothing to do with Joanna, I suppose?'

'For God's sake, Mum. That's Nicola and Lawrence's daughter you're talking about,' replied my eldest, his mouth half full of toast. 'She's two years younger than I am.'

'Perhaps that's why Peter's been making a bit of an effort recently,' I suggested, grinning.

Teresa pretended to have lost interest in talking about Joanna and turned back to the AGA.

'She's not my type, Dad,' said Peter, firmly. 'She's OK now but give her five years and the bloom of youth will be long gone.'

'That's unkind, but very few women have a lasting beauty like your mother's.' I could feel Teresa blush, even if I couldn't see her face. 'You know, boys, with her auburn hair and those lovely green eyes, she charmed me from the day we met?'

There was an embarrassed silence until Matt put his spoon down and looked up from his cereal. Teresa never tried to hide our pointless disagreements from the boys. They were only too aware of how difficult our relationship had become.

'You're right, Pete. I saw Joanna's mum in Morrisons last week. She's a right boozy old minger.'

Unlike his brother, Matt had not embraced academic study and had gone to work for a local plumber after he left school.

'You're not looking too good yourself, Matt,' I suggested. 'It wouldn't do you any harm to spend a bit less time hanging around the Punch Bowl with your mates. I mean, look at the state of those overalls.'

For a second, Teresa looked as if she were about to leap to Matt's defence and I was struck by how alike they looked. Peter didn't look like either of us.

'Anyway, as you're so interested, I'm all dressed up because I have a viewing of the Bentley this morning. It's all about presentation, isn't it, Pete?'

Peter nodded, scooping up what was left of his breakfast with his fork.

'And how did you get on yesterday, darling?' I asked Teresa as she brought my omelette over, trying to bring her back into the conversation.

'It's nice of you to ask,' she replied, a little surprised but smiling. 'Jackpot was in great form and we came second. We could win next week in Neston if he's anything like he was yesterday.'

'So how about going to that new restaurant in Hoylake tomorrow to celebrate. The Monte Carlo? Mike and Martine went there last week and said it was excellent. We haven't been out for months.'

Both boys looked over to see her reaction.

'Go on, Mum,' encouraged Matt. 'When's the last time you and Dad went to a restaurant together?'

Matt was right and I could feel Teresa's embarrassment as we all waited for her response. It felt more like asking someone out for a first date than planning an evening with my wife of over twenty-five years.

'That would be lovely, Simon,' she eventually replied. 'We'll take a taxi so we can both have a few drinks. And don't forget Mike's birthday on Thursday. Martine has invited us over for a surprise dinner.'

'You know, I had forgotten. I'll stick it in the diary as soon as I get to work, but you'd better get the aspirin ready for Friday morning.'

I got up from the table and turned to leave, only to find Teresa following me to the front door.

'Have a good day, darling,' she whispered, opening it for me and giving me a kiss on the cheek as I went to step outside. 'I'll have a nice dinner ready this evening for when you come home.'

TWO

THE HALLMARK
CARRIAGE COMPANY

'Isn't it a lovely morning?' greeted Mrs Williams as the door closed behind me.

I had no idea why my wife had been so pleasant. She had never seen me off in the morning and even a welcome home in the evening had become an exception.

'It certainly is. We're lucky here, when you see all the grey and drizzle they get inland,' I managed to reply.

'I do feel nostalgic when I can see all the way over to Snowdonia. I could sit looking at that view for hours on end,' she continued, her Welsh accent becoming thicker as her eyes took in the distant mountains. 'It's a wonder I ever get any cleaning done when I'm here.'

Mrs Williams liked to call herself our housekeeper and we had taken her on her from the previous owners. Sometimes it felt as if she were the owner of the house and we were her tenants.

Closing the door of her battered old Mini, she was dressed as usual in an old pink tracksuit that had become too big as her body shrank with age. White trainers and a baseball hat pulled over a greying mop of hair completed the look of an elderly athlete.

'Well, I'm sure you've got plenty to be getting on with,' I replied, a little rudely. She was always ready for a chat and I knew from experience that if I allowed myself to be trapped, I would still be there in half an hour. I wanted to get off to work.

'Now that is a beautiful car,' she said, ignoring my hint as I opened the garage doors to reveal the Maserati Cabriolet parked inside.

'It is, Mrs Williams. I sold this beauty to a football player from Manchester a couple of months ago, but he brought it back after someone tried to get in through the roof. He bought a Range Rover instead. Now, what was his name?'

'You don't need to bother telling me, Mr Duggan. I've no time for all these footballers and their antics. Money doesn't care who it belongs to these days.'

'You could say that about most of my clients.' I laughed, climbing into the car.

I turned the key in the ignition and grinned as I sat listening to the motor purring away. A couple of minutes later, I drew out onto the road and my grin became a full smile as the purr became a lion's roar.

Luxury cars had long been another passion of mine and I was very fortunate they were now my livelihood.

When I reached the main road, I turned to head up past my old grammar school towards where the garage stood at the top of the hill. As it rose, the road marked a boundary between the exclusive residential area of Caldy on one side and suburban Newton on the other. It was as if the school were a gateway between the two.

How different to when, as a seventeen-year-old schoolboy, I used to ride my old BSA Bantam up to the garage to spend my weekends working on the petrol pumps. My friend Mike and I would share the shifts and then lie about our age when we wasted our earnings on beer at the Ring O'Bells.

I never forgot how one afternoon, the driver of a big Jaguar pulled onto the forecourt. Handing over his keys with a smile, he promised me a good tip if I filled up both tanks, checked the oil, battery, radiator and window wash, did the tyres and gave the windscreen a wipe.

Ten minutes later, as he climbed back into the driving seat, I leaned over towards the car's open window asking, 'What about the tip, Sir?'

'Oh, yes, of course,' he replied. 'Never get married!'

*

'Good morning, Mr Duggan,' greeted Joanna from behind the reception desk, with a big smile, her long blonde hair shining in the sunlight.

'Good morning, Joanna,' I replied. 'I do wish you'd call me Simon.'

'I'll try, but doesn't Mr Duggan sound posher?'

'I'm afraid that word doesn't exist, but in any case, there's nothing posh about me. Ask your parents.'

'But you talk posh,' she retorted, grinning as she exaggerated her barely discernible Liverpool accent.

'That's because my mother was proud and Scottish and used to beat me if I came home speaking like the local scallies.'

Despite all the years I had known Joanna and her family, she had made me feel uncomfortable ever since she came to work at the garage. She was very conscientious and got on well with everyone, but there was something in the way she spoke to me that put me on my guard.

Having got past reception, I made my way past a shiny black Bentley Continental towards my large and tidy desk at the far end of the showroom.

I stopped for a moment to admire a bright red Ferrari we had bought the previous week.

I felt great pride in the row of gleaming, top pedigree cars lined up to face the main road outside. It almost felt as if they were on the starting grid of the British Touring Car Championships at Oulton Park.

Not that we had much passing trade. Most of our clients found us through our full-page adverts in the glossy *Cheshire Life* magazine, our website or by word of mouth.

Mrs Davies appeared from her office with a big mug of strong Yorkshire tea in one hand and a letter in the other.

She was dressed in a blue cashmere twinset and a pair of grey tailored trousers. Her dyed, chestnut hair was tied up in a bun.

'Good morning, Mr Duggan,' she greeted.

She could have been anywhere between forty-five and sixty, but she had been with us for years and I knew she'd recently passed her fiftieth birthday.

Her husband had been a Merchant Navy Captain until he was murdered by pirates in the Indian Ocean. She had seen very little of him during their thirty blissful years of marriage. A year later, she spent the insurance money on a beautiful Victorian house in West Kirby, where she lived alone.

I often wondered if my own marriage would have been happier if Teresa and I had spent less time together in the early days.

'Good morning to you, Mrs Davies,' I replied. 'What have you got for me today?'

I had given up trying to introduce any sort of familiarity into our daily routine; our exchanges were always short and to the point. Apart from the sad news about Captain Davies, I knew nothing about her at all.

'Not a great deal, Mr Duggan, only your appointment with Brian Arkwright for the Bentley at eleven and this letter that came in over the weekend. It's from Customs and Excise. They want to come in and look at the books again.'

'Let's hope it will be that charming young lady we had last year. What a pity she ended up in such a miserable job.'

'No, it's not from Liverpool this time. It's from the regional office in Manchester.'

'That's odd,' I replied. 'Still, you should get an appointment in the diary and let Mike know.' As well as a good friend, Mike had been my accountant ever since I took over the business. 'And could you ask Rob to pop into the showroom?'

'Of course, Mr Duggan.'

A true scouser, Rob oversaw the workshop and had two youngsters working under him. There was nothing you could teach him about luxury cars. He prided himself on getting used cars back into showroom condition, regardless of what state they were in when they arrived at the garage.

'Good morning.' Rob beamed as he arrived a couple of minutes later in his spotless overalls.

'Rob, we've got a buyer coming in for the Bentley at eleven. Could you get one of your boys to have a quick look at it for me?'

'Of course, Simon, I'll send young Darren through.'

Soon after he left, Peter came hurrying in, greeted Joanna and rushed over to his desk in the middle of the showroom.

There had been another salesman, but I got rid of him as soon as Peter had gained some experience. We used the space for a pair of matching black leather Chesterfields and a glass-topped coffee table.

It was hard to believe the garage's transformation since the days when Old Man Levitt ran it as a British Leyland dealership.

My friend Lawrence qualified as an architect at about the same time as Mike became a chartered accountant. I got him to help me with the renovation of the showroom once the business got going. Apart from the Chesterfields, everything was white, from the big, shiny floor tiles to the matt painted walls.

Spotlights shone down from the vaulted ceiling. Nothing was allowed to draw attention from the beauty of the cars. Lawrence had suggested painting the ceiling black to reduce the feeling of height, but I loved the bright sterility we had created.

Peter had joined us a year earlier and was already a great asset to the business, although I did struggle to get him to keep his desk as tidy as mine.

Teresa had wanted him to use his qualifications to do something more respectable, but he enjoyed his job. It gave him a lifestyle he would never have had in some big company in Liverpool.

We all knew the business would be his one day. My secret hope was that my grandchildren would take it over – a real family venture.

I could have had a different future. When I returned home from Durham University, I was disillusioned that a master's at Cambridge was no longer an option.

There had been little in the Liverpool jobs market for a twenty-one-year-old history graduate. I knew I was lucky Levitt was prepared to give me a chance as a junior salesman.

I turned out to be good at shifting Morris Marinas and Austin Allegros and it wasn't long before I'd been promoted to sales manager. My strength was that, unlike the others, I didn't take my clients for granted and many of them became lifelong friends.

Whatever problems I had at home, it was a good time and I never looked back.

*

Darren arrived in the showroom, carrying a box of cleaning products, brushes and dusters. In his mid-twenties, he was a tall, good-looking boy with a pleasant smile. As he walked around the Bentley, giving a quick spray and wipe here and there, Joanna followed his every move with her big blue eyes.

Eventually, the temptation was too much for her and she started to slither over towards him.

For God's sake, you can do better than that, I thought, but before she could get near him, Darren had finished and was on his way over to my desk.

'It's spotless and ready to go,' he said.

'Thanks, Darren. Let's hope that does the trick.'

THREE

BRIAN

It was almost eleven when a large S-Class Mercedes turned onto the forecourt. Although not a recent model, it was in excellent condition.

The driver climbed out, a tall man in his mid-sixties. He was wearing a battered trilby over long, straggly hair that was trying hard to be blond. Despite the gathering clouds, a pair of sunglasses adorned his craggy, lived-in features.

From the other side of the car appeared a young woman in her early thirties. She was tall and willowy and a younger version of her companion. Her blonde hair looked natural and she had a perfect, almost porcelain complexion.

I went to the door to greet them.

'Good morning, I'm Simon Duggan; you must be Mr Arkwright?'

'I am, but call me Brian. All my friends do,' he said, turning to his companion, who smiled, embarrassed, before introducing herself as Anne.

I led our visitors over to the Bentley and for a few minutes, they stood there, admiring its long black lines.

'She's a real beauty!' enthused Brian, breaking the silence.

'They don't make this kind of car anymore,' I added, opening the driver's door.

'Do get in, please. I'm afraid that we can't let you have a test drive, but we do at least allow our clients to pretend to be out on the road,' I joked.

'This is awesome,' he said, settling into the soft magnolia leather of the driver's seat. 'Do you have the full history?'

The car was one of the finest we had handled, but the Continental range had recently been updated and we were having no luck in finding a buyer.

'Yes, of course. She was built in 1998. A rare example of the Mulliner model, which delivers an exceptional 420 brake horsepower. When new, she would have cost over £200,000. What I love about this car is how she combines regal elegance with a true sporting pedigree.'

'And what about the mileage? I expect there's only been one careful lady owner,' continued Brian, looking towards Anne for support.

'She has only covered 10,000 miles. That's 1,500 miles a year. The first owner went to live overseas and sold it on when it was still almost new. Our client, a well-known Liverpool businessman, has several cars and used this one to impress, like when he had a horse running at Aintree.'

For a few minutes, Brian sat there imagining himself driving along with Anne at his side. I couldn't help thinking that the Trilbys and straggly hair were poor partners for the ageless class of the Bentley.

'Can we talk about the price?' he ventured.

'Yes, of course. As you will have seen in the advert, we are inviting offers from £110,000, to take account of the low mileage.'

As Brian slipped out of the driving seat, Anne's broad smile was willing him to reach inside his shapeless jacket and pull out a chequebook. I had my fingers crossed behind my back, counting on her to make it happen. 'Actually, Simon, I'm really taken with it. Can you give me twenty-four hours to speak to my bank?'

'Of course, Brian. Give me a call when you're ready. If I'm not here, you can talk to Peter,' I said, gesturing towards my son, who was sitting at his desk, keeping out of the way.

*

After they left, I stayed on the forecourt, looking over to where the pumps had been decades earlier. The area was landscaped with flowers and shrubs, and the warmth of the Gulf Stream meant there was always a colourful display.

Back in the showroom, Joanna was beside herself with excitement.

'Do you know who that was?' she asked.

'Yes, it's Brian Arkwright, soon to become the proud owner of one of our luxury vehicles.'

'No, he's the lead singer in The Mac. You must remember all their hits when you were young, back in the '70s. They did a national revival tour last month.'

'Joanna, when I was young, I was far too busy with my studies to have had the time to listen to rock bands. Anyway, after you've been with us a bit longer, you'll see we have many clients far more famous than Mr Arkwright. Most of them are a long way from needing any revival.'

FOUR

MRS GILMORE

'Come on, Peter,' I called across the showroom. 'Time for lunch!'

Our house was only two miles from the garage, but I preferred to eat out at midday.

Once in the car, we pulled out of the forecourt and set off down the hill towards West Kirby. The gathering clouds from when Brian and Anne arrived had dispersed and the sun was back out. Framed by the sandstone walls and luscious vegetation on both sides of the road, Hilbre Island stood defiant against the cold waters of the Irish Sea.

'It's a spring tide. Hopefully a good omen for your deal with Worzel Gummidge,' joked Peter.

'You need to be careful with these nicknames,' I warned him. 'Something's going to slip out one day and then it won't be funny.'

'I can't help myself with some of our clients. Still, do you think he'll do the deal?'

'I've no idea. He's keen and Vanessa Paradis was egging him on, but we shouldn't spend the money yet. For God's sake, now you've got me doing it!'

Minutes later, we were at our table in the Wro Lounge, a bright and trendy restaurant converted from an old Post Office building.

'This is the place to be for the ladies who lunch,' I said, looking at all the women with their fake tans, improbably blonde hair and whitened teeth. 'They're all playing with goat's cheese salads and sipping Gavi di Gavi. Could you imagine your mother coming in here?'

'I don't think so. They're not her type, but I'd rather be here than in a café on Banks Road, full of old biddies, counting out their pennies for a cuppa and a toasted tea-cake.'

'Peter, you've become the most hopeless snob. When I was your age, you used to beg me to take you to the Marigold for a sausage roll and a lemonade.'

'Well, you wouldn't catch me eating one of those horrible, greasy things now.' He smiled, leaning across the table towards me. 'Quick, look over by the bar. Some old bloke is trying to post a parcel. He thinks it's still the Post Office.'

A tall, attractive brunette arrived at our table.

'Are you ready to order?' she asked with a smile.

I knew her from somewhere, when the boys were younger and the house would have been full of their friends.

'It's Lisa O'Brien, isn't it?' I asked, finally putting a name to the face. 'John and Kerry's daughter. Weren't you in the same year as Joanna Gilmore at Upton Convent?'

'Oh, my God! Yes. You're Simon Duggan, aren't you? My dad was in your class at school.'

'He was, and this is my son, Peter. We haven't seen you or your parents for ages.'

'I've been away in Australia. I'm only working here until I can find something a bit more interesting,' she whispered.

'Well, it's nice to see you again. Are you still in touch with Joanna? Peter, why don't the three of you go out together one evening?'

'Yes, that would be great,' he muttered, looking down at the table to avoid making eye contact with Lisa.

*

'Dad, that was embarrassing,' said Peter, after we'd ordered.

'I'm sorry, but she's such a lovely girl. I was only trying to help. You know, her father is a senior partner in some big accountancy firm in Liverpool?'

Peter wasn't at all convinced and poured himself a glass of water.

'Dad, I wish you'd stop trying to match me up with every girl you like the look of. I'm old enough to make my own choices.'

'OK, I'm sorry. Anyway, how was your morning?' I asked with a forced smile. Between the blonde Joanna and the lovely brunette Lisa, my son could at least be interested in one of them. If I'd been twenty years younger, I would have invited them both out. I hoped he wasn't turning into some sad singleton, destined for a miserable, solitary life.

'Not bad. I had Nick French on the phone. He's flying out to Italy next week to pick up the Lamborghini I was telling you about. He'll stay over there for a week or so with his fiancée and then drive back through France.'

'Sounds like fun. I guess the profit will pay for the holiday. Didn't you say you had a buyer for it?'

'One of the Everton players has said he could be interested, but we'll need to get it registered as soon as it arrives.'

Nick owned a nightclub in Liverpool, and three or four times a year he would buy a top-end sports car, drive it for a while and then sell it on to us. He spent hours scanning the internet for deals, but it was a good way to make a bit of extra money.

'Peter, I've been wanting to talk to you about Matt. Your mother and I are worried. He should be setting up on his own by now, but he's over at The Punch Bowl every evening with his mates, spending everything he earns.'

'Not to mention the Plasterers Arms,' joked Peter, raising an eyebrow.

'It's not funny. Between your weekends in Liverpool and Matt out on the piss, I do wonder what it's all about. If we all spent some time together, it would help bring him back on track. How about a weekend up in the Lakes? We could go on walks, have a few good meals and a bit of a laugh, like when you were kids.'

Peter waited a moment before replying. 'If you want to go to the Lakes, why don't you go with Mum? It would do you both good.'

I ignored his suggestion, letting him continue. 'Look, Matt's fine. He's twenty-four. Can't you remember what you were like at that age?'

'Yes, we were up to our eyes in nappies and debt. You boys had a very different childhood to your parents and you've no idea what I have done to give it to you.'

We sat, eating in silence for a few minutes until I was ready to carry on.

'OK, you're right, but we should still try to do something as a family now and again. Your mother has been talking about selling the house and downsizing, and I don't think it's much to pay for being housed and fed.'

*

Back at the garage, Joanna had gone for lunch and Mrs Davies was looking after the reception.

'Anything to report?' I asked as we walked in.

'Nothing in particular. We had a couple in earlier, looking at the Ferrari, but I don't think they were serious.'

'Well, we can never be certain. That's a car that would have cost over £150,000 when it was new.'

'Don't worry, Mr Duggan, I took their details and I've sent an email to Peter so he can follow them up.'

'What would I do without you?'

She ignored my question. 'Oh, yes. I've heard back from the VAT office. They'll be here next Wednesday at about ten.'

'They? There's never been more than one person. Still, is Mike going to be here?'

'Yes, he's fine for Wednesday. He'll be here a bit earlier to make sure everything's ready.'

*

'I can't believe how different the showroom was when it was still Levitt's,' I said, as Peter and I drank coffee together at my desk.

I remembered when I had started over twenty-five years earlier. They had been good times to begin with; client loyalty was high and, for a while, there wasn't much competition.

Levitt only realised what was happening when it was too late. The supermarkets were killing the petrol business and he was finished as soon as the Japanese flooded the market with cheap cars.

With the rubbish British Leyland was turning out in those days, it was a miracle he kept going as long he did. At least it gave me the chance to buy the garage for next to nothing when it all went wrong.

I smiled, thinking about how lucky I had been.

'You did well to achieve what you did. I don't think I could have managed it,' said Peter, draining his cup.

'It wasn't easy, but I had the support of a couple of good clients and they're still with us today. They even lent me a bit of money to get started.'

'Was James Hennessey one of them? You've been dealing with him for years.'

'He's my oldest client and I owe him a lot, even if I did repay his loan years ago. There was only one other buyer for the garage when Levitt went into liquidation, but James had a word with him. I'm not sure what he said, but it worked.'

My son looked at me in astonishment and I raised my eyebrows and shrugged.

'It's just a pity he had to lumber us with the Bentley. Still, fingers crossed for Brian,' I added, giving the car a last, mournful look as Peter got up and went back to his desk.

*

The afternoon flew by. On my way home, I decided to call in at Morrison's to pick up a bottle of wine.

The car park was packed and I found a space on the Marine Lake promenade. I couldn't risk the Maserati being damaged by a carelessly opened car door and I always enjoyed the walk along the front, looking out over the estuary.

Once inside the store, I took my well-trodden route to the wine section and picked up a 1999 Duas Quintas, avoiding the temptation to take two.

As I turned, I didn't see the trolley in front of me and I was lucky not to end up on the floor in a glassy pool of Portuguese wine.

Shit, it's Joanna's mum, the Morrisons Minger, I thought, trying to keep my balance.

'Fancy seeing you here,' I choked. 'How are you doing?'

From the sight of her, not well. Her trolley was full of bottles, with only a bag of lettuce leaves and several chocolate bars to add some variety.

It was upsetting to see her in such a diminished state. Her eyes were red and watery, grey roots were invading her long dark locks, and her bright red nail polish was chipped. She had always been well presented, even when she was still a teenager. All our parents had modest white-collar jobs and struggled to make ends meet, but Nicola's father had a fancy job at Liverpool Town Hall. She used to think her family was a step up from the rest of us.

'I'm fine, Simon. How about you?'

I could smell the alcohol on her breath as she spoke.

'Great, thanks. Joanna's settling in well. She's a good girl. Always keen to help.'

'That's good,' she replied. 'Her father will be pleased.'

'And how is Lawrence?' I asked, immediately realising from her expression that this was not a good question. She didn't reply but stared at me, almost bitterly.

'Nicola? Are you still driving the Mercedes convertible I sold you last year?'

'Yes, of course. I love it. Why do you ask?'

She glared at me with her boozy red eyes.

'They've been having a few problems with the electronic key fob. May I take a quick look at yours?'

I pounced as soon as the key emerged from her handbag and slipped it straight into my trouser pocket.

'What are you doing?' she shouted.

'I'm sorry, but I'm not letting you drive anywhere. Let's go and pay and I'll give you a lift home. I can drop Joanna down to pick up your car tomorrow morning.'

She knew there was little point in arguing and followed me over to the checkout.

'Good evening, Mrs Gilmore,' greeted the cashier. 'I see you like that Fleury. I bought a bottle to treat my boyfriend and we had it with our dinner last night. It was lovely.'

'Yes, it is a good wine, dear. Simon, do you remember Becky's parents, Patrick and Siobhan Fitzgerald? You met them at that party last year over at Mike and Martine's house. They're good friends of theirs.'

'Yes, I do, but I need you to wait for me outside while I get the car. Will you be OK for a couple of minutes?' I asked.

Nicola nodded, staring down at the floor with an air of resignation. I was struck by how pathetic she looked. A pickled old trout, still in her house slippers.

'What's happened, Nicola?' I asked as I got her into the car.

'Ever since Lawrence won that award for the new community centre, we haven't seen either of you.'

She burst into tears.

'He couldn't care less about Joanna and me. He's not the man I married,' she sobbed.

'I was surprised when I saw him at the Sailing Club last Christmas. What has he done with his hair? I couldn't believe my eyes when I saw that ponytail of his.'

'That's only the start of it. He bought a flat in Albert Dock last year. He said he had to work all hours and didn't want to disturb me when he came back late. But I know he's got some little scrubber over there. No wonder he's always exhausted at the weekend.'

What could I say? Everyone knew what this doyen of the Liverpool architectural scene was getting up to.

'You're still young, Nicola. You could find someone else if you tried,' I said without conviction.

From her reaction, I could see I was only making matters worse and I kept the rest of my thoughts to myself as my passenger cried all the way back to Caldy.

'Why don't you and Joanna come over for lunch on Sunday?' I suggested as we pulled through the open gates onto her gravel driveway. 'I'll try and get Peter and Matthew there too.'

'That would be lovely. I'm sorry about this evening, but thanks for the lift. You've probably saved my life, not to mention countless others!'

'That's what friends are for,' I said, lifting her shopping out of the boot.

A light was on in the kitchen and I could see Joanna getting supper ready. She had a difficult evening ahead of her, but it wouldn't have been the first.

'Would you like to come in for a drink?' she asked, watching me carry her bottles over to the front door.

'I'd love to,' I replied. 'But I do need to get home.'

'That is a pity, but thanks again. Seeing you has cheered me up. I'm looking forward to seeing you all on Sunday.'

Nicola's news had affected me more than I realised and I sighed as I climbed back into the car, waiting a few minutes before starting up the engine.

Where were our lives taking us? I wondered.

Mike, Lawrence and I had been close friends since our teens; they used to call us the Three Musketeers. Then we all got married and, with our new partners, we became closer than ever. Three couples working together to achieve their dreams. Dreams that were now being shattered, one after the other.

Lawrence had run off to Liverpool and Nicola was on her own. Mike was embarrassed by his wife, Martine, and Teresa and I lived separate lives under the same roof.

Hardly the stuff that dreams are made of, I thought, as I finally turned the key in the ignition and set off on the short drive home.

FIVE

THE HARDCASTLES

Tuesday began with my usual routine and the familiar sound of Teresa emptying the dishwasher in the kitchen. I had been planning a quick half-hour in the gym after breakfast but, with Nicola's car to collect and the call I was expecting from Brian, it would have to wait.

When I arrived downstairs, the mood was much happier than the day before. Teresa was at her usual post, a spatula in one hand and her coffee in the other, but there were smiles everywhere and even a bit of banter between my sons.

'The apple never falls far from the tree, Pete. I'd be careful if I were you,' teased Matt, having heard the story about my rescuing Nicola Gilmore.

'I've told you, I'm not in the least bit interested in Joanna,' replied Peter, smoothing back his hair with his hand. 'Anyway, Dad's trying to set me up with Lisa O'Brien. She's working as a waitress in the Wro Lounge.'

'Another one your father's got his eye on, I suppose,' said Teresa, pretending to look at me suspiciously. Unlike the day before, she was laughing this time. 'Still, you should both be careful with what you say. Joanna and her mother are coming for lunch on Sunday and it would be nice if the pair of you could be here for a change.'

The boys both looked at me for my reaction.

'You've taken the news of my Sunday lunch invitation much better than I expected, darling. It will be good to put on a bit of a show, like in the old days,' I replied. 'And I agree with your mother; you boys should be here.'

Matt was grinning, but Peter didn't seem at all pleased.

'It'll be fun. Is Lawrence coming?' asked Teresa.

'Not from what Nicola was saying, but I'll check with Joanna later. We should invite Mike and Martine as well. If Nicola's in the state she was in yesterday, we're going to need a bit of support.'

'Let me think about it,' replied Teresa. 'There are already six of us and it's been a while since I've done anything like this.'

I nodded my agreement, smiling. I had no idea what was going on, but Teresa's whole mood seemed to have changed.

'Oh, and Simon, did you remember to book the restaurant for our date tonight?' she continued.

I was surprised by this comment. All I had been expecting was a nice meal in a good restaurant, but if Teresa was expecting a date, why not?

'Of course I did, darling. It's all sorted.'

*

Twenty minutes later, I arrived at the garage. As usual, Peter would be there soon after me, but Mrs Davies was already in her office, talking to Rob. I imagined they were ordering spare parts for a service.

I always found it reassuring to see everyone busy when I arrived, although I had given up trying to get Peter to get in on time.

I headed straight over to the reception.

'Joanna, did your mother tell you about her car? If you're ready now, I can drive you down to get it.'

'I'm ready when you are,' she replied.

A few minutes later, we were heading into West Kirby.

Joanna had been on edge since we got into the car. I imagined she was embarrassed about the state her mother had been in the previous evening.

'Have you driven the Mercedes before, Joanna? It's a lot livelier than that Clio you're used to,' I asked, trying to lighten her mood.

'It was kind of you to look after my mum last night, Simon. Goodness knows how much trouble she could have got herself into,' she replied, with a nervous laugh, ignoring my question.

'She looks as though she's been having a rough time. Do you not see much of your father?' I probed, already knowing the answer.

Joanna drew a deep breath before answering, as though she was preparing to get something off her chest.

'Not a lot. He says he's got loads of work on and that it's difficult for him to get back in the evenings. I reckon it won't be long until we don't see him at all.'

I should have changed the subject, but Lawrence and Nicola were two of my oldest friends and I couldn't believe they were separating.

'But what about the house? I expect you and your mother would have to move if she and Lawrence were to split up.'

Joanna nodded, tears welling up in her eyes. 'Mum's already been to see all the estate agents looking for something decent to rent. It's depressing.'

By the time we pulled up next to her mother's car, she was crying her eyes out and, for the second time in less than twenty-four hours, I was lost for words.

'It will all be fine. It always is, Joanna. You need to stay strong for your mother. She must be at her wits' end,' I said, trying my best to comfort her.

I left her to compose herself. She eventually dried her eyes with a tissue before somehow managing to rest her head on my shoulder.

In the tight space of the car, my left arm had become trapped between our seats and I wriggled to pull it free before passing it behind her back.

She moved closer to me and I felt the warmth of her body against mine. The top buttons of her crisp, cotton shirt were undone and I felt a stirring between my legs as my eyes guiltily settled on her breasts, cradled by a delicate, white bra.

Joanna turned her head towards me. Our faces were inches apart and I had to control a sudden urge to kiss her.

'Are you alright?' she asked. 'We ought to be getting back.'

'Of course,' I replied, relieved the moment had passed. 'But you must tell me if there's anything I can do to help. You mustn't keep things bottled up.'

'That's the last thing any of us should do, Simon,' she said, giving me a quick kiss on the cheek before she took her mother's key and stepped out of the car.

It was an odd comment and I wondered whether she had seen how I had been looking at her.

She glanced back as she opened the door of her mother's Mercedes and my fears were confirmed by the searching look she gave me.

I had betrayed Joanna's trust and it was going to be awkward when I got back to work. I had enjoyed our moment of closeness, something I had not had with Teresa for as long as I could remember.

Why did this have to happen? I asked myself. What would I do if a similar situation arose again? I was confused and it was a few minutes before I managed to clear my head and set off up the hill to the garage.

*

Back at the garage, Mrs Davies was waiting for me again at the reception desk.

'The couple who were looking at the Ferrari yesterday came back while you were out. They didn't want to speak to Peter. They said they had to deal with the owner. I asked them to take a seat and I've given them coffee.'

'Thank you. I'll go and see them. You never know, but we might have a sale after all,' I replied, smiling.

Mrs Davies smiled back, raising an eyebrow. I was forever the optimist, but she had a sixth sense that was rarely wrong.

They both stood up as I approached, smiling encouragingly. In their late thirties, the man was casually dressed and his partner looked like a model in a BHS advertisement. They were the sort of couple I would expect to meet at a school parents' evening.

'Hi, I'm Jim Hardcastle and this is my wife, Julie.'

'I understand you're interested in the Ferrari Modena? If you would like to come over to my desk, we can go through the details.'

As soon as we had all sat down, Jim got straight to the point.

'We are very interested, but we need to talk about the money.'

'Of course. We are looking at £95,000 on the road. One owner from new and only 22,000 miles on the clock. A fine example of this model.'

'Could we do £85,000 if we pay cash?' he asked, glancing at Julie.

'You know, it's all cash once it's in the bank. Very few of our customers take out a loan,' I answered, instinctively folding my arms.

'No, you don't understand. We've had a bit of luck recently and we'd prefer not to involve our bank in this.'

Instead of following the conversation, Julie looked as if she were trying to remember what she had in for supper. Her face bore none of the excitement I had seen from Anne the day before.

I now had to accept that Mrs Davies had been right, but why were they carrying on with this charade? If Jim was trying to impress Julie, it wasn't working.

'It's an interesting proposal, but not one I could accept. If you're able to pay by bank transfer, though, I could meet you halfway at £90,000,' I replied, reluctantly letting Jim continue his little game.

'But surely that amount of cash could come in handy,' he insisted.

By now, Jim and his dreary companion were starting to irritate me. I had better things to do than let them act out their fantasies.

'I'm sorry, Jim. I would be delighted to sell you the car, but not on the basis you propose. Now, if you don't mind…'

'OK, I understand. I guess we'll have to try elsewhere. Do you know another dealer who might be a little more flexible?'

'Not really. You could have a go with private advertisers, but you'll need to be careful. The people who own this kind of car can be very sharp and you could get your fingers burned. But thanks for coming to see us,' I continued, leading them towards the door. 'If you do change your mind, it would be a pleasure to do business with you.'

'Thank you, Simon,' replied Jim. 'Who knows, we may be seeing each other again very soon.'

I didn't like how Julie looked at me when Jim made this last remark and I was pleased to get them both outside.

SIX

TERESA'S NIGHT OUT

The taxi arrived on time at half seven and Teresa was first through the door, with me rushing to keep up behind.

She had spent what seemed like hours getting ready and looked fantastic when she came downstairs.

She was wearing a tailored black dress I hadn't seen for a very long time and a dark green cashmere cardigan that drew out the colour of her eyes. I immediately felt underdressed in my beige chinos and a blue polo shirt. I self-consciously tied the sleeves of the brown sweater draped over my shoulders as we climbed into the back of the car.

'How long is it since we were together like this?' she asked, edging towards me as I fastened my seat belt.

'I can't remember,' I replied, not sure where this was leading.

'Exactly! Then let's have a cuddle. The driver won't mind.'

I looked up and could see a big pair of eyes in the rear-view mirror.

'Don't worry, guys. If you knew half the things I've seen going on in that seat, you'd want to get out right now.'

Like two guilty teenagers, we pulled apart.

'The day I got my driving licence,' he continued, 'I took my girlfriend out for a few drinks to celebrate and afterwards, we went down to that car park by Caldy beach.'

Teresa and I exchanged knowing looks.

'She was a lovely girl but not too bright. So, after we parked up, I asked her if she'd like to get into the back seat. Do you know what she said?'

We both shook our heads.

'I can if you like, but I'd rather stay here in the front with you! Here we are, guys. If you need a lift home later, give us a ring and I'll be over in a couple of minutes. Tuesdays are usually quiet and I don't expect we'll be busy.'

We were welcomed into the restaurant by the manager, who introduced himself as Giancarlo.

Market Street in Hoylake had once been fashionable, but shoppers had deserted it for the region's retail parks. Now, bars and restaurants replaced the shops that had been there since Victorian times. The Monte Carlo Restaurant was no exception and had recently opened to replace an upmarket gent's outfitters.

Once we were settled, two chilled glasses of champagne in front of us, Teresa took my hands in hers and looked me straight in the eyes.

'I do love you, Simon,' she said. 'It may not seem like it at times, but I always have.'

'Darling, are you alright? You haven't spoken to me like this for years.'

Something about her reminded me of how she had been before all the relentless years of family life. Although we had been together for almost three decades, I felt oddly embarrassed; it was almost as if we were out on a first date.

'Or course I am, it's just...'

She took a moment to sort out what she wanted to say.

'Well, the thing is, I've been thinking a lot about us recently, what we've got, the boys, where we're going. I mean, things have been tough, but—'

'They have, but that was some time ago. It's not exactly difficult for us now,' I interrupted.

'It isn't, Simon, but it all leaves its mark. I mean, we hardly got off to a good start. You having to come back here after you had worked so hard to get away. And living at my mum's for the first few years. That didn't help.'

'It didn't help that my parents disowned me when they found out you were pregnant.'

I remembered what my mother said as though it were only yesterday. 'Why can't she have an abortion like all the other tarts on the Gilroy Road estate? Look at you, crawling back to play happy families with a bunch of papists. You should be ashamed of yourself.' It was awful.

'Your mother hated me from the day we met,' said Teresa. 'But she only has herself to blame if you didn't see her again before she died.'

I nodded, thinking how unnecessary it had all been. 'It's my father I felt sorry for, having to put up with all her shit for years on end. I only found out about his funeral because a neighbour called me.'

From her frown, I could see that Teresa found it unpleasant talking about my parents. It could all have been so different for everyone if they had given us some support, not that they had a great deal themselves.

'At least I didn't have any problems with your mum,' I continued. 'I got on better with her than you did most of the time.'

'You did, but you have to admit she became quite difficult after the first few months. Even with you. I'm sure she thought we were going to be living with her forever.'

I took a sip of champagne as I remembered how we had squeezed into Teresa's mother's three-bedroom semi. It hadn't been easy with a new-born baby and all the equipment that goes with it.

We never had any money and it was very different from the dreams we had shared as teenagers. Peter was not a good sleeper, and Teresa would spend half the night getting up and down to feed him and change his nappies.

It was no wonder she was shattered most of the time. At least I managed to get out to work, even if I gave most of what I was earning to her mother to cover our food and lodging.

'Tell me the truth, Simon, do you ever wonder what our lives would have been like if we hadn't had Peter?' continued Teresa.

'Of course not. It might have been difficult at first, but we were fine once I bought the garage,' I replied, grinning.

I had regretted giving up my plans for a life in academia, but my doubts disappeared when the money started rolling in.

'Yes, but we were only sorting ourselves out when Matthew came along. Then there was the house and all the renovations. Talk about gluttons for punishment,' continued Teresa, shaking her head and frowning.

'And what about when they were going through adolescence?' I added.

'Yes, Matt was a right little shit back then. He's lucky I didn't strangle him.' Teresa laughed.

'I guess we all are,' I joked, but I sensed she was more interested in working out how our marriage had arrived where it was today than talking about the past.

'But where do you think we would have ended up otherwise?' I asked.

'I don't know, Simon,' replied Teresa, shaking her head.

'Well, I'd be in Cambridge with some vegan leftie and you'd be stuck here, married to some dreary bloke,' I said, pulling an ugly face to emphasise the point.

I stopped when I felt my shins being gently kicked under the table.

'I would have you know, Mr Duggan, that I would have gone to university like you did, had it not been for Peter.'

'But then you wouldn't be spending three or four days a week riding Doughnut all over the county, a lady of leisure.'

'Jackpot!' she corrected with a smile. 'And don't try to tell me it was fun being stuck at home looking after two young children. Not when you were getting out, doing what you enjoyed. At least when we started renovating the house, I had something useful to do.'

'Now I understand why you always kept your eyes closed when we made love. You hated to see me enjoying myself!'

She pretended to ignore me.

'Seriously, though, we've been lucky with the boys, although I wasn't happy when Matt came home in that van with "If you need a plumber – call Ivor Leake!" painted down the side.'

'You did make me laugh when you asked if his boss was really called Mr Leake and told him to keep the van hidden behind the garage.'

Matt had always been Teresa's baby and, for all his faults, everyone could see he had a special place in her heart. He would never admit it, but he still needed her as much as she needed him. In contrast, Peter was strong and dependable. Sometimes, it felt as if his emotions were hidden deep behind an invisible wall. It had never felt like he needed either of us.

'Imagine if we'd ended up with Mike and Martine's kids,' I continued. 'That Sean is a right stoner.'

Mike made no secret of the fact he preferred Peter to his own son. He often asked me how he was getting on and made a point of chatting with him whenever they met. Not that he seemed particularly interested in Matt, though.

'And as for Tricia. Matt told me she's been working her way through all the lads at the Punch Bowl.'

'Him included, I should imagine,' joked Teresa. 'She's turned out to be a right little slapper.'

'But look at her mother. She was very popular when she was that age. Thank goodness she found Mike and settled down.' I laughed.

'It's been ages since we've talked together like this,' said Teresa, taking my hands again.

'It has and we need to keep on doing it.'

Teresa's dreamy look was interrupted by Giancarlo, who came to take our orders before heading off to the kitchen.

'The thing is, we need to make a new start. Let's try to enjoy living again,' said Teresa. 'We were lucky having the boys early. We're still young and there's plenty of time to do everything we missed out on.'

'Well, I'm ready if you are. I suggested a family trip to the Lakes yesterday when I had lunch with Peter.'

'And what did he say?' asked Teresa, one eyebrow raised.

'He suggested that you and I should go on our own. He would never do anything that stopped him enjoying his weekends in Liverpool.'

Teresa looked down at her plate for a second as though she were thinking about what I had said.

'So let's go to the Lakes on our own?' she suggested. 'We could stay at that pub next to Rydal Water. Do you remember what it's called?'

'The Ferryman's?'

'Yes, The Ferryman's; it always felt so romantic. We'll go midweek and Peter can look after the garage for you.'

Our food arrived and I ordered more wine. The evening felt like who we'd been before becoming young parents a quarter of a century earlier.

'Do you know what started me thinking about all this?' asked Teresa.

I shook my head.

'That bloody gym of yours.'

'Because you can finally see what a gorgeous husband you've got?'

'There is that, but it made me realise that we don't have to sleepwalk towards retirement.'

'You made enough of a fuss when I told you I wanted to convert the pool house.'

'I'm sorry, but that was the old Teresa. I want to forget about her and start a new life with my husband before it's too late.'

*

When we got home, I resisted the temptation of a Glenmorangie in front of the fire and went to make my way upstairs.

'Are you not having a nightcap?' asked Teresa.

'No, I'm fine. We did very well at the restaurant.'

'You usually enjoy a nice whisky at the end of the evening.'

'I do. A bit too much for my own good. It might be better if you stopped filling the decanter every time it starts getting empty.'

'But I hate to see it sitting there empty on the buffet. I always want to fill it up.'

'And I hate to see it full. I always want to empty it. We'll have to get rid of the decanter.'

She smiled and took my hand as we started up the staircase to our bedroom.

I had taken a shower before we went out and, once upstairs, I pulled off my clothes, slipped on a pair of boxer shorts and climbed under the giant duvet that covered our bed.

'It was hot in the restaurant. Do you mind if I have a quick shower?' asked Teresa, undressing and neatly arranging her clothes.

'Of course not. Take your time,' I replied. I was happy to lie there, mulling over what we had talked about at the restaurant. I had not for a moment been expecting what she had said and, if she did mean it, our lives would finally be complete.

Eventually, I heard her turn off the shower and I watched her emerging naked, still covered with little droplets of water.

As she stood there, framed in the bathroom doorway, I took

in every detail of her body. My eyes finally came to rest on a small patch of fine ginger hair above her pubic mound.

When we first met, we were both virgins and it took her some time to allow me to visit her "secret garden", as she called it. I was pleased to see she kept it manicured and regretted not having been invited back for such a long time.

She finished drying herself and came over to the bed.

Putting a finger over my mouth, she pulled back the duvet, reaching down and slipping off my shorts as quickly as I had put them on.

'You won't be needing those,' she whispered as she passed a knee over my body and sat astride my hips.

I had felt a stirring between my legs since being in the car with Joanna that morning and I was erect and inside her within seconds.

'Don't you worry,' she said as she settled into position. 'I won't be closing my eyes tonight. I want to see you enjoy every single moment.'

I put my hands behind my head and looked up into her eyes as my penis slowly moved in and out of her vagina.

Lifting her pelvis up and down, Teresa was doing all the work and the effortless pleasure was almost too much for me. I struggled not to burst when I looked down and saw my glistening shaft framed by her lips, half-hidden behind a curtain of soft ginger hair.

Finally, I felt her starting to climax and I let myself go, my heart pounding in my chest.

'It's a good thing you made me have that vasectomy, or that would have been twins,' I said as she climbed off me.

'And that wouldn't be funny, would it?' She laughed as she pulled the duvet back over us. 'Thank you for this evening, Simon. I've enjoyed every minute.'

'So have I, Teresa,' I replied. 'I'm looking forward to our new life together.'

SEVEN

MIKE'S BIRTHDAY

The next few days flew by. We had smiles at breakfast, a candlelit supper in the dining room on Wednesday and the promise of a weekend of passion once we were alone on Saturday evening.

'After last night, I can't wait until the weekend,' whispered Teresa on Wednesday morning as I left for work. 'All alone in this great big house. We can do whatever we like.'

The thought of it had me stirring again.

'Simon, I'm surprised he doesn't need a rest,' she joked, tapping the growing bulge in my trousers before giving me a quick kiss and pretending to push me out of the door.

By Thursday, Brian still hadn't come back to me, hopefully a sign that he was sorting out payment for the car.

I wanted to shift the Bentley and get some cash in. I had never expected it to sell overnight, but when James Hennessey offered it to me, I couldn't refuse. I could never have built the business without his support.

Meanwhile, Peter was progressing with his Lamborghini deal, having agreed on a sale with the Everton player. 'I'm waiting for

43

Nick to come back with a date and we should be good to go,' he told me with a satisfied grin.

*

Even at the garage, they could sense the change in my mood.

'You're very happy today.' Joanna smiled as she brought a handful of papers over to me on Thursday afternoon. 'Anything you want to share?' she asked with a cheeky grin.

I blushed as I felt what was happening between my legs, hidden away under the desk.

'No, not especially. This lovely spring sunshine is enough to put a smile back on anybody's face,' I said, grinning back at her.

'The spring gets us all blooming, doesn't it, Simon?' she replied, giving me an odd look before turning to head back to the reception.

Sunday lunch was going to be a nightmare.

*

Shortly after seven o'clock on Thursday evening, Teresa and I set off on the short walk to Mike and Martine O'Mara's house, a hundred yards or so up the road.

It was a fine evening and we were serenaded by a chorus of birds in the trees and hedgerows that lined both sides of our route.

'You know what I love more than anything else at this time of year?' I asked as we walked along, hand in hand. 'The sweet smell of gorse drifting across from the common.'

I was carrying a bottle of Glendalough thirteen-year single malt Irish whiskey in my free hand; it was one of Mike's favourites. Teresa had a small bouquet of flowers for Martine.

Mike's family had come from Ireland in the nineteenth century to join the navvies working on the Liverpool and Manchester railway. He still felt loyal to his roots.

Most of the houses in Caldy had been built between the wars by wealthy ship owners and industrialists escaping the noise and grime they had created on the other side of the Mersey.

Mike and Martine's house stood out from its older neighbours. An opulent example of the Greek Revival style, it was a triumph of money over taste, not that this had put them off buying it.

'You don't think it's a bit over the top?' I asked when they showed us around for the first time.

'Not at all,' came Martine's reply. 'If you've got it, flash it.'

Not that Martine had always had it to flash. She and Mike had faced the same challenges as the rest of us along the road to affluence, but then discretion had never been one of her strong points.

Martine was waiting for us at the front door and she looked as if she had already started the birthday celebrations.

'Come in,' she almost whispered. 'He isn't home yet. I wanted to get you over early so we could surprise him.'

Mike and Martine had been part of our group of friends, along with the Gilmores, since Mike, Lawrence and I had been at school. We now lived within a few hundred yards of each other in the exclusive area of Caldy, having made the difficult move from suburbia on the other side of the hill.

I often thought about how the move had made the bonds between us stronger than ever.

Martine was only sixteen when she left school to work as a waitress at one of our favourite haunts, the Pancake Kitchen in West Kirby. Although neither a great beauty nor very bright, Mike had been smitten by her experience and generosity.

To his embarrassment, she often reminded us that, although now in her forties and the mother of his two children, she remained as generous as ever.

She had an earthy, almost rustic way about her and an ability to make the most innocent remark sound crude and suggestive.

'Would you like me to give you something before my husband

gets home?' she asked me, a twinkle in her eye, ignoring Teresa, who was taking off her jacket in the kitchen.

'Here we go again,' I muttered, my eyes drawn to her ample cleavage. It was glistening with sweat and I suspected this was due more to the booze she had been putting away all afternoon than the heat coming off the AGA.

With her dyed blonde hair and outfits that tried to be glamorous, Martine fought hard to overcome the ravages of time, but the battle was already lost.

'No thank you, Martine. It's still early,' I said, glancing over at the half-empty gin bottle next to the fridge. 'I'll wait for Mike. How about you, Teresa?'

'I'm fine. Let's have some champagne when Mike arrives.'

'So long as you're both happy. I need to finish off the main dish. It's your favourite, Simon. Spanish chicken.'

This was what I had been dreading.

Soon after Mike and Martine met, they invited us over with Lawrence and Nicola to her family's house for dinner. The parents were out for the evening and she and Mike were playing at being grown-ups, even though she was only sixteen.

Her face had been alight with pride as she served up a tasteless concoction of chicken and tinned tomatoes on a bed of overcooked, sticky rice.

Luckily, we were hungry teenagers, and there was nothing left on any of our plates by the end of the meal.

I regretted having been so greedy on that evening long ago. Now we were adults, it was more difficult to hide my disappointment when the same dish kept cropping up at her dinner parties.

*

Despite years of overindulgence, Mike cut an impressive figure as he came through the door in a tailored suit and expensive-looking tie.

Martine would often say how proud she was to have such a tall, dark and handsome husband.

He was as surprised to see us as he was pleased.

'My God,' he said. 'I thought she'd forgotten. This is great!'

Wait until you see what's for dinner, I thought. Although, from the extra weight he was carrying, I guessed he was used to shovelling down whatever his wife put in front of him.

'I'm going up to change. Why don't you open a bottle of that champagne we bought at Christmas, Martine?' he asked as he headed off upstairs.

'Don't you worry, lover. I've already got a bottle chilling in the lounge. There'll be a glass waiting for you when you come down.'

'Are the children not with us?' asked Teresa as she helped Martine with the glasses.

'No, not this evening. We'll celebrate with them at the weekend.'

I had to try very hard not to catch Teresa's eye.

After about five minutes, Mike reappeared and I handed him the whiskey. 'Happy birthday and may there be many more.'

'Thanks, Simon. Only one more before the big "Five-O". Still, live for the day. We'll give this bottle a good run for its money after dinner!'

Martine passed around the champagne. 'The first of many,' she toasted, smiling at her husband. 'To the birthday boy!'

'To the birthday boy,' Teresa and I replied, raising our glasses.

It wasn't Martine's first of the day, but it should have been one of her last, I thought, watching her steady herself on the back of a chair.

*

Dinner was not as bad as it might have been, but the Spanish chicken was the same soggy mess it had been thirty years earlier.

'Come on, Simon,' Martine asked as she served, 'are you a breast or a leg man? Teresa never did tell me. I suppose you don't care so long as you get a big portion?'

She was getting worse. 'Keep the big portion for Mike,' I replied. 'After all, it's his birthday and he deserves a special treat.'

Mike pretended to ignore his wife and kept us entertained with shocking stories about some of his more dubious clients. His Liverpool accent made them seem even funnier.

As soon as we had finished the cheese, washed down with some port, he stood up and grabbed the Glendalough from the sideboard.

'Let's leave the ladies to clear up. We'll go and smoke a cigar in the conservatory.'

'Martine, can't I give you a hand?' I asked. 'There's quite a bit to do.'

'No, Simon, I'll help Martine; you go with Mike,' replied Teresa. 'It is his birthday, after all.'

The conservatory had been Martine's project and she had not held back.

Fully glazed, the roof was supported on Ionic columns and it had been decorated in the style of a temple.

The plastered walls were painted with creatures from Greek mythology. Giant minotaurs stood on both sides of the doorway through to the house as though they were guarding it.

On the right-hand side of the room, a marble sculpture of Dionysus, the Greek god of wine, hung over the bar, his head crowned in a mass of vine leaves.

'Let's sit here,' suggested Mike, pulling out two black leather cushioned metal stools.

Once seated, he reached inside a large humidor, pulling out two large and expensive-looking cigars.

'Try this,' he said, handing me one. 'It's Cuban and the best you're ever likely to enjoy.'

'Honestly, Mike. It's a lot bigger than I'm used to,' I replied, feeling quite intimidated by it.

'That's what Teresa said this morning when I popped round

to your house for my birthday present,' he joked. Even by Mike's standards, this was pushing the boundaries, but it was his birthday and he was already quite drunk.

I gave in and watched him pour two generous glasses of the whiskey as I struggled to light my cigar.

'I'll allow you one ice cube in your glass. Any more would spoil it,' Mike said as he handed it to me. 'You were a lucky bastard when you met Teresa. I hope you appreciate what you've got?'

I looked down into my glass, watching the alcohol melting the ice cube.

That had been the problem all along. Ever since the day Teresa had told me she was pregnant, I had never taken the time to appreciate what we had both worked so hard to achieve.

I told him about my night out with Teresa and how we were set for a new start.

'I'd swap with you any day of the week, Simon. A beautiful wife, the boys, a business you love. How would you feel about swapping with me? If Peter were my son and you had Sean? Be honest.'

He was right. He had an expensive but tasteless house, a generous but crude and sweaty wife, a job that gave him little pleasure, and two children he wished he had strangled at birth.

'Mike, it's your birthday, for God's sake. Let's have another glass.'

It would not be our last and it wasn't long until there was little to show of the bottle that had cost me the best part of seventy pounds.

Mike finally dozed off and I went through to the kitchen to find Martine asleep in her chair and Teresa reading a magazine.

'You should have come through,' I said as she got up to put on her coat.

'Don't worry, she's only just gone. I'm surprised she stayed with us as long as she did, but I could hear you were having a good time and I didn't want to spoil it.'

This was the new Teresa. Previously, she would have been through to the conservatory to drag me home long before Martine had started snoring.

It seemed to take us a lot longer to get back than it had to walk over, and when we did get home, there was no talk of a nightcap or a repeat of Tuesday's performance. It was straight to bed, a quick kiss on the cheek and off into a deep, drunken sleep, hoping that Friday morning would be kind to us.

EIGHT

THE BIG, BAD FRIDAY

The next day, I woke around eight, alone in the bed.

I could hear Teresa downstairs and pulled on a dressing gown before going down to join her.

'I've put a couple of aspirin on the table,' she greeted with a wide grin. 'I thought you might need them.'

I nodded painfully and washed them down with a mouthful of tea.

'Thank you, darling. My God, I feel terrible. Can you give me a lift up to the garage later?' I asked. 'There's no way I'll be driving today.'

'Of course. I'm going over to Frankby for a ride. It will clear my head. But why don't you have a day off?'

I looked across the Dee estuary and shivered when I saw how bleak it was.

'I'd love to, but it's better if I get out. I'll only be bored if I stay in bed, especially if I've only got myself to amuse.'

*

By ten o'clock, I was at my desk with another mug of tea, a box of aspirin next to it. It would be another two hours until I could take a second dose and I was nursing a monumental headache.

I was on the point of falling asleep when Joanna called me.

'I've got Mike on the line. Shall I put him through?'

'Yes, of course,' I replied, thinking he must have been in an even worse state than me considering how much he had drunk.

'Simon, how are you feeling?'

'Dreadful. How about you? I'm surprised you made it into the office.'

'You must be joking. I only woke up half an hour ago. I'm sitting in bed with coffee and a cognac. Martine's been throwing up all night. What did you do to us?'

'It's more what you did to us. Teresa had to drop me off on her way to the stables. Still, to what do I owe this call?'

I could hear the cogs turning in Mike's brain as he tried to remember why he had called.

'Oh, yes. I'd almost forgotten,' he replied after a couple of seconds. 'I've had a call from one of my guys at work. I'd asked him to do a bit of digging on who's coming for the VAT inspection next week.'

'And what did he tell you?' I asked, gulping. 'You wouldn't be calling me from your bed if it weren't serious.'

'They're from a Special Investigations unit. I have no idea what they're investigating, but once these people get their hands on you, they never let go.'

This was all I needed to hear on a Friday morning, struggling with a hangover.

'Mike, we don't need to panic. I've got nothing to hide, but we do need to make sure we haven't missed anything.'

'Don't worry. I'll be there before they arrive on Wednesday. Anyway, why don't you go home and have a lie-down?'

I was starting to wonder if I should take his advice when Joanna called again. 'I've got Worzel Gummidge on the line,' she said as I picked up the phone.

'Thanks. Put him through.' It might have been worthwhile coming in, after all. 'Hello, Brian. How are you?'

'I'm great, but unfortunately, I'm not calling with great news.'

I felt like going round to Mike's place and climbing into bed with him and the remains of the previous evening's whiskey.

'I've heard back from the bank and they're not going to lend me the money. It's taken a few days because the local guy needed to speak to his director.'

There was no point in getting upset and I tried to stay positive.

'Honestly, don't worry. If you like, I can get Peter to look for something with a few more miles on the clock. We should find a decent example for sixty to seventy thousand.'

'It would be great if you could. Anne's very disappointed. She's pretending not to be speaking to me!'

'Well, we can't have that. I'll get Peter straight on to it and we'll get back to you before the end of next week.'

I hung up and staggered over to Peter's desk.

'I didn't think he had the cash, but I'll come up with something. You stink of booze, Dad. Have one of these mints. In fact, take a couple. One won't be enough.'

'Thank you. It must feel good after all the times I told you off for coming home drunk.'

We both laughed. Matt had always been more of a party animal than his brother, but there was no holding Peter back when he let himself go.

'Joanna, is there any chance of another tea? I'm dying here,' I called across the showroom.

As she came over to my desk, a police car turned onto the forecourt and a couple of uniformed officers got out. Joanna turned to follow my gaze.

'This is all we need,' I moaned. 'You better go and see what they want.'

She reached the door as the police did and, after a brief exchange, she reluctantly brought them over to my desk.

'They would like to speak to you, Simon,' said Joanna, raising her eyebrows. 'It's a personal matter.'

I felt instinctively nervous as I stood to greet them. I could see from their expressions that this wasn't a social visit.

'How may I help you?' I asked, gesturing to the two empty chairs opposite my desk. 'Please take a seat.'

'Thank you, Sir. We won't be here long. I'm PC Wainwright and this is my colleague, WPC Carter. Is there somewhere private we could talk?'

There was only Mrs Davies' office, but she was busy getting the books ready for the inspection.

'Here will be fine. That's my son, Peter, over there and Joanna won't be able to hear us.'

'OK, Sir. That's no problem, but Peter should join us.'

I thought this was odd but waved for him to come over. They reminded me of the couple who'd come in for the Ferrari. Two dreary suburbanites. The only difference was the uniforms.

'Sorry, I should have asked,' continued the PC. 'Are you Mr Simon Duggan?'

I nodded in agreement.

'And you are Peter Duggan?'

'Yes,' said Peter, his eyes wide open with apprehension.

'And is Teresa Duggan your wife and mother, respectively?'

'Yes,' we both replied.

'Then I'm afraid we have some terrible news. Teresa Duggan was involved in a serious riding accident this morning. It would appear she lost control when a motorcycle spooked her horse on the Frankby Road; they were hit head-on by a passing truck.'

'Jackpot,' I muttered, shaking my head. I felt the adrenaline now surging through my veins, chasing the hangover from my body.

'I beg your pardon, Sir?' asked WPC Carter, with a puzzled look on her face.

From his expression, I had also aroused PC Cartwright's curiosity. The pair of them sat staring at me, waiting for my reply.

'The horse. He's called Jackpot,' I said, without emotion.

'Oh, I see,' said the WPC, looking relieved. 'Well, Jackpot, as you say, was killed at the scene. I'm very sorry to have to tell you that your wife has also died. They did everything they could to save her, but she had significant head injuries. My condolences to you both.'

She spoke in the strange, robotic way the police always adopt when announcing a disaster or a serious crime on the television. There wasn't a hint of emotion and it was as though she were reading from a script.

I was stunned and my mind couldn't even start to compute what I had been told.

After the happiness of the previous few days, it felt as if my life had come to an end with Teresa's.

I sat upright in my chair, shaking my head from side to side.

Nobody spoke for a minute or two until the silence was broken by the sound of Peter sobbing, his head gripped between his hands.

'I'm sorry, but we'll need one of you to identify her,' started the WPC.

'Y-yes. I understand. When do I need to go?' I asked, trying hard to remain focussed.

'As soon as you are ready. We wouldn't want to rush you, but it's always best to get this sort of thing over with.'

Tears welled up in my eyes as I wondered what state she would be in. Would they try and cover up her injuries, or would I be faced with a bloody, unrecognisable corpse? A tangled mass of flesh and bone. 'OK, but I'll need an hour or two to sort myself out,' I muttered, holding back my tears. 'You'll need to tell me where she is.'

'Of course, Sir. She's in the mortuary at Arrowe Park Hospital; it's well signposted when you get there,' replied PC Wainwright, with an affected air of solemnity.

Peter was now slumped in his chair, still sobbing, and Joanna came over with the box of tissues she kept at the reception for emergencies. Although she wouldn't have heard the conversation, she would have witnessed the scene of devastation as it unfolded and she looked quite shaken.

'Is it alright if I come too?' he asked the PC, clearing his throat and drying his tears.

'Of course, Sir,' he encouraged. 'Your father shouldn't have to go on his own.'

Our visitors rose to leave and Joanna went to escort them out of the showroom.

'I'd love to have a drive in that Ferrari,' whispered PC Wainwright to his colleague, as they walked past the row of cars.

They reminded me even more now of the Hardcastles and I was relieved to see them head off towards West Kirby.

'That was pretty insensitive, but I suppose it's part of their job,' said Joanna, pulling a chair close to Peter.

Mrs Davies had been watching from her office and went to lock the showroom door before coming over to join us.

'I'm so sorry, Mr Duggan, Peter. I remember when I received news of my late husband's death. I was devastated. But I tell you what, I'll pop out and get us all something to eat. The last thing you need at a time like this is an empty stomach.'

'Thank you, Mrs Davies,' I replied as I watched her head off, organised and purposeful as ever.

*

Joanna stayed with Peter and me, passing my son tissues as I sat upright and immobile, staring into space. The gleaming cars didn't mean anything to me anymore. Our lives would never be the same again.

As soon as she returned, we were all ushered into her office. 'I've got a selection of sandwiches and some crisps. It wouldn't do to have crumbs all over the showroom. Darren offered to sit at the reception. He's such a nice young man.'

'I can't eat anything, Mrs Davies,' I said, looking across at Peter, who had put his head back between his hands.

'That's nonsense, Mr Duggan. When Captain Davies was taken from me, I was in and out of the fridge for weeks. It was the shock.'

Looking for the champagne, more than likely. The sad news of Captain Davies' death would have been relieved by the fact that her well-ordered life would no longer be disturbed by his inconsiderate visits home on leave.

'Oh, my God!' said Peter, raising his head, his eyes red and bloodshot. 'What about Matt? We have to call him. I'll try to get him on his mobile.'

We all watched as he went outside and I could only imagine Matt's terrible reaction at the other end of the phone.

'He'll meet us at the hospital,' Peter told us when he came back into the office.

'Fine,' I muttered. 'We'll leave as soon as we've cleared all this up.'

'Don't you worry, Mr Duggan,' said Mrs Davies, forcing a smile. 'Joanna and I will deal with it. You both go and do what you have to.'

Once again, she had shown how loyal she was, and I was embarrassed by my uncharitable thoughts.

*

I was now in a state of shock, but Peter had brought his emotions back under control, for the time being at least, and offered to drive us to the hospital.

When we arrived, Matt was outside the mortuary, leaning against his van. He wasn't the happy young man eating his breakfast from only a few hours ago. His eyes were fixed on the ground and his face was a deathly white. As he took a last draw on his cigarette, he looked like a condemned man, minutes from death.

'How could this happen? Why now?' he shouted. 'It's not fucking fair. It's not right.'

All I could do was to shake my head in agreement.

'I mean, what had she done to deserve this?' he continued. 'Nothing; nothing at all. And then you see all those people who deserve to die living happily ever fucking after. Why can't they fucking die instead?'

A small group of people had gathered to watch from the other side of the car park and a matronly-looking nurse left them to come over to us.

'Is there anything I can do?' she asked, putting a hand on Matt's shoulder.

'Not if you can't bring my mother back to life, and I don't suppose you do that on the NHS.'

'I'm sorry, but we've all had a terrible shock,' I explained. 'It's best if we get inside.'

'There's no rush. It's not as though she's going anywhere,' snapped Matt before Peter took his arm and started to lead him away.

'Thank you for caring,' I offered as the nurse turned to go. 'But no one can help us right now.'

*

'Good afternoon, Gentlemen,' greeted a young nurse as we entered the mortuary.

Opposite the reception desk, there were several comfortable chairs and a table decorated with a vase of fresh flowers and glossy magazines. There was even a copy of *Cheshire Life*.

Everything possible had been done to provide a calm and reassuring sanctuary for the bereaved. Yet, I couldn't help thinking that this was spoilt by notices taped all over the walls telling us not to assault staff and everything else the NHS thought we needed to know.

'Good afternoon. We've come to identify my mother's body,' replied Peter. 'It's Teresa Duggan.' With me in shock and Matt out of control, he knew he would have to take charge.

'Oh, yes, our new arrival. Let me call the doctor. I'll only keep you a minute.'

He appeared almost immediately. He was my age, tall, slim and starting to bald, with a bearing that inspired immediate confidence.

'Hello, I'm Dr Murray. Do come this way. Have you brought some identification?'

'I haven't brought anything. I had thought it was only my wife who had to be identified. Peter, you usually have something,' I suggested, feeling completely useless.

'Will this do?' he asked, stepping forward and producing his driver's licence from his wallet. 'I'm her son.'

'Of course, Mr Duggan. We only need one of you to sign the papers. Please follow me.'

We arrived in a large, bright room, and we could make out the shape of a body, covered with a white sheet on a trolley.

'We haven't had time to put her into cold storage,' explained Dr Murray.

'Thank God for that,' I muttered. I wasn't ready to see my wife in a refrigerator drawer like a pack of meat.

'I am going to have to pull back the sheet,' he said, looking at each of us in turn.

We all nodded. Matt was shaking and Peter retook his upper arm while I grabbed him from the other side. My legs were giving way and I wanted to pee myself, but I could feel Peter's strength and it helped me keep control.

As I gulped and drew a deep breath, I heard Matt whimper like a lost puppy. Only Peter stood silent and motionless in front of his mother's lifeless body.

Her face was beautiful and she looked relaxed, almost happy. The damage must have been to the back of her head.

She looked so normal that I almost believed she would open her eyes, smile and ask us what we wanted for dinner.

The doctor looked at Peter, not saying a word.

'Yes,' said Peter. 'It's her. It's my mother.'

'I'm so sorry. My wife's a keen rider. She knew your mother well,' he continued before stopping himself. 'So, Peter. I suppose you're going to look after the formalities – that will be a great help to your father. Nurse Edwards will give you my medical certificate and a booklet explaining everything. I'm afraid there's a lot to sort out, but there's support should you need it.'

He was professional but pleasant and I could imagine how he and his wife could have been our friends.

We thanked him and Matt and I went outside, abandoning Peter with the nurse.

As soon as we were in the car park, Matt lit another cigarette and took a deep draw.

'For Christ's sake. Can't you stop that; at least for today?' I yelled. 'If you carry on smoking at this rate, it won't be long before you're alongside your mother!'

'I wish I was already there,' he blurted out, bursting into tears.

'I'm sorry,' I apologised, trying to stay calm. 'I shouldn't have said that. Come on; give me a fag. It will help my nerves.'

Matt waved the packet towards me and I pulled out a cigarette, lighting it and taking a deep breath.

'This is my first cigarette in almost twenty years! At least we'll die together,' I choked as the nicotine flooded my body.

The shock of seeing Teresa had left me numb and I waited in

silence with Matt until Peter emerged from the mortuary clutching a handful of papers.

'OK, Pete?' I asked calmly. He nodded.

'Come on then, lads, let's go home.'

NINE

THE DAY AFTER

Saturday morning marked the second time that week I had woken with a hangover.

It had been a difficult evening.

When we arrived home, Peter and Matt had gone off to their rooms, preferring to deal with their grief alone. I stayed in the kitchen with only my thoughts and a couple of glasses of Glenmorangie for company. Around 7pm, I went upstairs to wake the boys, telling them to take a shower while I got dinner ready.

There wasn't much in the fridge, so I heated up one of Teresa's pre-cooked dinners from the freezer. A lamb curry which I had bubbling away in the oven by the time I heard the boys' footsteps on the stairs.

'This is very tasty. It's odd to think of Mum cooking it, not knowing she wouldn't be alive to enjoy it,' said Matt, tears filling his eyes.

Peter looked at him, open-mouthed, but I waved for him to let it go; each of us would deal with his loss in his own way.

I was floating in a fourth dimension, detached from reality, but I sensed a fragility in Matt that I had never seen. My big worry was Peter, who was retreating even further into his protective shell.

It was the first evening I had spent with both of my sons in years. It had taken Teresa's death to bring us together, but I couldn't stop looking towards the back door, hoping she would appear. We were all trying to come to terms with what had happened. After Matt's comment, we sat in silence for a while, eating the curry and drinking red wine.

I was resigned to going off on my own to the study for a nightcap when Matt put down his knife and fork on his empty plate and looked up at Peter and me.

'Well, that's the end of the curry. What else has Mother got waiting for us in the deep-freeze?' he asked, with a grim smile, tears streaming down his face.

Peter looked at me for my reaction, but it was the icebreaker we had needed.

I opened another bottle of wine and tried to get the boys to talk about their mother.

I told stories about how she would cluck around like an overprotective hen, big, slobbering Bruno making sure they didn't get into trouble. He had been like a brother to them.

There had been a summer's day when they were young and we had all gone down to Caldy beach to play together in the sand. I had helped the boys build a castle with four towers and a moat.

'It needs some water to finish it off,' I suggested.

The tide was in and they ran off down towards the water's edge, only to be rounded up by Bruno and brought back to their parents, their buckets still empty.

'He's a bad dog,' cried Matt, in floods of tears.

It seemed so long ago and, of course, it was. There was a lot less to say about what we had all done together in recent years.

They started to share memories of their own, but we were all avoiding talking about the future. Matt was the first to summon the courage.

'Our lives will never be the same. We're not a family anymore, are we?' he asked, clumsily refilling his glass.

'It will be no different to how it's always been,' replied Peter, opening another bottle and pouring himself a glass. 'I'm sorry, Dad, but we've never been a family – not a proper one.'

For a second, I reeled with the shock of Peter's comment. This was a time when we should have been sticking together.

'But what about the running around your mother and I did for you both? You never wanted for anything. And the trips we've been talking about? I worked hard to make sure everyone got what they needed.'

'Yes, when it suited you, but what about love?' Peter pressed. 'All you cared for was your business and the bloody house. Everything else had to fit around that. Sometimes I even wondered whether you were my father.'

'Well, I'm sorry, but a real son would have appreciated everything you've been given. I've even handed you your career on a plate, for God's sake.'

Peter stared at me and shrugged. This had not been a helpful reply and I grabbed the bottle from him to refill my glass.

'The problem is,' he continued, not to be discouraged, 'you've got a selective memory. It's like remembering that summers were warm and sunny and that it always snowed on Christmas Day. But it wasn't like that, was it, Matt?'

His brother could only shrug a reply, looking across at me, his eyes filling up with tears again.

'I mean, it's no wonder Mum spent every weekend with Jackpot. What did she have here? You at the garage or shut away in that study of yours with your whisky and your precious books.'

I didn't have an answer for him.

*

It was ten in the morning and I was alone in the kitchen when the doorbell startled me from my musings.

I was not expecting anyone and I hurried to the front door.

It was Joanna, standing against a backdrop of darkening rain clouds, moving in from the Irish Sea. She looked radiant as ever, wrapped up in an immaculate trench coat that wasn't used to being out in bad weather.

'I hope I'm not bothering you, Simon? I wanted to see if you were OK. And Mrs Davies asked me to say she's thinking about you all – she didn't want to call.'

'Of course you're not bothering me. Come into the warm. You'll catch your death out there.' I immediately regretted my choice of words.

I put the kettle on and Joanna explained that Darren would be looking after the showroom. Mrs Davies would be there to support him.

'That's kind of them. I had been hoping to go in later, but I don't think I'll be up to it.'

'You need to spend time with your sons before thinking about anything else, Simon,' replied Joanna, giving me a puzzled look.

'You're right, but I want to get back to work next week. Sitting here feeling sorry for myself won't do me any good.'

She shook her head and forced a smile.

'I almost forgot. Mum said the three of you must come to ours for lunch tomorrow. She said about one o'clock.'

Peter appeared before I could answer, still perfectly groomed, closely followed by Matt.

'Hi, Joanna,' greeted Peter. 'How are you?'

'I'm fine, but what about you guys? I can't imagine what you must be going through. I was telling your father that Mum wants you all to come over for lunch tomorrow.'

Peter and Matt looked at each other, unsure how to reply.

'And why don't I take you to the Wro Lounge this evening for a meal? You too, Simon. It will be better than staying here, drinking yourselves stupid,' she continued, eyeing the empty bottles next to the back door.

Her invitation surprised me and I didn't know how to reply. There could be nothing wrong with having a meal out, away from the house and our grief, but somehow it didn't feel right.

'I'm not sure, Joanna. It's kind of you, but it's a bit soon.'

I looked towards the boys for support, but they didn't look back at me.

'Come on, boys. What do you think?' I asked.

'Well, I'm not happy about it,' replied Peter, glaring at me. 'How can I enjoy myself when Mum is lying in a mortuary? I mean, Sunday lunch at a friends' house, why not? But an evening out. It's not right.'

'And you, Matt. What do you want to do?' I asked.

Matt carried on staring at the floor and shrugged, shaking his head.

Joanna looked across at me with an embarrassed expression on her face, but I knew what I had to say.

'I'm sorry, Joanna, but Peter's right. It's too soon for us to be going out to a restaurant.'

Peter stared up at me again, with a look of triumph on his face. 'Yes, we'll be fine here. We'll manage somehow,' he said.

'Well, you and Matt can make supper this evening, or must I warm up another of your mother's frozen meals?' I shouted, not expecting an answer.

Joanna looked disappointed as she gathered up her coat and set off towards the front door.

'Joanna, wait,' I called. 'Lunch tomorrow. Tell your mother we'll be there. It will be good for us.'

'That's great,' she replied, forcing a smile. 'I'll see you all then but try not to drink too much this evening. You know what state my mother will be in and I may need some help.'

*

The doorbell rang again just as I went to sit down.

It was Mrs Williams, struggling to protect a bunch of roses from the rain.

'Good morning, Mr Duggan. I know I'm not usually here on a Saturday, but I wanted to come and give you a hand.'

'Of course. Come on through. We're about to have some tea and toast.'

As she shrugged off her heavy overcoat, I was pleased to see she wasn't in her pink tracksuit. She was wearing a smart dark grey dress, with a large rose brooch paying tribute to the flowers she had brought. Her hair was under the control of a bandeau and she looked as if she had arrived a few days early for Teresa's funeral.

'Mrs Davies telephoned me last night with your dreadful news but let me get these into some water. They'll cheer the place up a bit. Roses always were her favourite.'

'Teresa loved having flowers all over the place,' I replied, watching her getting a vase and filling it with water. 'I always complained about the cost, but they did make our home bright and happy.'

I went back to the boys at the kitchen table and Mrs Williams started emptying the dishwasher.

'There are a lot of empty bottles. Did you have friends over?' she asked.

'Not at all, but we were up very late. It was a difficult evening for us.'

'I can imagine. I was devastated when I heard what had happened. Teresa was such a lovely lady. She was very kind when my Arthur passed away. I've been thinking, though,' she continued, instinctively starting to wipe the worktops. 'My niece, Sarah, is staying with me at the moment. She's graduated from some smart cookery school. What's it called now? It's run by one of those celebrity chefs. Oh, yes, that's it – Marco Blanc.'

Out of the corner of my eye, I could see Peter and Matt looking at each other, wondering where this was heading.

'Well, she got her diploma. It cost her father a fortune. He owns a Caribbean art gallery in Notting Hill. It's quite trendy – you can imagine. How he ended up with my sister, I've no idea. A simple girl from North Wales. So where was I?'

'Your niece, Mrs Williams.'

This wasn't the time for one of her rambling stories, I thought, motioning to Peter to sit down as he started to get up.

'Oh, yes. She wanted to work in one of those fancy London restaurants, but they offered her jobs right at the bottom. She's only twenty-four, after all.'

'I suppose we all have to start somewhere,' I reflected.

'That's what everyone told her, but she expected to go in higher up after her expensive course. Anyway, it became too much for her and she's come here to spend some time away from London.'

She seemed to have finished and I breathed a sigh of relief. I was struggling with a hangover and, after the discussion with Joanna, I wasn't in the mood for conversation.

'Now that brings me back to what I wanted to say,' she started off again, after a brief pause. 'Don't think I'm taking advantage, but how about Sarah gives you a hand for a month or so? Until you get yourselves sorted out? I'll carry on as usual, but Sarah could do the cooking and everything else Teresa used to look after. She's a good cook. You can imagine.'

It made me think how much Teresa used to do without our notice or appreciation. The boys and I had always imagined that the house looked after itself and there was no way we would manage on our own.

'When could she start?' I asked.

'Don't you want to meet her first?'

'If you're vouching for her, that's good enough for me,' I insisted.

'That's settled, then. I did speak to her this morning and she's keen to give it a go. If it doesn't work out, she can always come back to stay with me.'

The boys and I exchanged worried glances.

'You mean she'll be living here with us?'

'Of course. If she's doing your meals, you can't expect her to be running backwards and forwards to West Kirby at all hours. It's not as if you don't have the room.'

'Let's not rush into anything, Dad,' said Peter. 'We should wait a couple of days to see where we all are before making any big decisions.'

Peter was starting to annoy me in his new role as the family's moral guardian. He did have a point, but as Mrs Williams had explained, her niece could always stay with her if it didn't work out.

'What do you think, Matt? Having another person around the house could be good for us,' I asked, trying to bring him into the discussion.

He shrugged his shoulders and I thought for a couple of minutes before turning back to Mrs Williams.

'Alright, we'll give it a try, but I hope she realises what she'll be getting herself into,' I replied. 'It's not exactly going to be Jolly Manor here.'

Mrs Williams must have found it difficult sharing a small, terraced house with her niece, and this arrangement would suit her as much if not more than us.

'There's one other thing, Mr Duggan. She'll need a car to run around in. In your business, I'm sure you'll have something available?'

This was a lot for me to take in at once. She would want paying as well, but we could agree on the details later.

'Of course, I'll sort it out.'

'That is kind. Shall I drop her over here later today, then? About four o'clock?'

'That would be perfect. We're going to Nicola Gilmore's for lunch tomorrow. Sarah can come along and meet her daughter, Joanna – they're the same age. Pete, you'll need to call Joanna and tell her there'll be an extra person.'

Peter nodded, looking at Matt with a raised eyebrow. Keeping him on side over the coming weeks was going to be a challenge.

'That's great. We'll see you at four,' replied Mrs Williams, picking up her handbag and heading back out into the rain.

*

After a mug of tea and a slice of toast, I was ready to go back to bed for a few hours.

'Peter, I would like to talk about what you said yesterday evening, but I'm not up to it right now.'

My son got up and took my mug with his over to the dishwasher before turning back to face me.

'I'm surprised you can remember, the state we were all in, but I did mean what I said, even if I'm sorry to have hurt you. Anyway, tell me when you're ready.'

He looked determined and Matt stared at the table with embarrassment.

'Thanks for that,' I replied. 'I'm going upstairs to rest for a while and you boys might want to do the same. I'll see you both later.'

*

I was woken by a bedroom door being closed. When I arrived downstairs, Mrs Williams was waiting for me in the kitchen.

'I hope you don't mind, but Sarah and I have come over a bit earlier. I wanted her to settle in before she makes your evening meal – she's upstairs unpacking her things.'

I smiled my agreement.

'I gave her the bedroom at the end of the corridor on the first floor, the one with a nice sea view. She's only brought one suitcase for the time being. She'll come back over to my house for the rest of her belongings in the week.'

I started to wonder how long she would be staying with us.

'That's fine,' I replied. 'I guess that, once she knew she was coming here, there was no point in staying over at yours all afternoon.'

'Thank you, Mr Duggan. Now, I'll make you all a big pot of tea. It's what you need on a cold, wet afternoon like this. I've brought a bara brith that I'll get into the toaster once the boys are here.'

Bara brith is a currant loaf Mrs Williams made to a recipe passed down through the generations. I loved it toasted and smothered in butter.

Our talking had woken the boys and a few minutes later, they were sitting with me at the kitchen table.

Matt was struggling to keep his eyes open. As he started to doze off, the door to the main hallway opened and in walked Sarah.

She had a lovely smile. We were captivated by her beauty, a fusion of the tropical Caribbean islands and the Celtic hills of Snowdonia.

Woken from his slumber, Matt was the first on his feet, followed by Peter and me.

'Come and sit down, Sarah,' I said, gesturing to an empty chair. 'We're having afternoon tea.'

'Thank you. I'm ready for a cuppa after all that unpacking and bed-making. It was a good thing I didn't have to bring everything over today, especially in this rain.'

She had an upmarket London accent and she wore Armani jeans, a crisp white shirt and black suede loafers that would have been at home on Sloane Square.

'I'm sure your aunt has told you a lot more about us than she's told us about you, but I'm Simon.'

'It's lovely to meet you, Simon. I'm so sorry about your loss. My aunt was beside herself when she heard the news. She went straight for the bottle of sherry she keeps in the pantry for medicinal purposes. There wasn't a drop left by the time she went to bed.' Mrs Williams eyed her uncomfortably.

She was charming, but I sensed the boys were intimidated by her confidence. It took Matt to break the silence.

'I'm Matt,' he said with an embarrassed grin. 'And hardly anything your aunt has told you about me is true.'

She looked at him with a raised eyebrow before turning to Peter, who introduced himself with his usual charm. He was watched enviously by his younger brother.

'So, you work with your father at that fab garage up on the hill? I'd love to own one of those cars. Will you take me out for a drive one day? We can cruise along West Kirby promenade in a beautiful convertible, waving to all the old ladies.'

Mrs Williams glared across the kitchen, ignored by her niece.

'If he doesn't, I'll take you out in my van, but I'll have to give it a good clean first,' joked Matt, not to be left out. We all laughed.

'That would be lovely, Matt. My aunt told me you're a gas and fluids engineer?' She gave a broad grin.

'That's the nicest description I've heard for a long time,' he replied.

'And you, Simon. What do you get up to when you're not selling cars or trying to keep these two under control?'

'Between work and what I do around here, there's no time for anything other than a quick whisky before bed.'

Peter looked at me as if I had confirmed everything he had said the previous evening, and this was not lost on Sarah.

'Well, we'll have to change that, won't we?' she answered, looking between Peter and Matt for their support.

I hoped it wasn't too late. I was sure Sarah would settle in with our reduced and dysfunctional family, and her presence in our home could only be for the better.

*

I was feeling quite tired again after the introductions. Once I had finished my tea, I left Sarah chatting to the boys and went off to enjoy the peace and tranquillity of my study.

It was too early for a whisky and I was not in the mood for any serious reading.

In my armchair next to the desk, surrounded by shelves full of books, I sat looking through the French door into the rain-drenched garden.

Everything was being blown back and forth in the wind. I smiled as I watched a green woodpecker hopping across the lawn, pecking at the poor creatures trying to escape a watery death down in the wet earth.

I had been staggered by what Peter had said the previous evening and his behaviour during Joanna's visit had been out of character.

Had he meant what he had said to me? I asked myself, or was it a reaction to his mother's death? Either way, we would still be living and working together, and I would need to deal with him as soon as possible.

I wondered what he had discussed with his mother and the image of her face on the mortuary table filled my mind.

What was she thinking about during those last few moments before she died? I wondered. Her wasted life, our new start?

As I sat there struggling with these thoughts, a wave of tiredness came over me and I closed my eyes. As Matt had said, I would have been better off if I had died alongside her and had finally found some peace.

*

There was a gentle knock on the study door and I opened my eyes as it slowly opened. It was Sarah.

'It's six o'clock, Simon. I've made some supper for us. You have to eat, you know,' she added when she saw my expression.

I nodded with a sigh, struggling to keep my eyes open as I got to my feet and followed her through to the kitchen.

The boys were already there, huddled together on the opposite side of the table.

I hardly recognised Matt. He had shaved and brushed his hair, and he and Peter looked like brothers for the first time I could remember.

'That's my shirt,' whispered Peter. 'You should have asked me first. And what about those shoes?'

'Stop moaning. I've never seen you wearing this stuff anyway.'

'That's not the point – ask next time!'

Sarah ignored them, getting the plates out of the warmer and putting them on the table next to a steaming bowl of pasta.

'My aunt and I popped out to get some supplies when you were all asleep,' she explained. 'There was nothing at all in the fridge.'

Teresa did her *big-shop*, as she called it, on a Friday afternoon, ready for the weekend.

'Let me get us some wine,' I suggested, now wide awake. 'If Peter doesn't object, that is.'

He gave me a look of contempt, but I ignored him as I sat down, placing a bottle of Chianti and four glasses in front of me.

'I'll pour,' he said, grabbing the bottle. 'Are you OK with red, Sarah?'

She nodded, reaching over to take the glass Peter had filled for her.

'Back in civilisation at last,' she said, taking a sip. 'I love my aunt dearly, but a week was more than enough. Have you been to her house?'

'No. I dropped her off once when she was having her car serviced, but that's as close as I've been.'

'It hasn't been touched since my uncle died years ago. It's like a museum.'

'It was kind of her to have you to stay, though,' I suggested.

'Of course, she's a kind lady, but we've nothing in common, even if we are family.'

The pasta was delicious, Penne Alfredo with ham and broccoli. The comfort food we all needed for a wet and miserable evening.

'I added some white wine to the cream sauce,' explained Sarah, as I put some green salad on the side of my plate. 'There's extra parmesan if you want it, but there's already quite a bit in there.'

I smiled before loading up my fork with another mouthful.

'It's delicious, Sarah. Thank you for making this for us,' I said. 'I guess the boys will be doing the washing up.'

Matt laughed, but Peter was silent. He was focused on eating and sending text messages from his mobile phone.

'Your aunt told us about your cookery course in London. What are you doing up here in the North of England?' I asked. 'Not that we aren't happy to have you here.'

Sarah sighed before answering. 'I had this idea of doing something interesting, not starting at the bottom, chopping vegetables. I couldn't find the right job anywhere.'

I tried to look sympathetic.

'But it's my fault and my dad is furious. He had to sell a couple of paintings from his collection to pay the school fees.'

'Your aunt said he has a gallery in Notting Hill,' said Matt, feeling a little left out of the conversation.

'It's more like Holland Park. He specialises in Afro-Caribbean painting and sculpture. Recently, he's been looking for some good examples of Afro-European fusion. A bit like me, I suppose,' she said, with a wide smile.

Even Peter laughed. Despite what he had said, having Sarah around was going to be a great help to us.

'And what are your plans now?' asked Matt.

'I don't know. That's why Dad sent me up here. He hoped the fresh sea air would help me to see things more clearly. I had wondered about asking him to help me open a restaurant near his gallery,' she answered.

'That would be cool,' added Matt.

'Yes, but it's not a good time to bring it up. I might have to stay here with you guys forever! You're all so nice.'

I choked as I emptied my glass and poured another one. We were all engrossed in Sarah's story, apart from Peter, who was still texting.

I gestured across the table to Matt, who elbowed him in the ribs, glaring at his phone. He apologised and put it in his trouser pocket.

'We all need a bit of luck sometimes, Sarah,' I said, grinning. 'That's how I managed to get into the motor trade.'

'Well, if you have any going spare, I could do with a bit coming my way,' she replied. She blushed as she remembered why she was with us.

There was an embarrassed silence and Peter started to send another text until he saw the look on my face.

'I don't know how you can all sit here chatting away as if nothing has happened. Your wife's body is hardly cold, for fuck's sake. Anyway, I'm off to my room,' he almost shouted, throwing back his chair and heading off into the hallway.

Sarah didn't know where to look and got up to clear away the empty plates.

'He'll be fine once he's had a good night's sleep,' I said without conviction.

Sarah would have to deal with more scenes like this over the next few weeks and I hoped that it wouldn't be too much for her.

Our home was never going to have been Jolly Manor, but how would she cope living at *Bleak House*, I wondered.

*

I was annoyed by Peter's outburst.

It had seemed odd to sit around a table and enjoy a good meal and wine with a stranger, but what did he expect us to do? Sit in silence or eat our meals in our rooms?

Resisting the temptation to return to my study, I took a waxed jacket from the cloakroom and headed out into the rain.

I didn't know where I was going, but I had to get away from the house to clear my brain.

I started to walk downhill towards Caldy beach, where Teresa and I had spent many evenings cuddled up in the back of my mother's car when we were young.

It was still daylight and my walk took me past some of the finest houses in the area, but this did nothing to improve my mood.

Why has all this happened? I kept asking myself. How have we arrived at this point?

The same questions kept turning in my head. Before long, my warm tears were mixing with the cold rain running down my face.

The gusts of wind had become much stronger and I was pushed from one side of the pavement to the other as I walked.

By the time I arrived at the beach, I was drenched and fed up. But now I was there, what could I do? Walk back home again?

A solitary Clio was parked at the side of the road, its windows misted up. As I drew alongside, the driver's door opened.

'Is that you, Simon?' shouted Joanna through the wind and rain. 'Get in, for God's sake.'

Without saying a word, I climbed inside in my wet clothes.

Joanna's eyes were red and she was crying. There were crumpled tissues all over the floor.

'What are you doing out in this weather?' she asked through her tears.

I shook my head but didn't reply. She understood.

I was shivering and Joanna started the engine and turned on the air-conditioning.

The sun was setting in the west and neither of us spoke as we watched day become night. We didn't need to.

The warm air coming through the vents cleared the condensation from the windows and I could just make out the lights on the Welsh coast, far away across the estuary.

How I wished I could be over there. Up in the hills of Snowdonia, far away from everything that was happening.

Eventually, Joanna put her hand on mine. 'I'm here for you, Simon. You know I am.'

'And I'm here for you, Joanna.'

*

Without another word, Joanna drove us back to the house. As we pulled into the drive, I saw the light go off in Peter's bedroom.

'Would you like to come in for a drink?' I asked before opening the car door.

'I'd love to, Simon. There's only so much crying I can do on my own,' she replied, trying to smile.

'We shouldn't stay up too late,' I said. 'We've got lunch tomorrow.'

'I shouldn't worry,' replied Joanna. 'Mother will be drunk as usual!'

'Well, she has always made us very welcome.'

Matt and Sarah had gone off to their rooms and I took Joanna through to the living room before getting our drinks.

When I came back, I sat next to her on a sofa.

After her silence in the car, the warmth of the room and the alcohol soon brought her back to life.

Sitting closely together, I felt strangely relaxed. I listened as Joanna explained how upset she had been that her father had not come back home for the weekend. Like me, she had been trying to escape from her house and all its memories.

I got some more drinks and it was Joanna's turn to listen. I told her about how Sarah had come to stay with us and about Peter's outburst over dinner.

'What a pair we are, she said, touching my arm. 'Don't you think you should go up and see if he's alright?'

'No, he'll be fine in the morning,' I answered, hoping I was right.

Joanna turned to stare into what was left of her drink as though it held the meaning of life.

'But how about you. Will you be OK?' I asked.

'I will, I promise. I'm worn out, I suppose. It's been a difficult couple of days.'

I started to feel very tired and put my empty glass on the table next to the sofa.

'It has. Anyway, you need to get home. I'll get your coat.'

'Would you mind walking with me? I don't want to drive after the vodka, but I hate to be out on my own when it's dark like this.'

'It's the least I can do. I could do with some fresh air.'

*

The wind had dropped. As we walked, I remembered how I would walk Teresa home when we were young, holding hands and stopping every now and again for a kiss at the side of the road. The memory made me smile, but when Joanna took my hand in hers, I felt very uncomfortable.

When we arrived at her house, it was in darkness, apart from two carriage lights that guided us to a pair of double oak doors, protected inside a sandstone porchway.

'Thanks for this evening, Joanna,' I said, as we sheltered together out of the rain. 'You need to be getting inside.'

In our attempt to keep dry, our bodies were almost touching and Joanna was still holding my hand. Her eyes were shining as they met mine.

'Goodnight, Simon,' she replied, smiling. 'I'll see you tomorrow.'

'Goodnight,' I replied, leaning forward to kiss her on the cheek.

She turned her head and my lips landed on hers, her hands pulling me towards her as her tongue entered my mouth.

I was in a state of complete panic.

'We can't do this,' I said, pulling away. 'It's not right.'

'Why?' she asked. 'We're both single.'

'Single! Think about what you're saying, Joanna? Teresa's only been dead for a day.'

'And?' she replied, looking me straight in the eyes. 'I know you find me attractive. I saw how you were looking at me in the car last Tuesday.'

Her comment caught me off my guard and I was too slow to resist as she pulled me back towards her, kissing me and running her hands through my hair.

Anyone passing by would have seen us in the light of the doorway; what if her mother had heard us coming up the drive?

I knew how wrong this was, but it was useless. It was as if I had lost control of the emotions I had been trying to suppress over the last twenty-four hours.

Eventually, I pulled myself free, breathless and full of shame.

'We shouldn't have done this. It mustn't happen again. I'm serious.'

She looked at me, smiling. 'Don't say that. It was lovely and don't pretend you didn't like it. From what I felt pressing against my stomach, I'd say you enjoyed yourself.'

I had enjoyed myself, but as I walked back home, I struggled to deal with what had happened. Had I been reliving the days when Teresa and I were young and carefree or was I looking for an emotional refuge? Either way, it was the worst thing I had ever done.

TEN

SUNDAY

It was Sunday morning and for once I didn't have a hangover.

I rolled over and felt for Teresa's warm body, but as soon as I realised I was alone, the memory of the previous evening came flooding back.

Saturday was to have been the beginning of her promised weekend to remember. Instead, I had snogged the daughter of two of my best friends in front of their home.

I had betrayed Teresa, the boys and my friends, but I couldn't ignore what was happening inside my pyjamas.

This was a dangerous situation. Although I had a genuine affection for Joanna, it could go no further.

When I saw her, I would make it clear that there could never be a repeat of what had happened in the doorway of her parents' house.

The smell of bacon was drifting up from the kitchen. As I lay there, wrestling with my conscience, my rumbling stomach told me it wanted feeding.

I pulled on a dressing gown and went downstairs, hoping I wouldn't be too embarrassed when I saw my sons.

Sarah was there at what, two days earlier, had been Teresa's post in front of the AGA, stirring a pot of baked beans. She seemed to be settling in very quickly – a bit too quickly, perhaps.

'Good morning,' she greeted. 'It's all ready. I'll do the eggs once you tell me how you like them.'

The table was already laid, with a large jug of orange juice next to Mrs Williams' roses.

'I thought you could do with a good breakfast this morning. It was quite late when I heard you come back last night.'

I couldn't help myself blushing but felt it was best not to try to explain where I had been.

'Thank you,' I replied. 'Teresa used to enjoy making us a cooked breakfast when the boys were younger, but the last couple of years, it's been rare for us to be together at the weekends.'

We were interrupted by the sound of someone coming down the stairs and we both turned to see Matt arrive.

He was looking bright and fresh in clothes I imagined he had borrowed from his brother, hopefully with his agreement this time.

'That smells great,' said Matt, looking over at the cooker.

'Thank you.' Sarah smiled. 'I'm enjoying cooking it for you.' He smiled back at her, awkward with embarrassment.

'Have you seen Peter?' I asked.

'He was fast asleep when I crept into his room. I guess he'll be down when he's ready.'

Peter didn't usually like to stay in bed in the morning and I feared this was the beginning of the breakdown I had been dreading.

*

The breakfast was what I needed.

'I can see I'll have to spend more time in the gym if you keep feeding us like this,' I said when my plate was spotless. 'Come on, Matt, let's give Sarah a hand tidying up before we get ready for lunch. We're due there at one.'

'Do we have to go?' he asked. 'It will be awful, stuck there with that pickled old trout moaning about her husband.'

'It will be fine, and stop being nasty about Nicola. Joanna will be there and Sarah's coming along too.'

I thought Sarah might keep Joanna occupied and we could pretend the previous evening had never happened.

'Are you sure?' asked Sarah. 'I don't want to impose.'

'Don't be silly. Peter called Nicola yesterday and she was delighted. Frankly, the more, the better, especially if she's under the weather.'

*

By ten o'clock, Peter still hadn't appeared and I went up to wake him. I had a good idea of the scene waiting for me and hesitated before turning the door handle.

My worst fears were confirmed as soon as I stepped inside the room. The lights were off and I could only just make out the form of his body, curled up in the foetus position under his duvet.

'Come on, Pete. It's time to get up. Do you want me to run you a bath?' I asked.

'Why don't you fuck off. I'm not coming to this stupid lunch. You and Matt can go with your girlfriends. At least one of us has some respect for our mother,' he replied, pulling a pillow over his head.

I panicked at the thought of my son seeing me arriving home with Joanna. Perhaps he had seen her car parked in the drive all night?

'Your mother would have wanted us to be with our friends,' I replied. 'But how dare you; since when have you had a monopoly on grief?'

'Grief? You don't know the meaning of the word. That's always been your problem. You're only interested in how much cash you've got in the bank,' he shouted from under the covers. 'There's something wrong with you; a big fucking disability. I'm surprised you haven't got a blue badge for the car.'

I had promised him a discussion, but there could be no reasoning with him in this frame of mind and I tried to keep calm.

'Now, look, you're upset,' I explained. 'We all are and this isn't helping anyone. You're going to get up, shower, get dressed and come to lunch with the rest of us. And you'll be nice to our hosts. That is non-negotiable. Nicola has her shit to deal with and she doesn't need you acting like a spoilt child.'

It was the first time I had spoken to Peter like that since he was a teenager. He threw the pillow to the floor before rolling onto his back, glaring up at me with a mixture of hatred and despair.

My face became hot with the blood rushing into my cheeks and my hands were shaking with anger.

It wasn't a question of whether Peter was right or not.

This was the breakdown I knew was coming, but I couldn't allow him to act like this, for his sake and his family's.

*

Peter joined us all downstairs several hours later. He was as well-groomed as ever and we set off in the spring sunshine, a sea breeze brushing the leaves of the silver birch trees that covered most of Caldy.

I was relieved that Joanna's car had disappeared; she must have come over to pick it up while we were having breakfast.

I expected some comment from Peter, but he was pretending I wasn't there and walking on the far side of the pavement. At least he's with us, I thought.

Before we could ring the bell, the door was flung open by Nicola. In contrast with Monday evening, she looked fantastic, dressed in a simple but stylish black dress with no sign of the grey roots or slippers.

'Hello, everybody. Thanks so much for coming over. You must be Sarah? Joanna's told me all about you. Welcome to our home.'

'Thank you, Mrs Gilmore. It was kind of you to invite me,' replied Sarah, smiling.

'Nonsense, it's a pleasure. And call me Nicola. Now go on through to the living room, the three of you. But not you, Simon, I need to see you on your own.'

I tried to smile, but I felt a sinking feeling in my stomach. I was certain she had seen Joanna and me kissing in the doorway the night before. There would be nothing I could say that could make that right.

I followed her through into her vast, ultra-modern kitchen. It was a dazzling composition in brilliant-white and stainless steel. The sterility was broken only by a fresh bunch of rosemary on the worktop and the delicious smell of roasting lamb.

Once we were on our own, she closed the door behind us.

Nicola turned to face me, standing with her back to the door as if to prevent me from leaving. She was holding her hands up in the air with a look of complete surprise and I braced myself for the worst.

'I can't believe what happened last night. It was the last thing I expected. I mean, my daughter was all I had left, Simon, and then...'

Expressionless, I looked her straight in the eyes, dreading what was to follow.

I went to speak, but she put her hands to her mouth as a sign for me to be quiet.

'He came back to me,' she continued, drawing a deep breath. 'He's left that little hussy and he's come back home.'

'What, Lawrence?' I asked, unable to hide my surprise.

'Yes, Lawrence. He arrived after Joanna stormed out of the house yesterday evening. He'd packed all his bags and he's selling the flat in Liverpool.'

'That was a bit unexpected,' I ventured, relieved at not having to explain why I had been snogging her daughter.

'Totally. He walked in and took me straight into his arms. He didn't say a word for the first few minutes. When he did speak, it was to say that Teresa's death had made him see how stupid he'd been.'

She realised how, in her happiness, she had been oblivious to my feelings.

'Oh, I'm sorry. I didn't mean to—'

'No, it's fine. I'm very pleased for you both,' I said.

I was pleased for Nicola and especially for Joanna. No more evenings down at the beach, crying her eyes out, alone in her car. But selfishly, I was ready for a bit of sympathy myself.

She continued, smiling. 'The next thing, I went upstairs to help him unpack and within seconds, he had me on the bed. We were at it all night. I didn't think he still had the stamina, let alone the imagination! It was like before we had Joanna.'

'And what about the little hussy?' I asked.

'To be honest, if he means what he said last night and sticks to being a loving husband and father, I'm prepared to put it all behind me. It won't be easy, but it's better than losing him and everything we've worked for. You men are all the same once you get into your forties. Sometimes we have to let the past be the past.'

Listening to Nicola, I wondered whether an affair might have improved my relationship with Teresa. There had been plenty of attractive women coming into the garage over the years. A few of them made it clear that they were hoping for more than a new car to give them some excitement.

'And if his little indiscretion was what he needed to put the lead back in his pencil, it may have been a price worth paying. I can't remember the last time we made love like that. When I got out of bed this morning, he said I was walking as though I'd been astride a horse all night!' She laughed before realising her blunder.

'Oh, there I go again, and I haven't even asked how you're coping.'

'Don't worry, Nicola. I'm fine. I've had the boys to keep me occupied and everyone has been helpful. It's next week I'm worried about. Once I get back to work.'

'Well, you've always been strong and determined. Once you put your mind to something, nothing gets in your way, but remember, we're here for you. Come on, let's go through to the others. I've got another surprise for you.'

*

The living room was as traditional as the kitchen was modern, with antique furniture that had cost a fortune. Exquisite paintings filled every bit of free space on the walls and Persian rugs covered the parquet floor. Lawrence was a master of his art and everything spoke of his money and taste.

'This house is our rock. Whatever we do, wherever we go, it will start and finish here,' Lawrence explained, after moving his family from their more modest home in Newton. That was a long time before he discovered new pleasures on the other side of the Mersey, but at least he was true to his word and came back.

The large room opened into a spacious conservatory, arranged as what Nicola called her summer dining room.

Two women, dressed in black, with spotless white aprons, were busying themselves around the long dining table. It was covered with a crisp, white cloth and decorated with two enormous vases of daffodils.

'I asked Mrs Gillespie and her daughter, Tracey, to help us out,' whispered Nicola as we passed through the double doors into the room. 'There's no way I'm going to be stuck in the kitchen while you're all in here.'

The merry chatter stopped as soon as we entered and everyone rose to their feet.

'Simon, how are you doing? Joanna was telling me you're bearing up very well,' greeted Lawrence, still sporting the ponytail we had first seen at Christmas. He was tall and athletic and pulled it off, but I wondered how long it would take before it ended up on a hairdresser's floor.

'I'm OK, Lawrence, thanks. It's all been a terrible shock, but the boys and I are doing the best we can. We don't have any choice.'

I could feel Peter's glare on me but avoided his eye.

'And Mike, Martine, how good to see you both here. Nicola didn't tell me you were coming over today.'

'I told you I had a surprise,' chirped Nicola. 'It will be like the old days!'

'Not exactly,' muttered Martine, looking darkly at our hostess.

Nicola broke the silence that followed by taking orders for drinks before disappearing off to the kitchen.

I was relieved that Joanna was keeping her distance, chatting with the boys and Sarah. I sat down next to Lawrence on a leather chesterfield in front of a finely carved sandstone fireplace.

Despite the sunshine outside, several small logs were burning away and I felt immediately at ease with my friend.

'So, how did the family birthday party go last night, Mike?' I asked, trying to get the conversation going again.

'Shite, to be honest,' he replied, looking across at Martine. 'The restaurant was great; good food, lots of great wine. We went to Scoglino's in West Kirby. I'm just sorry we took Sean and Patricia.'

Martine nodded in agreement.

'I mean, Sean spent half the evening in the lavatory; God knows what he was doing in there. Patricia was messing around with her mobile from the minute we sat down. Neither had a thing to say to us,' continued Mike. 'I've run out of patience with the pair of them and I'm fucking fed up with having them use our house as a hotel.'

Mike's comment reminded me of what I had said to Peter less than a week earlier over lunch; now that Teresa was gone, I would need my sons at least as much as they needed me.

'Language, please, Michael,' said Nicola, as she arrived back with a tray of drinks. 'Now, Simon, it's a beer for you, whiskies for Lawrence and Mike and a gin for Martine. Here you are, dear. I've brought you the tonic in the bottle – would you like it all in?'

'I normally do, don't I, Mike,' replied Martine.

'Please, Martine, it is Sunday,' chastised her husband.

'I'm sorry. I was only trying to have a laugh.'

We had all found Martine amusing when we were in our teens but, now we were approaching fifty, it wasn't quite the same.

Eventually, Mrs Gillespie asked us to take our places for the first course.

Nicola liked to do things properly and the table was laid with neat, handwritten name places, arranged "boy-girl, boy-girl".

Lawrence was in his old place at the head of the table with Nicola, Mike, Sarah and Peter on his right. Martine was on his left along with me, Joanna and Matt.

This meant that I found myself exactly where I had not wanted to be. Right next to Joanna. I had been ignoring her occasional glances from the other end of the room when I had been sitting with Lawrence, but now I had no choice.

'How are you doing?' she asked, looking me straight in the eyes and putting her hand over mine as though to comfort me.

I was aware of Mike watching us through the daffodils from the other side of the table.

'I'm good, thanks,' I replied, trying not to sound nervous.

As I had feared, it didn't take long for her to bring up what had happened the previous evening.

'Thank you for walking me home. I didn't expect you to be so passionate,' she said under her breath. 'I can't wait for the next time. But not in our doorway. I've got some exciting places I'd like to show you. Private places you haven't seen before.'

The dark pupils of her light blue eyes were dilated and I felt an uncontrollable swelling between my legs.

Nicola was also looking at us and I must have blushed because Joanna giggled as she took her hand away and started to butter a small bread roll.

I took a large swig of beer from my glass.

'Don't be embarrassed,' she whispered in my ear. 'It's important to grasp the moment; *carpe diem*. And let's not pretend I don't know what's happening inside your pants.'

I choked on my beer and only just managed to use my napkin to stop a full mouthful from flying across the table towards Mike.

'Let me get you another of those, Mr Duggan,' offered Mrs Gillespie, who was making her way around the table serving the starters.

'No, don't worry, Mrs Gillespie,' I replied, unsure if she was referring to the beer or the napkin. 'It looked much worse than it was.'

I found sitting next to Joanna exciting, but she was provoking me in front of everyone and I was relieved when Nicola invited us to eat.

'Enjoy the starter, everyone. It's a *tarte fine* of wild mushrooms and roasted garlic on a bed of rocket, with a sour cream drizzle.'

We all tucked in as Tracey went around the table pouring a well-chosen Pouilly Fuissé.

The condensation on the outside of the chilled, green bottles glistened in the April sunshine. After everything that had happened over the last few days, I felt strangely comfortable, surrounded by friends and family.

Martine could see that I was far away in my dreams and tapped me on the arm to attract my attention.

'Mike doesn't go in much for starters. He likes to go straight for the main course. He's a hungry boy.'

She was off again, but this time I was determined not to let her get the better of me.

'So he has told me, Martine. I'm the opposite. Often, Teresa and I would spend so much time on the starters that we couldn't manage anything else afterwards.'

'No, that's not for Mike. It's not his thing. Although he usually likes to come back for seconds right after he's finished with his first big helping,' she added thoughtfully.

It was becoming like a match at Wimbledon and I needed to throw her with a grand slam.

'You must tell me what you do to help him keep his appetite. Many of us coming up to fifty struggle to finish a whole serving, let alone ask for more.'

'You shouldn't ask a golden oldie like me. I'm sure Joanna could give you an idea or two if you wanted,' she replied before turning to Lawrence.

She had won. Game, set and match.

*

Nicola had excelled herself yet again and the first course was delicious. Getting Mrs Gillespie and her daughter to help was extravagant, but the service was seamless. Shortly after they had cleared away the empty plates, there were steaming serving dishes running down the length of the table.

'Help yourselves, please,' said Nicola. 'There's more of everything in the kitchen. We've done roast spring lamb, loads of different vegetables and my special rosemary and garlic gravy. It's all local and all homemade.'

As we served ourselves, *à la Française*, as Nicola liked to remind us, Tracey filled the larger of our glasses with a deep red, 1998 Châteauneuf-du-Pape.

'We must be doing a bit of damage to your wine cellar today, Lawrence,' I said to our host. 'You're spoiling us rotten.'

'Rubbish,' he replied. 'It's there to drink, not to keep hidden away until it turns to vinegar.'

'As long as we don't have you over too often,' joked Nicola, looking at her husband, who smiled back at her.

Everyone had got over the awkwardness I had sensed when I first arrived. That's the good thing about old friends, I thought. It doesn't matter how long it is since you last saw them – when you do meet up again, it's as if you'd never been apart.

To my relief, Joanna had turned her attention to Sarah and the boys.

'No more family birthdays then, Mike?' I asked.

Since his outburst, he had not joined in with the conversation. Considering what he would have had the previous evening, the whiskies and now the wine, he was already quite drunk.

'No more family anything,' he replied. 'I'm selling the house. Martine and I will buy a little love nest on the promenade and we'll live there happily ever after. Isn't that so, darling?'

'Let's not rush into anything,' she replied. 'It's a phase.'

'A phase, you reckon? It's a phase that started the moment the two of them could speak. I've had enough; I really have. Now, where's that wine? It's rather good.'

Mike was almost foaming at the mouth in his excitement, and Lawrence gestured to Tracey not to be too generous in filling his glass.

Turning back to the table, he stood and raised his glass in a toast.

'To my wonderful wife, to our guests and our dear, departed friend,' he toasted. 'Thank you all so much for being with us today. Our families have lived through difficult times. There will be challenges ahead, but together, we will succeed as we always have; ever since we met as teenagers.'

Chairs scraped on the floor as we all rose and returned the toast.

'Wasn't that meant to come at the end of the meal, Lawrence?' asked Nicola.

'It was, my darling, but it felt like the right moment.'

Reunited, Nicola and Lawrence made an impressive couple and I hoped it would work out for them. If only Teresa could have been there with us, I thought.

It was the first time she had been mentioned during lunch and I wondered if my friends were waiting for me to say something.

A fresh fruit salad and homemade vanilla ice-cream, with an excellent dessert wine, made way for British and continental cheeses and a 1980 Fonseca Port.

'What do you think of their conservatory?' asked Martine, tapping me on the arm again. 'It's very traditional.'

'It's Edwardian, like the house,' I replied, looking at the finely crafted cast-iron frame supporting the sun-filled windows.

'I prefer ours, though,' said Martine. 'It's a shrine to overindulgence.'

I could remember Mike telling me how he had wanted Lawrence to help Martine with the plans, but she would hear nothing of it.

'Mike loves getting in there for a few drinks and a cigar,' she joked. 'Like the other evening, when you and Teresa were over.'

She realised how tactless she had been as soon as she saw the dark expression that had taken over my face.

'Oh, Simon. I'm so sorry,' she whispered, taking my hand in hers. 'I can't believe I'll never see her again, after all those years. Nicola was so snooty when I started seeing Mike, but Teresa—'

'I know. We're all going to miss her.'

It wasn't long before Lawrence was back on his feet. 'Come on then, Mike, Simon. How about a cigar out on the terrace?'

The sun was still high in the sky and I was ready to get outside, even in a cloud of cigar smoke.

Nicola and Martine had disappeared into the kitchen to sort out the coffee, leaving Mrs Gillespie and Tracey to clear the table. Lawrence went off in the other direction in search of cigars and cognac.

I followed Mike as he stumbled his way outside and we settled into cushioned chairs arranged to overlook the Welsh Hills.

There was no sign of Joanna and the others. I imagined she had taken them off to a hidden corner of the garden that was already a vibrant mass of flowering shrubs and colourful borders.

I was not at all surprised when Mike dozed off and I was enjoying a few moments alone, taking in the view, until his snoring woke him from his dreams.

'I was in love with her,' he muttered, still half asleep. 'She was the only woman I ever loved.'

'Sorry,' I replied. 'What was that?'

I couldn't believe what I'd heard, even if Mike was drunk.

'I loved her. I always did. You were such a lucky bastard,' he continued, ignoring my glare.

I knew Mike had been fond of Teresa, but I had always taken his occasional, odd remarks as bad jokes. They were usually fuelled by a few drinks.

I wanted to get to the bottom of what he was saying, to find out if he and my wife had been more than friends, but he was off again.

'Look at me with that sweaty old cow and our care-in-the-community children. It's in her genes,' he continued, his eyes swivelling in their sockets. 'You haven't met her family, thank God. They don't come to see us very often. They feel intimidated. The whole lot of them are so fucking rough.'

'So, why did you marry her?' I asked angrily, trying to keep my voice down. 'You could have had whoever you wanted.'

'Martine was so available. You remember what it was like in those days, our hormones raging? Teresa might not have been ready for you, but Martine was gagging for it.'

'Yes, but that's not everything,' I suggested.

'You don't need to tell me. I dread it when she drags me off upstairs, slobbering all over me, but it was different when I was seventeen. I'm sorry. I don't know why I've told you any of this.'

I didn't either and I looked towards the door, hoping Lawrence would be on his way back, before turning towards Mike.

'It's alright, Mike, you're tired; we all are. It's not as if you've been to bed with her or anything.'

'Well, only the once, but we were both very pissed,' he mumbled, trying unsuccessfully to pull himself up in his chair.

'For fuck's sake, Mike, where are you going with all this?' I asked. 'If you think you're funny, I can tell you you're not.'

Thank God Lawrence and the others weren't there, after all, I thought, shaking my head.

'Don't worry, it was nothing,' he replied. 'We were at a party in Meols, at that nerd's house. Do you remember? Mark Howarth. I haven't seen him in years.'

'Fuck Mark Howarth. Where was I? And what about Martine?' I was starting to lose patience with him and struggling to keep my voice down.

'You'd gone back to university and Martine had the flu. Teresa was missing you. She had far too much to drink and threw up all over the bedroom. It was a hell of a job getting it cleaned up.'

I remembered her hangover when she told me about the party on the phone the next day. It had been the start of my final year at Durham.

'And what was your excuse?' I asked.

'I guess I was horny. With Martine being ill, I hadn't been getting my rations,' he replied, drunkenly trying to look disappointed.

'Your rations. Is that the best you can do? You fucked your best friend's girlfriend because you were horny? Tell me at least you used a condom.'

'Never have, mate. I come out in a rash if I even look at one of those things.'

'But you know when Peter was born? You're meant to be his godfather, for Christ's sake, not his bloody father?'

I was trying to work out the dates in my head. Teresa told me she was pregnant when I went home for a weekend at the end of October and Peter was born at the beginning of June.

Before I could tell him he was Peter's father, Mike was asleep again. Seconds after he had fucked up my life, already destroyed two days after earlier by Teresa's death.

I wanted to be sick, to hit someone, to get up, go home, get drunk and pretend that none of this had happened. To pretend my wife was still alive, that Peter was my son and that my neat and tidy life was as it had been a few days earlier.

*

'Leave him. It's best if he sleeps it off,' said Lawrence as he stepped outside with the Cognacs. He was followed by Nicola and Martine, carrying a tray of coffees and a silver dish of chocolates.

I reluctantly took a glass. However much I now wanted to leave, I couldn't risk upsetting our hosts and losing their support.

I tried not to think about what Mike had told me, but my stomach was churning at the idea that Peter may not be mine. That I had been betrayed and had given up everything to come home and look after another man's child.

My mother had been right and I had wasted my life on another tart from the Gilroy Road estate.

'He'll feel terrible tomorrow,' said Lawrence, pulling a sad face and looking over at Mike.

He had no idea how terrible. How could anyone drift off to

sleep in the middle of giving his best friend the worst news of his life, however drunk he was?

I didn't realise how late it was until Peter and Matt reappeared, followed by Sarah and Joanna. It reminded me of when they were still children. Their parents enjoying a Sunday afternoon drink while they played in the garden.

'Dad, I need to go home,' said Peter. 'It's getting chilly and I've got things to prepare for next week.'

Warmed by the cognac, I hadn't felt the drop in temperature.

'You're right. We should all go. We've had a good day, but it's time to leave our generous hosts. I'm sure they've got things they need to be doing as well.'

Nicola giggled and kissed her husband on the cheek. I was pleased to see how happy they seemed to be together, but it made me realise how lonely my life would become.

Peter was standing behind Mike's chair and my eyes flicked between the two of them, looking for signs of resemblance. Could Peter have brown hair, if mine was brown and his mother's was auburn? Mike's was black.

'Are you OK, Simon?' asked Nicola. 'You're looking a bit odd.'

'No, I'm fine,' I replied, doing my best to force a smile. 'I had something in my eye, but it's gone now. Anyway, thanks for everything. It's been great. A real boost for us.'

'You can all come over to ours next time,' said Martine. 'I'll dig out some of my recipes.'

Lawrence glanced over at me, grinning.

'You've all been welcome. We've had a lovely day, haven't we, Lawrence?' replied Nicola, looking very pleased with herself.

'See you tomorrow, then,' said Joanna, taking my arm as she walked with us to the gate. 'It's been a lovely day. What a pity it's almost over, Simon.'

*

After walking home in silence, I went through to the kitchen with Matt and Sarah, and Peter headed upstairs.

After the scene earlier in his room and what Mike had told me, I was relieved I wasn't going to see him again that evening.

I still felt sick and poured myself a whisky to take through to the study.

'We'll see you tomorrow morning then, Dad. Thanks for being there for us. This has been one of the best days I've had for a long time,' said Matt.

'Matt! Think about what you're saying,' I blurted, shocked he could think such a thing two days after his Mother's death.

'I'm sorry,' he cried, bursting into tears. 'It doesn't seem real; none of it, and with you and Peter arguing all the time. It's too much for me. I'm sorry. I wanted to be strong for you, Dad.'

He sat down at the table, his whole body shaking with the emotions he had been keeping pent up inside him.

'It's alright. Have a good cry. It's what you need,' said Sarah, drawing a chair up next to his and putting an arm around him.

I was struggling to hold back my tears and left Sarah to look after my son. It was going to be hard enough for me to deal with my own emotions, let alone trying to comfort someone else, even Matt.

'Thanks for everything,' I said to her as she looked up at me and smiled. 'It will be some time before we come to terms with what's happened, but we have to carry on. Your being here will help us pull through.'

*

There was no moon that evening and the bright, sunny day had given way to a dark and chilly evening. Once in the study, I drew the curtains, switched on the table lamp next to my armchair and settled into its warm leather upholstery.

The study had long been my escape from life's stresses. It had always been "Dad's Room", and there was an unspoken rule that no one was allowed in there other than me – not even Teresa. Everything had changed since I had been here the previous Sunday. In the seven days since then, I had found and lost my wife, snogged the daughter of two good friends and discovered that my eldest son wasn't even mine. Not that such a revelation would devastate Peter. I had been a rotten father.

My head was turning as I sat there, digging over every detail of what Mike had told me. That he had shagged my girlfriend because she was pissed and lonely and that betraying me was OK because Martine had not been available. In his rush to get his leg over, he hadn't even stopped to ask if Teresa was on the pill.

What was it my mother had said? That I had come 'crawling back to play happy families', but with little thought that it was for a baby that wasn't even mine.

I'd completely wasted my education. Three years at Durham, an offer of postgraduate study from Cambridge and all for what? To come back to a nest where my cuckoo friend's egg was waiting to hatch. No wonder he had always taken a close interest in Peter and ignored Matt. All the expensive gifts at Christmas and for his birthdays. I can't have been the only one who'd noticed.

It wasn't long before I heard Matt and Sarah heading off up the stairs. I was about to grab another whisky when I was startled by a tapping on the glass of the French door.

I pulled back the curtains to see Joanna shivering in jeans and a light shirt.

Thinking back to what she had said at the gate earlier, I knew she had been planning this all day.

'Let me in. I'm freezing,' she mouthed at me through the glass.

'What are you doing here?' I asked, opening the door.

She grabbed me with both arms, holding my body close to hers.

'Oh, that's better,' she said. 'I was so cold.'

Her face was close to mine and I could smell her sweet breath as she spoke.

'I had to see you. It was like torture this afternoon, having to go off with Sarah and the boys like naughty children, leaving you chatting with my parents and the O'Mara's.'

'There wasn't much chat coming from Mike,' I replied, sourly, 'but isn't that the problem? I was with your parents and you were with my children.'

'Don't start all that again. Kiss me.'

I felt her hand move up to the back of my head as her lips met mine.

'Let's go somewhere we can be together,' she said, releasing me from her grasp, her mouth only inches from mine. 'Not upstairs. What about that room off the kitchen?'

There was a room that would once have been the servants' parlour, but which we used for guests. More than once, we had tucked Mike up in there when, after a good evening, he had been incapable of walking home.

I hesitated for a second or two but felt freed from my inhibitions by everything Mike had told me.

'Come on then. We'll have to be quiet. Matt and Sarah only went to bed a few minutes ago.'

We took off our shoes and tiptoed through to the back of the house like truant schoolchildren.

Once inside the room, I turned the key in the lock.

'There's a bathroom through there,' I said, pointing to a closed door on the far side of the bed.

'OK. I'll only be a minute.' She grinned. 'Don't start without me.'

I ripped off my clothes, throwing them into the corner of the room, before pulling off the covers and throwing myself onto the mattress.

Joanna came out of the bathroom, completely naked, and within seconds she was lying down on the bed next to me.

We lay on our sides, facing each other, and I pulled her close to me, our tongues touching playfully as we kissed.

It was as if the nightmare of the past two days had never happened; all I could think about was making love to Joanna.

I was erect and my penis had taken on a life of its own, pushing and probing in the soft down between her legs.

'Not so fast,' she whispered, pulling herself away from me and sitting up. 'I want you to lie on your back, with your hands behind your head and your eyes closed.'

I did as I was told, guiltily thinking about when Teresa had said Joanna would be able to teach us a thing or two.

She had taken control. I didn't dare open my eyes and gasped as I felt her pull back my foreskin and take me into her mouth.

One hand was moving up and down my shaft and she cupped my balls in the other.

I desperately tried not to burst and motioned for her to come up alongside me, rolling her onto her back before kneeling between her legs. My eyes took in every detail of her perfect body; now it was my turn to take control.

Joanna's eyes opened wide as I pushed myself inside her and I lowered my head to kiss her hungrily. All my energy was focussed on giving her pleasure.

It was not long before I exploded and collapsed, sweating and exhausted, onto the bed.

We lay there for a few minutes, getting our breath back before our lips met again for a last, lingering kiss.

Any guilt I had was gone. As Joanna had said over lunch, I have grasped the moment, and I didn't want that moment to end.

'I love you, Simon,' whispered Joanna, pulling herself closer to me and putting her leg over mine.

'No, you don't, Joanna.'

'Yes, I do, and you love me too.'

She was asleep before I could answer, a smile on her face as though she were the happiest girl in the world.

ELEVEN

THE RETURN TO REALITY

Daylight began to filter through the curtains, and I glanced over at my watch on the bedside table.

It was almost time to get up, but I was happy to be lying there in the warmth of the bed, listening to the sound of Joanna's breathing.

I turned my head to look at her face, still smiling as she slept. It would soon be time to return to reality, but for these few last moments, nothing else mattered to me.

I had already been awake for a couple of hours. What little sleep I had managed had been shallow and fitful. Teresa's death, what Peter had said to me, Mike's betrayal and now Joanna had all happened in the space of two days. I had no idea how I was going to even start dealing with it all.

I was brought back to the present by a hand working its way down my stomach under the covers. 'He's up nice and early,' she whispered as her fingers curled around what they had been seeking. 'Come over here and show me how much you love me.'

Before I could move, we were disturbed by the sound of Matt and Sarah arriving in the kitchen.

'Oh, shit!' I whispered.

Joanna started to giggle and pulled the duvet over her face so she couldn't be heard.

'I have to get you out of here. Thank God I locked the door last night.'

Eventually, she poked her head out and looked across at me, a big grin on her face.

'I have to go to the loo. I'm going to wet the bed.'

'Well, go quietly. And don't flush!'

She pulled herself from under the covers and tiptoed, naked, across to the bathroom, gently closing the door behind her.

When she emerged a few minutes later, she was dressed.

'Don't worry, I'll climb out of the window. With a bit of luck, my parents will still be in bed when I get home.'

She sat back down next to me and picked up one of her shoes.

'The other one must be under the bed,' she whispered, but, as she reached down to get it, the first one dropped onto the floor with a heavy thud.

From the grin on her face, I wasn't sure this had been an accident.

'Is that you in there, Dad?' called Matt from the kitchen.

'Yes, I'll be out in a minute.'

'Would you like me to bring you a cup of tea?' asked Sarah.

'No, it's alright. I'm putting on some clothes.'

I was glued to the bed in a state of panic, but Joanna found it all very funny, smiling as she managed to find the missing shoe.

'I enjoyed last night. Thank you. I can't wait for the next time. I'll see you at work.'

She gave me a kiss on the cheek and, seconds later, I closed the window behind her and quickly got dressed.

*

Joanna had left her watch in her hurry to leave and I slipped it into my trouser pocket before going through to the kitchen.

'What were you doing in there?' asked Matt as I sat down at the table.

Unlike the previous Monday, he was a picture of health, dressed in a smart pair of jeans and a spotless white T-shirt. I had not realised what a toned figure he had been keeping hidden under his shapeless tracksuits and I was sure this had not been lost on Sarah.

'You know, I couldn't bear spending the night upstairs without your mother. It was better for me down here.'

'Well, you look as if you got a good night's sleep,' he replied.

'The second whisky helped,' I lied, 'but how did you sleep?'

He glanced over at Sarah, who turned away to open the top of the AGA.

'Good, Dad. I'm not used to all that fresh air.'

'But aren't you a bit smart for a workday?'

'Thanks to Peter!' he replied. 'I nicked this stuff from his wardrobe.' Sarah smiled as I raised my eyes to the ceiling. 'Oh, I forgot to tell you – he's already left. There's a note for you on the table.'

I picked it up and read it.

"Dad, I'm sorry to leave you now, but I have to get away. I'll give you a call later today about the funeral. I should be back this evening, or I'll come straight to work tomorrow, Peter."

I was relieved I had some time to get my mind around Mike's news before seeing him again. Until proven otherwise, he was still my son.

'So, what are you up to today, Matt?' I asked, as Sarah poured me a mug of tea.

'The boss has got me working on a new site over in Birkenhead.

A big block of flats. It should be more interesting than blocked drains and leaking taps.'

'And a lot better paid, I hope,' I added.

'I expect so, but I'm not pushing it for the moment.'

'My aunt's coming over this morning to give the house a good clean and sort out the laundry,' said Sarah, trying to join in the conversation. 'I said I'd give her a hand – we'll do a bit of shopping when we've finished.'

'Thanks, that's great. That reminds me. I have to sort out a car for you.'

'What about Mum's Discovery?' asked Matt.

It was still over at the stables and I didn't know how I would feel seeing it being driven by someone else.

'It might be too big for Sarah,' I lied. 'Let me see what else we've got over at the garage.'

'I could come up and pick something out. A nice red Ferrari?' joked Sarah, and we all laughed. It was good having her around.

*

Making love to Joanna had been a turning point.

What I had gone through over the last couple of days should have left me incapacitated, but I could see that nothing in the past was how it had seemed. My relationship with Teresa had been even less perfect than I'd thought.

My survival was the only thing that mattered now. Not only was I going to have to start sorting out Teresa's affairs, but I also had the visit by the Special Investigations Unit to deal with.

Peter would organise the funeral. My relationship with my sons could be dealt with later and I hoped that Mike had been so drunk that he wouldn't remember what he had told me. I would be lost without his support and the stakes were high.

As for Joanna, I would take her support and whatever else she was prepared to give me. Yes, I would be using her, but I didn't think this would be one-sided.

What if I were emotionally disabled, as Peter had said? It was what I needed to get through the next few weeks.

✳

When I arrived at the garage, I was greeted by Mrs Davies, who was standing next to a smiling Joanna at the reception desk.

'I'm glad you've come in, Mr Duggan. Darren is waiting to see you. I'll bring him through when you're settled.'

'Could you bring me some tea at the same time?'

'I'll get your tea,' offered Joanna. 'I've just boiled the kettle.'

Mrs Davies disappeared off to the workshops. As soon as I had sat down, Joanna was over at my desk.

'I had a great time last night. You weren't doing too much resisting, were you?' She laughed.

I smiled, taking her watch from my pocket and passing it to her.

'I found this next to mine.'

She grinned, slipping it on.

'I'm afraid that's it until the weekend, though; I've started my lady time,' she whispered.

'Probably for the best,' I replied. 'I need a couple of days to pull myself together.'

'Be careful what you're pulling, Simon. You'll need to be on top performance for what I've got planned.'

We both smiled as she turned to leave. I should have been pushing her away, but I would have given anything to take her in my arms.

My reflections were interrupted by the arrival of Mrs Davies and Darren. He was dressed in a suit and tie and was unrecognisable as the young mechanic who had been in the showroom the previous Monday, polishing the Bentley.

'Here he is, Mr Duggan. Go on then, Darren.'

'The thing is… You know I was looking after the garage on Saturday? Well, I've sold the Ferrari Modena.'

'How do you mean, sold?' I replied, looking him in the eye.

'A couple came in. Middle-aged, smart-looking. They said they'd seen our advert in this month's *Cheshire Life* and wanted to have a look at it,' said Darren, playing with his fingers.

'Carry on,' I encouraged.

'I like to read up about the cars that come in and I was able to take them through the history, performance and everything else. They seemed very pleased and we agreed on a sale,' he replied.

'But what about the money?' I asked, trying not to panic.

'They agreed to pay the full price of £95,000. I told them I couldn't negotiate because of that other couple who were here last week.'

'So why are you all dressed up like you're going to a wedding?' I asked as Mrs Davies gave me a reproachful look.

'They promised to send the money to our bank this morning and I said they could collect the car as soon as we'd received it.'

All dressed up and neatly groomed, there was something about Darren I hadn't seen before. He was good-looking and would polish up nicely, as Teresa would have said.

'And you want to be here when they come in?'

'I was hoping so, Mr Duggan. It's best if they keep dealing with the same person.'

'You're right. Well done. You'll need to get the Ferrari out onto the forecourt and put the Maserati in its place. When you've finished, you can take Peter's desk – he's not coming in today. You might even sell another car for us.'

*

I wasn't in the mood to concentrate on my work. After helping Darren get the Ferrari outside, I started leafing through the classified adverts in the *Sunday Times*.

When I had finished, I flicked through a catalogue Peter had left on my desk for the following week's BCA car auction in Manchester. Auctions were not my favourite place to buy cars, but sometimes there was something worth a bid and I found an interesting TVR Tuscan.

For the first time since Friday, I had time to think and I found myself replaying everything over in my head.

I felt as if I were floating in a rowing boat without oars out on the Irish Sea. A hostage to my waves of emotion.

I couldn't bear to think that I would never see Teresa again, but I hated her for betraying me with my best friend. I would never be able to ask her why. I felt sick at the possibility that Peter wasn't mine. That I had sacrificed everything for him, only to be told that I had never been a true father.

My dark thoughts were disturbed by Joanna giggling as she leaned over the desk in front of Darren, showing him how to use the telephone system.

'So, Darren, to get an outside line, press zero; if you want to pick up an incoming call, dial 72 and to transfer a call to another person, dial their number and then T.'

'And what if I want to have a chat with you?' he joked. 'Do I dial your number, or should I come over to reception?'

'Neither,' she said, looking over at me. 'You're here to work, not mess around. I'll be keeping a close eye on you and giving a detailed report to Mr Duggan later on.'

They both laughed. It was good to have a bit of laughter in the showroom.

The time dragged by until about eleven o'clock, when Mrs Davies came over with a fresh mug of tea.

'The money's in, Mr Duggan. Should I ask Darren to call his client? I've got all the paperwork ready.'

I nodded my agreement. 'Thanks, Mrs Davies.'

As she left, there was a call on my direct line.

'Hi, Dad, it's Peter.' I felt my muscles tense up as soon as I heard the sound of his voice. 'I've had the coroner's office on the phone. There has to be an inquest, given the circumstances. Still, they are prepared to issue an interim death certificate and release the body.'

'The body? That's your mother you're talking about, for Christ's sake,' I almost shouted down the phone.

After his moralising over the weekend, I was annoyed by Peter's lack of sensitivity.

'I'm sorry, I wasn't thinking,' he apologised. 'My brain is all over the place. The good news is that I've managed to book a slot at Frankby Cemetery for noon on Friday.'

'That is good news, but how are you feeling?'

'To be honest, I've been a lot better since I got away from the house.'

'And your heartless father, I suppose. Still, you've been busy. I hope it won't all be too much for you?'

'I'll be fine, but I'd like to stay over in Liverpool for a few more days. I can deal with everything from here; all you'll need to do is turn up on Friday.'

'If you're happy with that, I've got Darren helping me out in the showroom. He sold the Ferrari on Saturday. If he carries on like this, you might be out of a job.'

'Not me. It's always first in, first out, Dad! You know the rules,' he joked.

There was hope for my relationship with him after all.

'Could you follow up on that Lamborghini deal? Now that Brian's let us down on the Bentley, we should try to get another sale tied up.'

'I've got it under control. It's all confirmed for next week. If there's anything else, call me.'

We both hung up. He was a good lad, but there was going to be a lot to discuss once the funeral was over. At least the hatred of the last few days seemed to have vanished, now he was away from the house.

The phone rang again before I could reach over to take a sip from my mug of tea.

'I've got Frankby Stables on the line. Can I put them through?'

'Of course, Mrs Davies,' I replied, knowing I had no choice.

'Hello, Mr Duggan. It's Lesley from the stables. I wanted to say how sorry we all are. Your wife was very popular with everyone here and a great inspiration to the younger riders.'

'Thank you, that is kind. I hope what happened won't put any of them off,' I replied frostily. 'You might want to tell them all that the funeral is at noon on Friday at Frankby Cemetery.'

'I'll certainly do that. The other reason for my call is that we need you to come over to the stables. Your wife's car is still here. I've got her handbag with the keys and there's the final account to settle. Of course, we had to dispose of Jackpot. It was all terribly sad.'

She was only doing what she had to, but it worried me that this was only the start of everything I would have to deal with.

'I understand, Lesley. How about tomorrow morning at ten?'

'That will be fine. I look forward to seeing you then.'

I wasn't looking forward to seeing her at all and my mood was not helped when I looked up and saw Darren chatting away with Joanna over by the reception desk.

She sensed my gaze and called me on the phone.

'We're waiting for Darren's client,' she explained. 'They live in one of those big houses in Stanley Road in Hoylake – they'll be here any minute.'

'That's fine. Thanks for letting me know.'

I was surprised at how jealous I felt, seeing the two of them together.

Minutes later, a taxi pulled up in front of the entrance and Darren went out to greet its passengers.

They were quite ordinary-looking, compared with most of our clients. A smartly dressed couple in their fifties; he looked like a solicitor and I reckoned she had never done a day's work in her life.

Darren took them to look at the Ferrari before they all came back into the showroom and over to Peter's desk.

Mrs Davies brought the paperwork and keys over to the couple, and the man took the pen Duncan was offering him to sign. I rose from behind my desk and went to introduce myself.

'Good morning,' I said, shaking hands with them both. 'I'm Simon Duggan. I wanted to thank you for your purchase and wish you many safe and happy miles of motoring.'

'Thank you, Simon. Anthea and I are pleased to meet you because we wanted to tell you what a pleasure it has been dealing with this young man. You're lucky to have him.'

Mrs Davies put a hand on Darren's shoulder and he smiled self-consciously.

'I'm delighted to hear that. We do try to treat our purchasers as fellow enthusiasts and not just customers. Hopefully, we can help you with a car for Anthea in the not-too-distant future,' I joked.

From the look they gave each other, this was not the first time the subject had cropped up.

*

I couldn't face eating in a restaurant on my own and I decided to have lunch at home. When I arrived, Sarah and her aunt were already at the kitchen table.

'Come and join us,' said Sarah. 'We've only just sat down. My aunt's had me working flat out all morning.'

Mrs Williams smiled. 'I've given the house a good clean, top to bottom. We've changed all the sheets and towels, and this afternoon

Sarah will give me a hand with the laundry. Then we'll go to the supermarket.'

I was grateful for her help, but I was not in the mood to listen to her giving me a detailed account of everything she'd done.

'Thank you, Mrs Williams,' I replied dryly. 'I'm sure once you've got everything under control, it will be a lot easier for you.'

'It will, but it's going to be a big house for the three of you,' she added with her characteristic insensitivity.

'Perhaps, but who can see what the future has in store?' I replied, trying not to catch Sarah's eye.

I was sure I wasn't the only one to have slept in someone else's bed the previous evening. Although it was a bit sudden, I was comforted by the thought that Sarah was there for Matt.

'Talking of which,' continued Mrs Williams, 'would you like a hand sorting out Teresa's clothes? In my experience, it's best to get it over with as soon as possible.'

This was something else I hadn't started to think about; one of many things to do that would remove all signs that Teresa had existed.

'If you don't mind, Mrs Williams,' I replied. 'I couldn't do it myself. Why don't you and Sarah go through her wardrobes in the dressing room? You can take anything decent to one of the charity shops in West Kirby and the rest can go to the tip.'

'Is there nothing you'd like us to put aside?' asked Mrs Williams, with an almost mischievous look in her eye. 'A favourite dress or something?'

I shook my head, trying to hold back the tears.

'No, but thank you. I'll go through her jewellery and personal belongings when the time is right.'

As soon as lunch was over, I started to feel very tired again. 'Why don't you go and have a lie-down?' suggested Sarah. 'It would do you good.'

She was right, but the way I was feeling, if I went to bed, I would never want to get back up.

'I need to be getting over to the garage. I can't stay here on my own. I'll see you both later.'

I would sooner have gone upstairs and shut myself away, but that wasn't going to achieve anything. It was my survival instinct that was telling me to get back to work.

*

Darren waited until I was back behind my desk before coming over.

'What do you want me to do now, Mr Duggan?' he asked, with a hopeful smile.

A smiling Mrs Davies had moved to the door of her office and I could see Darren wasn't the only one waiting for my reply.

'Do you have another suit?' I asked.

He grinned. 'I have several. I may spend the week covered in oil and grease, but do I like to put on a bit of a show at the weekends.'

'I can imagine you do, but Peter won't be back this week, so why don't you carry on with us in the showroom? We'll see how you get on.'

'And what about Rob?' he asked with a frown, afraid his dreams were about to be shattered. 'Will he be OK with this?'

'I'll sort him out, Darren. He's still got Alan to help him. You concentrate on selling cars!'

Darren went back to Peter's desk, where he was joined by Mrs Davies and Joanna, both full of smiles. I hoped it would work out for him.

The rest of the afternoon dragged by and there were only a couple of visitors to the showroom. I left Darren to handle them and I was on the point of going home when Mrs Davies came over with yet another mug of tea.

'Sorry to bother you, Mr Duggan,' she said. She looked troubled as if she didn't quite know what to say.

'That's alright, Mrs Davies. What is it?' I asked, trying to reassure her.

'I've had a call from the owners of the truck that was in the accident. It was badly damaged and they need to make an insurance claim; it had to be towed away.'

I sighed before answering. 'OK, I'll dig out the papers when I get home this evening and let you have them tomorrow.'

It was the start of what was going to be a long week.

*

On Tuesday morning, I took my time getting up and, after a late breakfast, I set off to Frankby stables.

I had arranged for Rob to meet me there to pick up the Discovery and take it back to the garage for a service and a good clean. Despite keeping any car I drove spotless, the inside of Teresa's hadn't seen a vacuum since we bought it.

It almost brought me to tears to see her car in the yard when I arrived. I parked as far away from it as I could before making my way to the office.

Rob and Alan were already there, talking to Lesley. She was a podgy girl with cropped hair and there was straw and horsehair all over her filthy, army-issue pullover.

'Hello, Mr Duggan,' she greeted. 'Thank you so much for coming over to see us. It must be a tough time for you.'

She reached into a drawer and pulled out Teresa's handbag, passing it to me as though she were in a rush to be rid of it.

Her hands looked red and raw, and her nails bore witness to the hours she spent mucking out the stables.

'Thank you, Lesley,' I replied, taking the bag from her and checking inside.

There was a heart-shaped silver fob attached to the car keys. I had given it to Teresa a few days after discovering she was pregnant with Peter.

I struggled to hold back my tears when I read the engraving –

"*Simon and Teresa forever – 1979*". I took it off the ring and put it deep into my trouser pocket before handing the keys to Rob.

'Can you take these and hitch up the horsebox? We can store it at the garage until we find a buyer.'

'One of our riders has said they're interested in buying it, Mr Duggan,' interrupted Lesley. 'You can leave it here and I'll call you once I've had an offer.'

'It's not a week since the accident and the vultures are already circling,' I sighed. 'Still, that's one thing less to worry about.'

'And what about all the tack?' asked Lesley as Rob and Alan headed back out to the yard.

'You may as well hang on to that as well,' I replied. 'I'm sure you'll have someone for it.'

'That is kind, Mr Duggan. Now, about the money, with the removal of Jackpot and our livery fees, there's a total of almost £2,000. There's also the vet's bill. He had to confirm that Jackpot was dead.'

'That's fine,' I replied, as Lesley passed me a sealed envelope. 'I'll get these paid. And thanks for everything. I hope we'll be seeing you on Friday.'

After Mrs Williams wanting to clear out Teresa's clothes and my meeting with Lesley, all traces of my wife were being washed away like footprints in the sand on West Kirby beach.

I was impatient to get back to the garage, but as soon as I was back in the car, I felt my strength leave me and I was overcome by a feeling of complete helplessness. It was uncontrollable. As I cried, I could taste the salt in the tears running down my face onto my shirt.

There was no way I could go to work and I accepted that I would need more than the support of my friends to make it through the next few weeks.

*

Usually, appointments had to be made days, if not weeks in advance, but as I entered my GP's surgery in West Kirby, the receptionist took one look at me and rang through to the doctor.

'Good morning, Mr Duggan. Dr Evans will see you as soon as he has finished with his patient,' she said, gesturing towards an empty chair before I even had a chance to open my mouth.

Minutes later, I was sitting in front of Dr Evans' massive oak desk, unchanged from when my mother used to take me there for my childhood jabs.

He was a tall, well-built man, close to retirement age, if not already past it. As usual, he was dressed in a tweed suit that exuded a faint smell of pipe tobacco.

'Listen,' he said in his avuncular tone once he had listened to my story, 'I could prescribe you antidepressants, but they'll take a month to kick in and I'd hope you'll be feeling a lot better by then. The reason you didn't feel this bad at the weekend is that you were keeping yourself occupied.'

I nodded my agreement.

'What you need to do is concentrate on your work during the day and try not to be alone in the evenings. Get out with friends, enjoy a drink or two, but don't get carried away. That's my job.'

He was a man who enjoyed good food, good wine and all the other things he told his patients to avoid. '*Do as I say, but not as I do,*' he always used to joke.

Of course, I hadn't learned anything I didn't already know, but he was very reassuring and I felt better already.

Thanking him, I left, and on my way back to the car, I called the garage. As I had hoped, it was Joanna who answered.

'Hi, it's me. What are you doing for lunch? I'm in West Kirby; we could get a bite together.'

'I'm sorry, but Darren is taking me for lunch at the Farmer's Arms. He's had a good morning. He reckons he might have sold the Maserati. I've never seen him so excited.'

'I hope that's as excited as you'll ever get to see him,' I muttered, but she didn't hear. 'What about this evening, then? We could go out for a meal.'

'I'd love to, but Mum's doing this family dinner thing and I've been told I must be there. Now that Dad's back and everything. But why don't you come over to us? They'd be delighted.'

'To be honest, that might be a bit strange after last weekend. Still, don't let Darren have anything to drink. I need him to do that deal this afternoon.'

*

On Wednesday morning, I was up and out by eight-thirty, and unusually, I was the first to arrive in the showroom.

I had not been at work at all the previous day. After seeing the doctor, I had a light lunch in West Kirby and then took myself off for a walk across the sands to Hoylake for a pint of lager at the Green Lodge.

I strode forward purposefully, taking deep breaths of the cool sea air. I could feel my body being recharged after the stress of the previous few days.

The tide was starting to go out and Hilbre Island, with its flocks of birds and colonies of seals, stood marooned in an unmoving sea of sand.

I stopped to look at the line of gentle dunes running all the way to Red Rocks, a sandstone outcrop marking the end of the Wirral peninsula. Still in our teens, Teresa and I would spend whole afternoons snuggled up together, keeping each other warm against the sea breeze.

'We have four seasons in a day,' she would say as we lay there. We'd watch the billowing clouds race past to make way for the sun, only to be followed by more clouds and then the rain.

We would talk for hours about our plans for when I had finished my studies, unaware of what lay ahead.

As my mind slipped back to those happy and innocent times, I reached into my pocket and pulled out Teresa's silver heart, holding it up to my lips.

I was more determined than ever to be strong, if not for Teresa's sake, then for mine.

*

Mrs Davies arrived soon after me, followed by Mike, and I went through to join them in her office.

Mike was his usual, cheerful self. It seemed he didn't remember what he had told me on Sunday afternoon.

I wanted to have it out with him, to find out what happened twenty-seven years earlier. Still, I couldn't risk falling out with him until the investigation was over.

The three of us went through everything that Mrs Davies had prepared, and once I was sure nothing was missing, I left them and went over to see Darren.

'How did it go yesterday?' I asked, taking a seat in front of his desk. 'Joanna tells me you might have a buyer for the Maserati.'

'Yes, Mr Duggan. I had a nice gent come in before lunch. He asked lots of questions and was quite interested. He was going to think about it overnight and come back to me this morning.'

He had a broad smile across his face and I was aware that he was being watched by Joanna, who was smiling too.

'And you, Joanna. What have you got planned for today?' I asked, not wanting her to feel left out.

'Nothing special. Making your tea, greeting clients, helping Mrs Davies.' The way she smiled, her blue eyes sparkling, I couldn't help thinking back to our adventures on Sunday evening.

'That all sounds good. You could start with a nice mug of tea then. You make it so well; good and strong.'

'How I like my men,' she joked, glancing at Darren before heading off to the kitchen.

I struggled not to show any sign of jealousy, but was she interested in him or trying to get a reaction from me?

Either way, I realised I was going to have to be very careful.

*

Our special investigators arrived a few minutes before ten o'clock – a miserable-looking couple in their mid-thirties.

He was tall and pleasant, introducing himself as Kenneth Roberts. His female colleague looked like an oversized, ill-tempered rodent and didn't even bother to give us her name.

After all, she had already decided that I had done something wrong and it was only a question of finding the proof. Being surrounded by luxury cars she could never afford would only have made her more determined.

I went over to greet them and took them through into Mrs Davies' office, which felt very crowded.

Once everyone had taken a seat, it was agreed that Mike would give an overview of our accounting systems and then leave them with Mrs Davies.

I wasn't needed and I returned to my desk. When Mike finally emerged twenty minutes later, I followed him out to the car park.

'I've no idea what they're after, but I don't like the look of them,' he said once we were out of earshot.

'That Roberts character seems OK; it's her I'm worried about,' I replied.

'That's how they get you. She's like that because she's short, fat and ugly and knows it. It's the friendly ones you have to watch,' joked Mike, grinning. 'Anyway, give me a call when they're finished. We can go for a beer at the Moby Dick this evening if you like.'

I would have to keep Mike onside until the investigation was out of the way and I accepted his invitation. I also reminded myself that a few beers with a friend was exactly the medicine Dr Evans had ordered.

I stopped to speak to Joanna on my way back to my desk.

'So how about lunch today?' I asked. 'Got time in your hectic schedule for your long-suffering boss?'

'That would be lovely,' she replied, smiling. 'We can talk about how we'll reorganise the showroom, now there are three of you,' she added, glancing over at Darren.

I felt a growing attachment with her. Although I was honest enough to accept that this was a reaction to what I had been through, she was the only good thing left in my life.

I just didn't want to think about how difficult it would be if our relationship were to develop. I would lose the boys and my friends, and I could only guess how Mrs Davies and Rob would react.

*

The sun was out as we drove along the tree-lined Meols Drive back to the Green Lodge, where I had been the previous day.

It was a large and attractive building that looked like an Edwardian country house, sitting in its own grounds. During the summer heatwave of 1976, Teresa and I would spend our evenings in the gardens in front of the pub, drinking beer and relaxing to the sound of other people's laughter.

I was already eighteen, but she was two years younger. Publicans worried less about such things in those days.

'We can sit outside,' I suggested. 'It would be a pity not to on a day like this.'

'Yes, I could do with some fresh air after being at work all morning. I haven't been here for years. I see it's one of those two-for-one pubs,' Joanna said.

'Why do you think I brought you here? I pay and you get to eat for free.'

'Talk about a cheap date.' She laughed.

I had not thought of our lunch as a date. Still, it was happy and enjoyable, and we talked about everything other than the reorganisation of the showroom.

Joanna told me how pleased she was to have her father back home and how she hoped her mother would let him put his Liverpool adventures behind him.

'And how's Darren doing?' I asked, waiting to see her reaction.

'He's getting on well,' she replied. 'He has a way with the clients – they all seem to like him.'

'And a way with the ladies?' I asked, despite myself.

'He probably does, but we should never mix business and pleasure, should we, Mr Duggan?' she teased, squeezing my hand.

Seeing the time, we got up to leave, and as soon as we were in the car, Joanna retook my hand and looked me straight in the eyes.

'Kiss me, Simon. I wanted you to kiss me the second we left the garage.'

Our lips joined without hesitation and we kissed as we had on that first night outside her parents' house.

'I can't wait for the weekend. I want to feel you deep inside me. Last Sunday seems so long ago.'

'We have to get back,' I said, trying to break away. 'If you get me any more excited, there'll be a major explosion.'

'If you'd like me to give you a hand, you only have to ask,' she teased, feeling the hardness of my penis through the thin fabric of my trousers. 'I may be out of action this week, but there's no reason why you shouldn't have some fun.'

'I'm not joking,' I replied. 'That thing could go off at any minute.'

'I never like to start anything I can't finish,' she complained, pretending to look disappointed as I started up the car.

*

When we returned to the garage, I put my head into Mrs Davies' office.

'Everything all right in here?' I asked, trying not to seem too interested in the reply.

'Fine, thank you, Mr Duggan,' she replied, as her guests both managed a polite smile.

The three of them were huddled around Mrs Davies' desk and there were papers and open books everywhere. Accounts had never been one of my strong points. I couldn't imagine how they could even start to make sense of it all.

'We should be finished shortly. Can we come over and see you once we're done?' asked the tall, pleasant one.

'Of course. I'll be here all afternoon.'

Darren was at my desk as soon as I sat down.

'That guy for the Maserati came back while you were out,' he said, almost breathless with excitement.

'Then it's a good thing I was the one who took Joanna out for lunch today,' I replied, not even trying to hide my sarcasm.

'I guess so,' he replied, not taking the bait. 'Still, we've agreed on the deal and he wants to come in to pick up the vehicle tomorrow afternoon.'

'That's fantastic news, Darren, but was he difficult on the price?'

'Not at all. I had to take off £2,500 to push him over the line. I hoped you wouldn't mind?' he asked, looking at me questioningly.

'Of course not. We'll take it off your commission,' I joked. 'And listen. You'll need to get Rob to finish off the preparation of the Cadillac Escalade. Once the Maserati leaves, it should go straight into its place. At this rate, we won't have any stock left by the end of the month.'

He went off to the workshops and I was joined by our visitors and Mrs Davies, who brought over an extra chair.

'And how are we doing?' I asked with a smile.

'On the VAT side, you are fine, Mr Duggan. There were a couple of minor accounting issues, but we've sorted them out,' explained Mr Roberts. He looked at Mrs Davies, almost appreciatively.

'That is good news,' I replied, but I could sense he hadn't finished.

'It is, but that's not why we came here, I'm afraid,' he continued.

Mike's worries had been justified. I braced myself for what was coming next.

'You see, our interest is money laundering,' said Mr Roberts, fixing me straight in the eye, looking for some expression of guilt.

I could hear the sound of my own heart beating.

The oversized rodent nodded her head in agreement, a grim look appearing across her already depressing face.

'Take that Bentley over there,' he continued, pointing to where it was on display. 'There is a lot of unhealthy activity in the luxury car market these days and we believe that you are heavily involved in it. That car is only the tip of the iceberg as far as we're concerned.'

'I don't understand,' I spluttered. 'All of our dealings are documented and pass through the usual channels.'

'As you explained to our colleagues last week, but it's a bit more complicated than that.'

I had been right about the Hardcastles. I had not for a minute been fooled by their pathetic play-acting over the Ferrari.

'Imagine your client, James Hennessey, who is currently on police bail for tax fraud, has cash he wants to get back in the system. What does he do? He buys an expensive car, uses the cash to pay some of the price, drives it for a month or two and then sells it to you.'

He turns towards his companion with a look of self-congratulation before turning back to face me.

'If he buys and sells at the right price, it doesn't even need to cost him anything.'

'But where do I come into all this?' I asked, trying hard to remain polite.

'It affects you because when you buy cars from the likes of Mr Hennessey, you are acting as an accessory to money laundering,' replied the rodent, smiling as though I had made her day.

Their accusations were baseless and I knew there wasn't the slightest bit of proof. Hennessey could have won the Bentley and all the other cars he had sold me over the years playing poker, for all I could care. What did that have to do with me?

'I'm sorry, but I can't accept that,' I almost shouted. 'If I'm buying a car registered in the name of the vendor, how they came to be the owner is none of my concern.'

Roberts was looking at me as if he already had all the proof he needed.

'We believe it is, and you should get yourself a lawyer. In the meantime, here's a card with my mobile number. If you have anything you want to talk to me about, give me a call. It might help you later on.'

Later on? I wondered. Where the hell were they going with this? Innocent or not, I was going to need Mike, whoever's father he turned out to be.

*

As soon as they left, I called Mike and we arranged to meet at seven.

'I'm sure there's nothing to worry about, but we can discuss it in the pub. We should have a bite to eat while we're out; it will be good to get you out of Chateau Duggan,' he added light-heartedly.

'That would be great,' I replied, already feeling better. 'I'll get Matt to drop me off.'

As I put the phone down, Rob came through to tell me that the Discovery was ready and I followed him back to the workshop.

I didn't recognise the car. Now all the mud and grime had been cleaned off, it looked a different colour.

'You've done a hell of a job. We could almost put it in the showroom.'

'Don't thank me; Alan did all the work. Don't take him off me as well, or I will be in the shit.'

The glint in his eye told me he was joking. As useful as Darren would have been in the workshop, it would be easier for him with only one extra pair of hands to worry about.

'I tell you what, if you get Alan to bring it round to the front, I'll drive it home once I'm finished.'

Back in the showroom, Mrs Davies was whispering to Joanna and from their expressions, I guessed it was about the investigation.

'Now, don't worry, Mrs Davies,' I said as I approached them on my way out. 'Mike reckons it can all be sorted, and if there is any worrying to do, leave that to me.'

She forced a smile onto her face, but the visit had upset her.

'I almost forgot, but it looks as if Darren has sold his second car. Could you help him out again with the paperwork? We can't afford any mistakes.'

This cheered them both up and as Mrs Davies wished me a good evening, I only hoped she had not seen the mischievous look Joanna was giving me.

*

Matt's van was parked outside the house and I found him and Sarah sitting in the kitchen drinking coffee.

'You're back early, Matt,' I said, joining them.

'I wanted to give Sarah a hand with dinner,' he replied, glancing at her as if they were hiding something from me.

'That is kind of you,' I said, raising an eyebrow and smiling. 'But haven't you got other priorities? Like your work, for example?'

'Calm down, calm down,' he said, imitating a thick, scouse accent. 'I was joking, actually. The material didn't turn up on site and the boss sent us home.'

Sarah was glaring at me as if to say I was bothering them.

It was out of character for her, but it showed how close they had become over the last few days.

'Sarah, when you've finished worrying about my undeserving son, you might want to come outside. I've got a car for you.'

They both jumped to their feet and followed me out to the front of the house, where I had left the Discovery.

She was overjoyed and gave me a kiss on the cheek as she took the keys.

'You don't still think it's too big for me?' she asked, looking down from the driver's seat.

'Not at all. You'll need something comfortable for all the running around you're going to have to do.'

'And lots of space to pick up the rest of my stuff. There's an awful lot of it.' She laughed when she saw my expression.

'There are two snags, though,' I added.

'Oh, yes, and what are they?' asked Matt with a broad grin.

'The first is that I need one of you to give me a lift to the Moby Dick, and I'm not getting into the Mr Leaky van! As you'll be busy peeling vegetables, Matt, it will have to be Sarah.'

'Very funny, Dad. And the second?'

'I'm afraid the two of you will have to spend the evening here alone, without me. I'm meeting Mike, and I expect to be getting back very late and very drunk.'

Sarah giggled, hiding her face behind her hands, and Matt pretended to look the other way. My instincts had been right again.

Now he no longer had his mother to rely on, Matt would need a lot more support than his brother. I was glad that Sarah was there for him, but I doubted his breakdown of Sunday evening would be his last.

*

Sarah dropped me off outside the pub, showered, changed and pleased to be getting out of the house for the evening, as Dr Evans had instructed.

Her driving had been better than expected. Although nervous at first, because of the size of the vehicle and me watching her every move, she soon relaxed.

I had been uneasy about letting a stranger drive Teresa's car, but I felt a lot happier when I saw it shining like new, with nothing to remind me of its previous owner.

The Moby Dick was typical of a suburban pub built in the 1960s; it was in the West Kirby conservation area and had replaced a hotel dating from the nineteenth century.

From the outside, it was unremarkable, but the sumptuous lounge bar, with its whaling frescos and memorabilia, drew everyone who wanted to be seen from all over the Wirral peninsula.

In the summer months, rows of flash cars would be lined up in front of the entrance; many of them would have been bought up the road at the Hallmark Carriage Company.

Mike was already sitting at a table with two pints in front of him.

'I've got you a pint of lager. Come and sit down. You look like shite.'

'Thanks a lot – I was starting to feel better,' I replied, trying to smile.

'Don't worry, mate. Get a few of these down you and you'll be as right as rain. So, tell me about these bastards. Did they give you a hard time?'

I took a sip of the ice-cold beer before giving him a full account of my discussion and handing him the business card I had been given.

'Ken Roberts – Senior Investigating Officer. OK, let me handle it. I'll email him tomorrow telling him to deal with me from now on,' said Mike.

'But do you think they can build a case? This is serious stuff they're going on about,' I replied.

'You never know with these boys, but I suspect they're on a fishing expedition.'

Mike was trying to look reassuring, but there was something about his expression that worried me.

'How do you mean?' I asked.

'Unless they can prove you have a history of buying cars from jokers like Hennessey, they've got fuck all on you. They're hoping you'll panic and tell them something they can use against you.'

'But I don't have anything to tell them,' I insisted.

'Then you're fine. If the Bentley deal was a one-off and they can prove neither motive nor collusion, I don't see where this can go.'

'And if they can prove something?'

'Then you are in the shit. I had a client who got mixed up in this kind of business a few years ago. They threw the book at him. Ten years inside and they took everything he had. The house, car, the whole fucking lot.'

'So what do we do?' I gulped. Was that how I was going to end up when all this was over? I wondered.

'We keep quiet and wait until they find an easier target, but if you do have anything to tell me, now's the time. I'm bound by client privilege and it will stay between us, but it would help if I had some idea of what I'm dealing with.'

I tried to hide my pained expression as I remembered what Ken Roberts had said before he left.

'Anyway, where's my second Guinness, Simon? I'm dying of thirst here!'

*

I had a feeling the investigation was going to become very difficult and I would have to rely heavily on Mike over the next few months.

At the same time, not being able to ask him about Peter was driving me mad.

What choice did I have? I already knew the answer. None at all.

When the children were young, a couple of beers after work had been an almost daily ritual. The excuse was that it allowed us to talk about business, but we were never in a rush to get home before our offspring were tucked up in bed.

That evening, we had far too much to drink, with only a bit of food to soak up the alcohol.

Just when he looked as though he was finally running out of steam, Mike leant over and gave me a deep, questioning look.

'Tell me about you and Joanna?' he asked in a whisper.

He had taken me by surprise. How could anyone have known what was going on?

'I've no idea what you're talking about,' I replied, trying not to show any embarrassment.

'Come on, I've been your best friend for years. Everyone thinks I'm oblivious to what's happening around me, but I saw the spark between the pair of you on Sunday.'

'Mike, what are you trying to say?' I asked.

'And it was as obvious to me at the garage this morning,' he insisted, ignoring my question.

'Look, it's crap at the moment. Teresa and I may not have been close for years, but it still feels like I've lost a part of me and Joanna's been giving the boys and me a bit of support.'

'I suspect she'd like to be giving you a lot more than that if she hasn't already. Still, be careful. I'm speaking to you as a friend, that's all. I don't want to see either of you getting hurt.'

He was right. What I was doing with Joanna was dangerous on every level, but was that part of what made it exciting? Probably, but it was all I had left.

TWELVE

THE FUNERAL

Peter finally made it home for dinner on Thursday evening. He looked fresh and well-rested, even though he must have been kept busy with all the arrangements for the following day.

'I'm really grateful for everything you've done,' I told him. 'I'm only sorry I haven't been more of a help.'

I did wish I'd been more involved, but it had been a relief to have had everything taken care of by my son.

'Don't worry, Dad. I've had Mrs Davies working away alongside me. She's been brilliant, as always. Anyway, to confirm, the hearse will be here at eleven-forty and you, Matt and I will then follow it to the cemetery in the funeral car.'

I shuddered at the thought.

'Can't Sarah come with us?' asked Matt. 'There'll be room for her.'

Peter looked at me for my reaction, and I remembered how he had been the previous weekend.

'Why not?' I replied hesitantly. 'She's only been here a week, but she seems like family already.'

I saw Matt take her hand under the table.

Peter looked down at his plate for a moment and took a sip of wine before carrying on. He wasn't happy, but it would have been difficult for him to say anything.

'The ceremony in the chapel will last about twenty minutes and afterwards, we'll go over to the grave. The funeral directors will manage everything. They've laid on a priest; he's non-denominational. I thought that would be best.'

I nodded, thinking back to my Presbyterian mother's comments about Teresa's family years earlier. A bunch of papists, she called them; for her, the pope was the antichrist.

'And what about afterwards?' I asked.

I had been expecting a few cases of wine from Morrisons and some finger food thrown together by Matt and Sarah.

'I've got caterers from Liverpool to come and serve a buffet here at the house for anyone who wants to come back. I said there'd be about thirty of us.'

I did a quick calculation in my head. 'Yes, that should do it. You've got it all sorted, haven't you, Peter?'

'It's nothing, but I will need your help with two things. The first is the eulogy. I thought you might like to read "Funeral Blues" by W H Auden. It was in *Four Weddings and a Funeral.*'

He handed me a folded piece of paper and I remembered how Teresa had been in tears when we saw the film together.

Now, I would be the one crying my eyes out when I read it and I wondered how I'd manage. 'Thanks. I'll rehearse it later when I have my whisky. And what's the second thing?'

'Can you try and keep Mike under control? He had a soft spot for Mum and we've all seen how he can get after a few drinks.'

More of a hard-on than a soft spot, I thought to myself, trying not to get upset again.

'I'll do what I can, but I'm not promising anything. Anyway, it's me you should be worrying about. I've no idea how I'll make it through the day.'

'You've got us, Dad – we'll get through it together.'

Peter's smile was as surprising as it was reassuring, but Matt was starting to crack and I was on the point of joining him.

Did Peter know I wasn't his real father? Why was he being so nice after everything that had been said? Was it all a show? Would the truth come out after the funeral?

These questions were whirling around in my head. I drew myself up, holding on to the back of my chair for a couple of seconds before heading off to the peace and quiet of my study.

A couple of whiskies and then off to bed for an early night, I told myself. I had to be on form for the funeral for Teresa's sake and for the boys.

*

The house had been alive all morning with everyone getting ready and the sound of Matt running backwards and forwards to Peter's room as he put together a suitable outfit.

I didn't think we would ever be ready on time. Still, everyone managed to get downstairs seconds before the hearse arrived on the driveway, followed by a classic Daimler Landau.

I felt my legs buckle as I went to lead the way out to the car.

'Come on, Dad,' whispered Peter, taking my arm. 'You'll be fine.'

He was trying to smile, but I knew that, underneath his calm exterior, he was as nervous as I was.

The rain was pouring down, and as soon as the driver opened the door for us, we lost no time scrambling into the limousine.

'Have you got the speech, Dad?' asked Peter, sitting beside me.

'Of course,' I replied, tapping the outside of my jacket pocket. 'But I've committed it to memory. It was the least I could do.' He nodded approvingly.

Matt's face was completely white, which accentuated the redness of his eyes, and he looked as if he had passed a difficult night. I was thankful that Sarah was with us because seeing Matt break down would have set me off.

The drive to the cemetery took no time at all but seemed to go on forever. My eyes were fixed on the hearse in front, thinking all the time of my wife lying inside.

When we arrived at the cemetery, we had an agonising few minutes in the car park as we waited for the previous funeral party to leave.

'How long are they going to be?' I asked Peter, holding back the tears.

He didn't answer but squeezed my hand. He must be my son, I told myself, turning to smile at him.

'Thank you,' I whispered as the driver got out of the car and opened the door.

Teresa had always loved Frankby Cemetery, which is laid out on a hillside with views over Liverpool Bay. Her parents were buried there and she would often visit their grave to clear the weeds and leave flowers before the headstone.

Under the clouded sky, the sea was almost black, save for the white crests of the waves, through which the Isle of Man ferry struggled towards the Mersey Estuary.

The imposing Victorian sandstone chapel was beautiful when it was sunny, but it took on a foreboding character in the rain, further crushing my spirits.

Our group was bigger than I had expected and there were a few faces I didn't recognise. It reminded me again how we had been living separate lives.

Once we were all inside, the funeral director and three of his team carried in the casket.

Thank God the family didn't have to carry the coffin, I thought with a grim smile. With the state Matt and I were in, we would all have ended up on the floor.

The priest gave a moving and detailed account of Teresa's

interrupted life, the details presumably supplied by Peter, followed by several readings from the Bible.

We were then asked to stand.

It was time for the hymns and I struggled as we sang "Morning Has Broken".

I had never been able to hit the high notes and I mumbled my way through, wishing every verse were the last. Peter, as ever, was in top form and led the singing with some enthusiasm, his voice rising well above everyone else's.

When I glanced to my side to check how Matt was getting on, however, I could see it was all he could do to silently mouth the words, tightly holding Sarah's hand.

We sat back down and the priest led a recital of the Lord's Prayer before making a sign for me to come to the lectern at the front of the chapel.

"Funeral Blues" is a very moving poem and I struggled to contain my emotions as I made my way through its four short verses. Only my words broke the silence and I could feel the weight of the grief that filled the chapel.

'And before we go outside,' continued the priest after I had returned to my seat, 'I would like to welcome Miss Deborah Gibbons from the Liverpool Philharmonic Orchestra. She will sing "Time to Say Goodbye", by Andrea Bocelli.'

This was a complete surprise and I took a sideways glance at Peter, who looked embarrassed.

My eulogy had already reduced some of the congregation to tears and the song finished them off; even the priest seemed moved.

*

The calls of rooks from the trees were like cries of the dead as we hurried out into the cemetery.

When we arrived at the open grave, I had my first chance to look around the faces of our guests.

Joanna was with her parents, Lawrence and Nicola; there was Mike with Martine, Mrs Davies and everyone from the garage. I could see Lesley from the stables at the back, surrounded by a group of horsey-looking types. Sarah was standing with her aunt on one side and someone I assumed to be her father on the other.

The expensive-looking black overcoat Mrs Williams was wearing reminded me of one that Teresa used to wear. I wondered what else hadn't made it to the charity shop in West Kirby.

Peter and I both spotted Ted, our gardener, next to the grave, dressed in his filthy work clothes.

'He could have made a bit more of an effort,' I whispered to Peter.

'He's one of the gravediggers, Dad,' he replied, giving me a stern look.

The priest arrived with the last guests and, as he started his reading, the coffin was lowered into the ground.

'Earth to earth, ashes to ashes,' he continued, passing me a small trowel with which I was to throw a handful of soil into the grave.

I couldn't help thinking back to my father's funeral when Teresa had said to keep the gravedigger's spade away from my mother. 'If she gets her hands on anything bigger than a trowel,' she said, 'she'll shovel all the earth back in herself.'

I started to tremble and Peter stepped forward with me, holding the top of my left arm with his hand as I threw a small amount of soil onto the shiny wooden lid of the coffin.

Having completed my last worldly duty towards Teresa, I passed him the trowel and he added his soil to mine before Matt stepped forward to take his turn.

'Amen,' said the priest finally, immediately echoed by everyone present. It was over.

*

I felt drained and I was relieved to be heading back to the house with Peter and Matt; Sarah was to follow in her father's car.

'You know, Peter,' I whispered, 'the whole thing took little over half an hour. Your mother's life accounted for in half an hour – is that all she was worth?'

'It's all any of us are worth, I'm afraid, Dad,' he replied, touching my hand.

Waiting for us at the front door were two uniformed servers, one with a tray of sparkling champagne glasses and the other with orange juice and water.

'Christ,' I stammered. 'What's this all going to cost?'

'Don't worry. A lot less than you might imagine. I've called in a few favours.'

'A few favours? I had always imagined you spending your weekends dossing down on a sofa in some student flat in Liverpool. Not rubbing shoulders with opera singers and fancy caterers.'

He blushed and looked away.

I felt a sense of relief now that Teresa had been laid to rest and the reception went smoothly, with a mix of old friends and people I had never met.

'It's good to meet you at last. I'm sorry it has to be in these circumstances,' said an attractive woman of about Teresa's age, holding out her hand to shake mine.

'And I'm pleased to meet you,' I replied, looking at her questioningly.

'Oh, I'm sorry. I'm Christine Murray. The wife of Dr Murray, who you met at the hospital last week.'

'Of course. He mentioned that you and Teresa were friends.'

'We were great friends. We went to a lot of events together and we'd often have lunch when we weren't riding.'

How sad that she had kept all this from me, but then I had never asked.

'Good afternoon, Simon. I'm Angus Sinclair,' greeted Sarah's father as he joined us through the crowd. 'I'm so sorry about your wife. This must be such a difficult time for you and your family.'

He sensed my surprise at his name and carried on before I had a chance to reply.

'The other side of the Sinclair family are wealthy landowners in Jamaica. My great-grandad was the fruit of the sowing of some wild Scottish oats and my mother was a strong believer in tradition.'

'And are you in touch with any of them?' I asked.

'What do you think?' he answered with only the slightest hint of a West Indian accent.

'Well, Angus, I'm pleased you've been able to join us today.'

'Thank you. I'm sorry I didn't tell you I was coming, but I only managed to free myself up at the last minute. Sarah's told me so much about you and the boys.'

'Especially one of them,' I muttered, taking a sip of my drink.

Matt and Sarah were standing next to Angus, holding hands and smiling.

Now the funeral was behind him, my younger son seemed to have made a full recovery. The blotches were gone from his face and his red and puffy eyes were almost back to normal.

'I hope you'll be staying with us for a few days, Angus?' I asked.

'I would love to, but I don't want to be any trouble,' he answered.

'It will be no trouble at all. We've got a nice bedroom with beautiful sea views that's free upstairs,' I replied, grinning at Matt.

Sarah's happy smile started to turn into a glare until I put my arm around her shoulders and pulled her towards me.

'Your daughter has settled in very well, haven't you, Sarah?' I asked.

Almost too well, I thought, as I saw Matt blush. I hoped for his sake she wouldn't let him down.

*

The two servers had moved in from the front door and were gliding around the room, one carrying platters of finger food and the other topping up drinks.

Our living room was perfect for the occasion, even if there were more guests than we had expected and the views over the Dee estuary were spoiled by the weather.

When my own glass of red wine was refilled, I remembered the promise I had given Peter to keep Mike under control. I had not seen him since we left the cemetery and managed to track him down to the kitchen.

'What are you up to?' I asked him with a grin. 'I've been looking for you everywhere.'

'A sad day, very sad, but you're doing well. A brilliant eulogy – organising all this,' he said, coming over to give me a hug.

'It's not me; it's Peter. He's done everything. He even chose the reading. I'm very proud of him.'

I looked for some sign of embarrassment from Mike, but there was none. Either I had nothing to worry about, or he couldn't remember what he had told me.

'You've got a good lad there, Simon. And what's happened to Matt? I hardly recognised him last Sunday, all smartened up, his hair washed. Is he shagging that Sarah girl?'

I didn't reply. 'Come on, let's get back to the guests. You can't leave Martine alone – God knows what she might be telling them.'

Mike followed me back to the living room, where Peter was waiting for me.

'Dad, this is Stanley Jones. He wanted to have a word with you,' he said, presenting the person standing beside him.

'Hello, Stanley,' I said. 'I'm pleased to meet you.'

He was in his late fifties and dressed in a dark suit and black tie, but his face had the weathered look that came from a lifetime of heavy smoking.

'Can we go somewhere private to talk?' he asked.

I glanced at Peter, who shook his head and shrugged. I didn't have much choice and I took our guest back into the kitchen where I had been minutes before with Mike.

'I'm sorry, Mr Duggan,' he started before I had a chance to speak. 'I haven't had a night's sleep since it happened. I'm only a few months from retirement and me and the wife had been counting the days until we pack up and go off to Spain.'

He began to cry, the tears running down his cheeks, getting lost in the craggy folds of his skin.

'There was nothing I could do when that horse bolted out in front of me. I'll never forget the look on your wife's face. She stared straight into my eyes through the windscreen. It was as if she was pleading with me, begging me not to kill her. It was horrible.'

My body went cold; I was with Teresa's killer. He was the last person to have seen her alive and my primal instincts were telling me to punch him in his miserable, self-pitying face. To drag him outside and kick the shit out of him.

I took a deep breath and unclenched my fists as I told myself that it hadn't been his fault. That he was a victim, as much as we all were.

'No one's blaming you for what happened,' I managed to stammer. 'It was brave of you to come here.'

'I wanted to pay my respects, Mr Duggan. To tell you how sorry I am.'

Despite my own despair, it pained me to see a man in such a state and I put my hands on his shoulders, steadying myself as I tried to comfort him.

'Look, it was an accident. You were in the wrong place at the wrong time. People get killed on the roads every day of the week and this time, it was my wife's turn.'

He was speechless, the tears still pouring down his face, but there was nothing more for either of us to say.

'Stanley, I'm going to have to leave you now, but you must promise yourself not to let this ruin your and, more importantly, your wife's retirement.'

'I understand, Mr Duggan. You must get back to your guests. I hope I haven't taken too much of your time, but I needed to do this.'

I patted him on his shoulder as he turned to leave. As I watched him shuffling off out of the front door, it made me think how a single, random event could change so many people's lives in an instant.

I was strangely pleased he had come; it had brought an element of finality to Teresa's death.

I drew another deep breath and headed back to the living room to find Nicola and Lawrence standing next to the doorway.

'Hello, Simon, how are you doing?' asked Nicola, giving me a kiss on the cheek.

'I'm bearing up, thanks. You're looking fantastic; you must tell me your secret.'

'It's best if it stays a secret. Isn't it, lover?' she replied, turning towards her husband and giving him a kiss on the cheek.

He smiled and I hoped he would keep his promise to Nicola.

'I see someone's barber has been busy,' I joked, noticing that the ponytail had finally gone, as I had predicted.

'I couldn't put up with it any longer,' he replied. 'Every morning, I was there with the shampoo, conditioner, hairdryer. I don't know how women manage. Thank God I don't have to shave my legs!'

I left them to top up my red wine at the bar and bumped into Joanna, who was talking to her colleagues from the garage.

Darren was standing next to her, looking very smart, as usual, and Rob was on her other side, chatting away with Mrs Davies. It was only the second time I had seen him wearing anything other than overalls. The first was when I had interviewed him.

'How are you all getting on?' I asked as I joined them.

'Very well, thank you,' answered Rob. 'It was kind of you to invite us.' The others all nodded their agreement.

'I'm pleased you're all here, despite the circumstances.'

The awkward silence that followed was broken by the sound of a spoon clinking against a glass.

'Ladies and gentlemen, friends,' Peter began with surprising confidence. 'If I could have your attention for a minute or two, I would like to say a few words. First of all, I want to thank you for being here with us today. More importantly, I would like to say how much my family appreciates the support you have given us over the past week. I don't know whether it's worse watching a loved one dying of a terrible disease or losing someone in the blink of an eye, but it will take my father, brother and me many years to overcome our sudden loss. But with your continuing friendship, I know we will because where there is death, there is also life and that life must continue. So, thanks again for being with us and please stay for some wine and a bite to eat.'

Peter glanced over and I could feel the eyes of everyone in the room fixed upon me. I had not prepared for this and it took me a few seconds to put something together in my head.

'Thank you for those words, Peter, and for organising everything for today. It is often said that people can never see what they have until they lose it. Although not a religious person, since losing my beautiful wife, Teresa, I thank God every day for my sons, Peter and Matt.'

There was a spontaneous round of applause.

'I only wish she were here with us today to celebrate a quarter of a century of marriage.'

There was total silence in the room.

'Some of you were there twenty-six years ago. Do you remember?' I asked. 'A quick service at St Bridget's and on to the Moby Dick for a couple of pints.'

'I was there,' shouted Mike. 'I remember Teresa wasn't allowed to drink for some reason.'

It was what I had been dreading.

'Thank you,' I replied, avoiding my son's angry glare. 'And now, I join Peter in asking you to stay with us for as long as you wish this afternoon.'

*

'I need a drink after that,' I said, turning to Joanna.

'Me too,' she replied. 'I'll come with you.'

She was crying and I passed her a paper napkin so she could dry her eyes.

'Are you all right?' I asked.

'No,' she replied. 'It's all been a bit much for me. Can we go outside for a minute? I need some fresh air.'

It was pouring with rain and I led her over to an ornate sandstone structure Teresa used to call the folly.

I needed to get us out of the rain, but it was a special place for me, a place full of memories.

'I'm sorry, Simon, but I can't see you this weekend,' she said nervously, as soon as we were inside. 'I know I said I never start what I can't finish, but I'm confused; I don't know who or where I am anymore.'

We were out of sight of the house and I took her in my arms.

'You're Joanna, here with me, in the folly, and I love you,' I told her.

I had said it and it was true. Whatever the dangers Mike had warned me about, whatever it was going to cost me. My family, my friends. I couldn't care less anymore.

'And I love being with you, Simon,' she replied.

A sense of shock went through my body. Less than a week ago, she told me she loved me, but now she was playing with words.

'I'm sorry, but with Teresa being killed, my dad coming back and seeing everyone today, my mind is all over the place. I want to be with you, but for all the right reasons.'

'And the handsome Darren?' I asked.

She looked at me without smiling. 'I need a week or so to sort my head out. Can you live with that?'

This should have been a relief to me, but it wasn't. I had been counting on her and now she was dumping me.

'I suppose I'll have to, but don't worry. I'll get on with it the same way I'm having to get on with all the other shit that's coming my way at the moment.'

I looked at her, searching for a reaction, some sort of reassurance, but there was nothing.

'It's lucky I'm a battered and bruised old dog,' I continued. 'Not some sensitive little puppy.'

I kissed her on her forehead.

'Perhaps that's it, Simon. Maybe I need a young pup.'

PART TWO

BACK IN THE LAKES

ONE

A NEW START

It was almost midday on the day after the funeral. I got up, brushed the grass off my trousers and started back towards the wooden footbridge that crosses the River Rothay as it leaves Rydal Water.

I found myself walking down the road towards Ambleside and the Ferryman's Inn. Less than two weeks earlier, Teresa and I had been planning to celebrate our new start there.

The building looked like a typical granite Cumbrian farmhouse, built to withstand the unforgiving northern winters, with only a few small windows here and there to let in some light. In contrast with the stark exterior, the log fires, wood panelling and timber beams inside created a cosy sanctuary. When bad weather cut short our family walks in the hills, we had often found shelter there from the wind and the rain.

It was comforting to be back and I smiled as I turned the heavy cast-iron door handle.

There was a large, handwritten note stuck to the door with tape. "Experienced bar staff required – Apply within."

Rain had blurred the writing and the weathered paper looked as if it had been there for some time.

How strange, I thought, as I stepped inside. It shouldn't be too difficult to find someone to work in such a beautiful pub.

*

'Good afternoon, Sir. Lovely spring day, isn't it?'

There was only one small window in the room and, from inside, it could have been any time of the year.

'It certainly is,' I replied, smiling.

The bar was as I remembered from my visits with Teresa and I felt a sudden pang of grief that she wasn't here with me, as we had planned.

Whatever paintwork had once been white was brown after years of smoke. The decorations were limited to several paintings of coaching scenes and an assortment of horse brasses.

It felt as if I had stepped back in time to when it would have been packed with thirsty travellers hundreds of years earlier.

Several illuminated lager taps were the only concession to modernity.

The publican was standing behind his bar as a ship's captain might stand on his bridge, master of all before him.

He was a man well into his sixties, stout, shorter than average, with a ruddy complexion partly hidden by an impressive moustache and a neatly trimmed beard.

'What can I get you then?' he asked. 'We have an excellent guest ale this week. Drivers' Dipper?'

'It sounds good, but I'm more of a lager man, I'm afraid. I'll take a pint of Heineken.'

'No accounting for taste,' he joked with a wink as he started to pour me a pint.

'I suppose you'll be wanting to eat something,' he continued, exchanging glances with a woman in her mid-forties at the other end of the bar, arranging a tray of glasses. She was a little past the bloom of youth, with her long, dyed blonde hair loosely tied up on top of her head and the buttons of her white blouse straining under the weight of her generous breasts.

It was still early and there was only one other customer in the bar: an older, balding gentleman, dressed in a tweed suit and well-polished, brown brogues, sitting with his pint, reading a newspaper. There was something familiar about him. Perhaps he had been there during one of my visits with the family.

'Do you have a menu?' I asked.

'A menu? This is a pub, not one of those family-friendly, wait-while-I-microwave-it-for-you types of establishment,' replied my host, almost as if he were telling me off.

I thought back to my lunch with Joanna at the Green Lodge.

'So, what do you have then?'

'We have pork pies, scotch eggs, ham or cheese ploughman's and ham or cheese baps. If you ask nicely, you could even have a ham and cheese bap. Mind you,' he continued, 'everything is sourced locally and my wife, Shirley, makes the pickle for the ploughman's.'

'How about a ham ploughman's then?' I asked, smiling.

'A wise choice, young man. Let me call that through to the kitchen.'

When he had finished placing the order, he turned to look at me as a magistrate would size up a new arrival in the dock.

'Malcolm Flint,' he offered, holding out his right hand to shake mine. 'Pleased to meet you.'

Our tweed-suited companion raised his head from his paper to see my reaction.

'Simon Duggan,' I replied.

'The regulars call him the Major,' added the barmaid with some pride. She had a soft, almost comforting, Lancashire accent.

'Thank you, Pauline,' reproached the Major, stroking his moustache. 'Are you staying nearby?' he asked.

'No. I've come for the day from Liverpool. I walked up from Ambleside.'

'What, in those shoes? I'd be careful, or you'll get terrible blisters.'

Everyone was looking at my feet and I realised I was wearing a pair of leather-soled loafers. Not ideal for a long walk.

Our discussion was interrupted by the arrival of a couple in their thirties. There was a growl from a small Border Terrier, who had been asleep on a cushion next to a roaring log fire.

'Quiet, Gunner,' cried the Major. 'No biting our guests, or you'll be straight outside. It's bad for business.' The dog gave one last half-hearted growl and went back to sleep.

The couple watched Gunner nervously as they approached the bar but were reassured by the Major's broad smile.

'Pauline, would you mind attending to Paul and Linda while I speak with Mr Duggan?' he continued.

'So, you live in Liverpool?' he asked, turning back towards me.

'No, I'm staying with friends.'

I had no idea why I was lying to him, but I was pleased to be having a conversation that had nothing to do with what I had been through over the past two weeks.

A buzzer rang and the Major disappeared to get my lunch.

'How about this, then?' he asked, placing my ploughman's on the bar in front of me.

'It looks delicious,' I replied, looking down at my plate.

The Major smiled in appreciation and waited while Paul and Linda took their drinks and headed off into the lounge.

'There's a funny couple,' he continued once they were out of earshot. 'They're married, you know!'

'Major, not now,' interrupted Pauline, glaring at him.

'Don't worry, they can't hear us in there. Anyway, when I say married, I mean to other people. Linda's hubby is a firefighter and works shifts over the weekend. Paul's from Grasmere and his wife thinks he's playing golf. Gunner can't stand the sight of them.'

'Do they come here every Saturday?' I asked, enjoying the gossip.

'And the rest of it. Last weekend they came in with grass stains on the knees of their jeans. Goodness knows what they'd been up to.'

'Looking for mushrooms,' suggested Pauline, giggling.

There was now a steady flow of customers and the bar started to become quite crowded.

'I see you're advertising for staff,' I said, during a brief lull.

'We have been for a month or two. It's a tragic story, isn't it, Pauline?'

She nodded and pulled a sad face.

'You see, we had this old barman, Leo. He'd been here for as long as anyone can remember, certainly from before I arrived. He was a good old chap and a great storyteller. He drank more than he served towards the end; it was because of the pain from his injuries.'

'What were those from?' I asked.

'He'd been a steeplechase jockey when he was younger. Tiny, he was, but he fell in the Grand National back in the fifties and never recovered. He drifted around for years before he ended up here.'

'He lived in the mobile home we've got behind the pub. Never went out, did he, Major?' said Pauline.

'Not often, but he'd walk into Ambleside to put a bet on if he had a good tip. It used to take him all day to get there and back.'

'So, what happened?' I asked.

'It was terrible,' answered Pauline, shaking her head.

'It could have been a lot worse,' added the Major. 'You see, he was serving John here a pint one lunchtime when he suffered a massive heart attack and dropped dead on the spot.'

The man I now knew to be John put down his paper and waited for what he must have heard many times before.

'How could it have been worse than that?' I asked.

'I'm glad you asked,' said the Major, looking very serious. 'He had poured a pint of Badger's Luck and was still holding it when he started to fall.'

I wasn't sure I wanted to hear what was coming next.

'There he was with the pint in one hand and the other hand clutched to his chest, and as he went down, he somehow managed to place the glass on the bar without spilling a drop,' he continued.

'A fine ale,' said John as he spoke for the first time. 'It would have been a tragedy if he'd dropped it.'

The Major, Pauline and John burst out laughing.

'Everyone in the bar started to clap. They thought he was messing around,' added the Major.

'It's what he would have wanted,' spluttered Pauline, tears running down her cheeks.

I smiled politely. It didn't feel right to laugh at jokes about death, but the story was amusing, especially the way the three of them told it.

'How's your pint?' asked the Major, taking away my empty plate.

'I'm fine, thanks. I need to be getting back.'

'Have a half, then. We'll be sorry to see you go, won't we, Pauline?'

'Alright, but just a half.'

I looked around the room, taking in the centuries of history, and I felt very much at home.

'I could be interested in the bar job?' I heard myself ask before I even had a chance to think about what I was saying.

'It only pays six pounds an hour, I'm afraid, but you could stay in the mobile home and we'd provide you with food and beer. We might even get you drinking proper ale.'

'So when could I start?' I asked.

I was acting on an impulse, something I hadn't done for far too long. How would the garage survive if I wasn't there? What about the boys? At that moment, I couldn't have cared less. All I wanted was a new life, far away from everything I had been through.

'I take it you have experience? We've got the May bank holiday in a few weeks and it's going to be very busy. The good weather always brings them out, doesn't it, Pauline?'

She nodded her head, smiling.

'I did six months in a bar on the Costa del Sol a few years ago,' I lied again. 'I'd get back into it in no time.'

'That's fine then. Can you start on Monday? Don't worry about references. You seem like a good chap and that's what counts, hey, Pauline?'

She nodded her head again. 'I tell you what, Simon,' she said. 'When you're ready, I'll give you a lift back to Ambleside. We can't have you doing another couple of miles in those shoes.'

'No, honestly,' I replied. 'I'm fine.'

'We insist,' said the Major. 'I don't want my new barman starting work with bad feet. And lunch is on me, by the way. Just make sure you turn up on Monday.'

*

'Did you see that car?' asked Pauline as we passed the parked Bentley, a few hundred yards from the pub. 'Whoever owns that must be minted.'

'Yes, you don't see many of those around,' I replied wistfully. I should have been climbing into it instead of being driven miles away.

'He's not a real Major,' confided Pauline. 'It's something that John made up and it stuck.'

'Very few of us are what we seem, Pauline,' I replied, wondering what I had got myself into.

After we pulled up in Ambleside, I thanked her and climbed out of the car, waiting until she was gone before heading off to look for a taxi.

I eventually found one down by the pier. 'Can you take me up towards Rydal?' I asked. 'I've left my car up there.'

'No problem, Sir – how did you manage to get yourself stranded here?'

'It's a long story.'

TWO

TWENTY-FIVE YEARS

'You're going to do what?' asked Mike when I told him about my visit to the Ferryman's. 'If the boredom doesn't kill you, the booze will.'

I had called him from the Bentley on my drive home and we had arranged to meet the following day.

'Look, Mike, I've spent the last twenty-five years at that garage. Do you realise? Twenty-five fucking years.'

'But you told me you enjoyed it?' he asked, shaking his head. I could see from his expression that he thought I had lost all sense of reality.

'I do, but I need to get away. A change of scene will do me good.'

'So go to that place of yours in France, or why not go on a cruise? There are some great offers at the moment. You could make new friends, even get your leg over.'

'A new relationship is the last thing I need, especially after...'

Mike grinned as he looked at me.

'As I've already said, I'm not here to judge.'

'I've always loved the Lakes,' I continued. 'Lots of walking and fresh air. I'll come back a new man.'

'A new man with a new woman, I bet,' suggested Mike with a raised eyebrow.

I ignored him. 'The thing is, you mustn't tell anyone, especially Martine.'

'If your mind's made up, I wish you all the best; I'm even a little jealous. They don't need anyone else, I suppose? It would be like the old days at Levitt's,' joked Mike.

'I'm afraid not; I need you here,' I replied. 'Peter's going to be running the garage, but you'll need to keep an eye on him. I'll have my mobile if you need to get in touch.'

'Just don't get too settled up there. You'll have to come back to deal with Teresa's will once the solicitors are ready,' warned Mike. 'And they'll be calling us in for this money-laundering thing sooner or later.'

'Don't worry, I'll be there. We don't want them thinking I've gone into hiding,' I replied. I was reassured that Mike had said "us". My future depended on him, but I knew it was in good hands.

'One last thing; can you give me a lift to Lime Street Station tomorrow morning?' I asked. 'I'll be dropping the Bentley off at the garage at about nine.'

*

I loaded two heavy suitcases into the boot of the car and headed off without even looking back at the house.

I didn't know when I would be seeing it again, but I wouldn't be in any rush to return.

My feelings of hope and optimism from Saturday were now mixed with apprehension. I was rarely at my best on a Monday morning and today was no exception.

I had called Peter to ask him to come home early on Sunday evening and, as soon as he arrived, I gathered everyone together in the kitchen.

'The last ten days have been a terrible ordeal for us,' I explained. 'And I thank you all for helping me, and each other, to cope.'

I could see Sarah looking at the boys' faces, waiting for a reaction.

'But Dad…' started Peter.

I raised my hand to stop him.

'Especially you, Peter. You've been incredible and that's why I'm asking you to run the garage for a while.'

His reaction was not what I had been hoping for.

'And take the blame for what you've been getting up to with Hennessey and his cronies?' he asked.

Peter had been in Liverpool when Kenneth Roberts and his ghastly colleague had been at the garage and I had explained the money-laundering accusations as a big misunderstanding.

'I haven't been getting up to anything, Peter,' I replied. 'Mike has assured me he will have it all cleared up in no time at all.'

He didn't seem convinced and sat, deep in thought, looking down at the table in front of him.

'And what will you be doing, Dad?' asked Matt, giving Sarah a worried look.

'I'm going away for a few months. After losing your mother, I need time to heal and it will be best if I'm on my own for a while.'

Of course, I couldn't tell them about the other reasons I needed to get away.

There was a look of panic on Matt's face.

'But how will we manage here on our own without you?' he asked.

'For God's sake, Matt; how old are you?'

He thought for a second before answering.

'Twenty-five.'

'And your brother's twenty-six. There are guys of your age with families of their own to look after. Look at Alan at the garage. He's only your age and his wife had twins a couple of months ago.'

Sarah's father had left earlier in the day and my news had upset her.

'It's like I've lost two fathers in one day,' she said tearfully. 'I hope I'm not going to have to leave as well.'

'Of course not. Somebody's going to have to look after these two.'

'That's right, Sarah,' said Matt, brightening up. 'I'll need you to get me up in the morning.'

'You'll be getting yourself up on your own if you make any more comments like that,' replied Sarah, giggling.

'Anyway,' I continued, pretending to ignore Matt's comment. 'It's not forever and you can call me if there's anything important.'

'But why won't you tell us where you're going?' asked Peter, looking up from the table.

'Because I need a complete break,' I replied. 'But don't worry; I'll be back as soon as I'm ready.'

*

When we arrived at Lime Street, I was reminded of when my father used to drop me off to take the train back to university after the holidays.

'Thanks, Mike. I don't know what I'd do without you,' I said, lifting my bags onto the pavement.

'I expect that this is one of the easier things I'll be doing for you over the next few months. But look, have a great time and keep out of trouble,' he replied, giving me a big hug.

It was a difficult moment. Despite what he had told me a week earlier, he had always been a good friend. We hadn't been apart for more than a few weeks at a time since I came back after my studies.

The train journey took about two and a half hours, with changes at Preston and Oxenholme, and the weather became cold and bleak as I headed northwards.

What had been a good idea in Saturday's sunshine was less appealing under the darkening clouds and rain. I had to remind myself that it would soon be summer.

When I arrived in Bowness, I thought about taking a lake steamer up to Ambleside but dragged my cases over to the taxi rank outside the station.

'Where've you left the car this time, Sir?' asked the driver of the first taxi in line. 'I picked you up two days ago.'

'Don't worry. It's safely locked up in the garage. Can you take me up to Rydal? The Ferryman's Inn,' I asked.

'Of course, Sir. Let me help you with those bags,' he replied, climbing out of the car and only just managing to squeeze my bags into the boot.

'From the weight of those bags, I would say you're planning to stay for a while.' He laughed as we headed off towards Ambleside.

'Only for a week or so. I'm hoping to do some walking up in the hills if the weather improves.'

'You've picked a good place to stay; it's a nice pub, the Ferryman's. The Major bought it about ten years ago. He's transformed it since the death of the previous owner. It was all very sad. He couldn't breathe in the end.'

'Had he been ill for long?' I asked.

'He had asthma, but it was all very sudden. One winter evening, he took a rowing boat out onto Rydal Water to do some fishing. It's illegal, but he'd been drinking all afternoon.'

'And the cold air was too much for him?'

'No, he fell overboard and drowned,' he replied, laughing at his own joke. 'So here we are; we've arrived. And here's my card. I'm Derek Bradshaw. Give me a call if you need a taxi.'

The Ferryman's had looked warm and inviting two days earlier.

The building was now in darkness, with only the small window in the bar showing any light. It looked sinister in the pouring rain and I felt a sense of discomfort as I approached the front door, especially after Derek's story.

I found the Major and Pauline standing behind the bar when I entered.

Their warm smiles put me at ease and dispelled my doubts of the previous few minutes.

'Welcome back to the Ferryman's, Simon,' greeted the Major, as I put my bags down in front of the bar.

'Thank you, Major. It's good to be back,' I replied. 'I'm looking forward to getting settled in.'

'That's what I wanted to hear,' said the Major, looking down at my suitcases. 'I'm glad to see you've got lots of luggage – it means you're planning to stay.'

'Yes, we've been looking forward to having you here, haven't we, Major?' added Pauline.

'We have, Pauline,' he replied. 'Now, would you be good enough to take Simon through to the mobile home to unpack his bags? We'll be opening the bar in half an hour or so.'

The mobile home was in a small copse behind the main building.

It was smarter than I had expected and quite spacious. There was an open-plan living room and kitchen area, two double bedrooms and a shower room.

Although far from new, it would be comfortable, even if some of the furnishings showed signs of wear.

'We've made up the bed and left you fresh towels,' explained Pauline. 'There's milk, butter and orange juice in the fridge and bread and cereal in the cupboard next to the sink.'

'Thank you. That's very kind of you,' I replied. It was going to be very different from the house in Caldy.

*

It took me no time to unpack and get back to the bar and the Major took great pride in giving me the grand tour.

'Shirley and I own the freehold. We are not tied to one of those blood-sucking breweries like most of the pubs around here,' he explained.

We started off in the kitchen, followed by Gunner. It was surprisingly modern and well equipped, given the limited food on offer.

'It's all this Health and Safety nonsense,' said the Major when he saw my look.

He then took me through a door into the residential part of the building.

'This won't concern you, but we have eight guest rooms. Shirley looks after that side of the business. It can be very profitable. The staircase by the reception desk is for the guests; our quarters are up the stairs by the bar.'

He gestured towards a door marked Private next to the one we had come through.

'Of course, our overnight guests are welcome in the bar, but I don't want them sitting there all day, drinking lots of tea. It upsets the regulars.'

I thought back to when we had stayed as a family all those years ago. Teresa and I had been no strangers to the bar, but I couldn't remember much tea being drunk.

We were about to head off to the cellars when we bumped into Shirley, carrying a pile of ironed sheets.

'Shirley, let me introduce you to Simon. He's coming to help out in the bar.'

She extended a hand from underneath her load. 'It's nice to meet you,' she said in a soft, well-spoken voice. 'We certainly need some help. My husband's been working far too hard since Leo died.'

Well into her sixties, she looked pale and grey, but I sensed a hidden toughness born from years of hard toil.

'Now, let me show you the engine room of this establishment,' offered the Major, gesturing for me to follow him down a narrow flight of stairs.

The cellars were indeed like a ship's engine room. Rows of beer barrels were lined up on one side. On the other, wine racks, cases of spirits and all sorts of cans and bottles were stacked as high as the ceiling.

There was a distinct and pleasant smell, a mixture of ancient timbers, fine whisky and stale cigar smoke.

At the far end of the cellar there was an office, separated from the alcohol by a pair of old glazed oak doors and illuminated by a solitary desk lamp.

'No one gets through this door without an invitation, not even Shirley,' the Major explained.

He took a key from his pocket and opened it.

'Come inside and sit down,' he said to me, pointing towards a chair in front of a small wooden desk. 'We'll have a welcome drink.'

As we sat, he reached into a drawer and pulled out a bottle and two crystal tumblers.

'Highland Park, eighteen years. You don't find anything better. Not that we'd sell it upstairs. It's too expensive.'

I swirled it around my glass before taking my first sip. I had read about this whisky from the Orkney Islands, but it was not one I had tried.

'It was Shirley who drove me to drink,' he joked, raising his glass, 'but it wasn't a long drive. Welcome to Rydal, Simon.'

The Major was right about the whisky. As its rich aromas filled my senses, I already felt at home.

*

Back in the bar, it was coming up to six o'clock and there were already a few customers taking seats around the tables.

'Thanks a lot for coming to give us a hand,' joked Pauline, looking at her watch.

Although it was a Monday, there was a steady stream of drinkers throughout the evening. Enough to let me learn the ropes of my new job. Thankfully, the till was simple to use. At the student bar I used to work at in Durham, we had to add up the prices ourselves and no one ever paid the right amount.

It had been a long day and by eleven o'clock, I was ready for bed, but the Major had different plans.

'Goodnight then, boys,' said Pauline as she closed the till for the last time. 'I'll leave you to it. Don't keep him up too late, Major!'

She knew him well.

'Pauline's a good girl,' he told me as the door closed behind her. 'I couldn't manage without her. She's been with us pretty much since we arrived. Her husband ran off with some little tart about six months ago. He used to knock her about a bit, but it still came as a shock to her.'

'Any children?' I asked.

'Fortunately not. Now, I can see you're ready to turn in, but we should have a quick nightcap to celebrate your first service. It's not as good as the Highland Park, but I do have a fifteen-year Knockando behind the bar.'

Shirley had gone off to bed an hour or so earlier and I was starting to wonder whether my role was to be the Major's drinking companion.

'Second of the day,' he said, raising his glass.

'Cheers,' I replied, doing the same.

'It's a good life up here. You'll enjoy it and Gunner's very excited. I struggle to get him out as often as he deserves. I hope you've got decent walking boots?'

I nodded positively.

'Good. Now let's have one more for the road,' said the Major, as he topped up our glasses.

He smiled as I took a sip.

'You know, Simon, I saw my doctor last week and he asked me why I drink,' he said, winking at me.

'And what did you say?' I asked.

'I told him it was to forget.'

'What are you trying to forget, Major?'

'I've forgotten!'

We both laughed.

I had enjoyed my first day at the Ferryman's and as I finally headed off to my new home, I was already looking forward to Tuesday morning.

THREE

THE FIRST DAY

I was woken by the sound of heavy rain on the metal roof above me and reached for my watch. It was half six.

Luckily, I'd made it to bed before midnight after refusing a second, or was it a third "one for the road"?

I opened the curtains and quickly closed them again. The Ferryman's back door was hardly visible through the downpour, and the trees around my new home were moving violently in the wind.

This was not how my first day was supposed to be. I pulled the duvet over my shoulders and tried to go back to sleep. There was no chance of a morning walk with Gunner.

Perhaps I should have gone on a cruise after all.

I was soon bored with feeling sorry for myself. I climbed out of bed, made tea and toast, and got showered and dressed before running across to the pub under an outstretched raincoat.

'Good morning,' I was greeted as I entered the kitchen. 'How did you sleep?'

'Morning, Shirley. Very well until this rain started. Is it like this often?'

'I won't spoil your first day by telling you the truth, but don't worry, you'll get used to it. Let me get you a nice mug of tea?'

'No thanks, I've just had one. Now, what can I help you with?'

There was an older woman on the other side of the room struggling under the weight of a large tray laden with cooked breakfasts.

'Oh, don't worry. I've got Mary here giving me a hand with the overnight guests. She keeps the place clean and tidy for us, don't you, dear?' She smiled.

Mary smiled back, resting the tray back on the worktop. 'Welcome to Rydal, Mr Duggan. Mrs Flint has asked me to change your sheets and towels and give the mobile home a good clean every Monday if that's alright with you.'

'That's really not necessary. I'm happy to do it myself.'

'I won't hear of it,' replied Shirley. 'You've got more important things to do here, like keeping my husband out of trouble.'

'And what sort of trouble is that?' asked the Major, grinning, as he entered the room. He was dressed in a double-breasted blazer, blue shirt, patterned navy cravat and dark grey trousers.

'You're all dressed up,' replied Shirley, ignoring the question. 'Are you going out?'

'Not at all, but now young Simon's here, I'll have to up my game a bit. We might even start attracting a better class of customer.'

'So long as you don't start putting off the locals,' replied Shirley. 'Your posh friends are all well and good, but it's the farmers and the hikers who do the drinking that keeps this roof over our heads.'

'But Shirley—' started the Major.

'And don't try to tell me you do your own fair share,' she interrupted, raising her hand. 'That doesn't put any money in the till, unfortunately.'

'Thank you, my dear. Talking of posh friends, John said he'll call in at lunchtime on his way back from Kendal. You met him on Saturday, Simon,' he reminded me.

I did remember him. The smart gentleman I had half recognised.

'The Right Honourable John Asquith,' explained Shirley. 'His family owns half the farming land around here – he's got a big house in the village.'

'Charming gent. If only we had more customers like that. Anyway, young man,' he continued, turning his attention to me. 'Pauline's in at eleven and you can start work at twelve. That will give you plenty of time to get out for a good walk with Gunner.'

'In this weather?' I asked.

'What weather?' replied the Major, raising an eyebrow. 'In half an hour or so, it will all have blown over.'

And with that, he disappeared off towards the bar.

Putting off the moment when I would have to get myself soaked in the rain, I accepted Shirley's second offer of a mug of tea and settled into an armchair in the corner of the room.

Gunner came sneaking in, sniffing the air for Mary's freshly grilled Cumberland sausages, but as soon as he saw me, he was at my feet, looking up with his dark brown eyes.

I pretended to ignore him and continued to chat with Shirley until the rain did eventually stop and the first rays of sunshine started to break through the clouds. Gunner also noticed this and got up, wagging his tail.

'Time to go then, Gunner,' I said, thanking Shirley for the tea and heading out through the bar.

*

It was the middle of the lambing season and the Major warned me to keep Gunner on a firm lead.

'Take this,' he said, as he offered me a leather-bound hip flask. 'It can get cold up there. You saw how quickly the weather changed earlier.'

'Thanks, but it's OK,' I replied. 'I don't expect we'll be going too far. If I do need warming up, I'll have something when I get back.'

Between late-night drinks, Mary keeping my new home clean and tidy, and now the offer of whisky for my walk with Gunner, I was being thoroughly spoiled.

Out on the lower slopes of Nab Scar, I was careful to keep to the footpaths and avoid the open moorland, which could become boggy after heavy rain.

There were small groups of sheep everywhere, but I followed the Major's advice to keep Gunner on his lead. Although he would have been only too happy to have sunk his teeth into a nice, tasty rump of lamb, he walked dutifully alongside me and was no trouble at all.

We managed to climb high up and my breath was taken as I saw Rydal Water for the first time from the north, framed by a rainbow.

This was why I had come to stay at the Ferryman's, I reminded myself. Teresa, the garage, the boys, even Mike and Joanna; they all seemed a lifetime away. I was here to start a new life. A life where I could find out who I was and what I wanted to become.

I would have liked to have stayed up in the hills all day, but I remembered I had to get back for the lunchtime service. Glancing at my watch, I saw it was already eleven o'clock.

'Come on then, Gunner. Time to go home,' I told my new best friend, and he followed me on his lead as I started to head back down into the valley.

*

There were a couple of customers talking to the Major at the bar when I arrived at midday. The log fire was burning away, with Gunner fast asleep on his cushion beside it.

'Simon, welcome back. Gunner tells me he had a great time this morning,' greeted the Major with a wink.

'We both did,' I replied. 'Now, who needs a drink?'

Everyone had a full glass and Pauline, who had been watching me from the end of the bar, stepped forward.

'Can you give me a hand changing a barrel?' she asked. 'The Heineken is finished.'

I had been dreading this but followed her out of the bar and down into the cellars. The taps above each barrel were labelled with the beer it contained and I went straight to the one we needed.

'Why don't you have a go, Simon? I'll keep an eye on what you're doing. I know it's been a while, but once you've done it, you never forget, do you?' she asked, with an amused look.

She was putting me to the test and I was determined to get it right.

It seemed obvious that the first thing was to disconnect the barrel, but when I turned the coupler, a jet of beer shot out of the pipe and Pauline threw herself on top of me as she rushed to relock the keg.

'You forgot to close off the gas supply,' she shouted, her beer-soaked breasts pressed against me. 'Have you done this before?'

I looked at her sheepishly as she pulled herself back onto her feet. It hadn't taken long for my lies to be found out.

'Let me do it. You can clean up the mess you've made. We don't need to say anything to the Major, though, do we?'

I shook my head like a naughty schoolboy being told off by his teacher.

'Don't worry. I'm going to enjoy having you here, even if you are useless in the cellars.'

She smiled at me, rearranging herself under her soaking blouse and straightening her hair with her hands.

'It's a good thing I always keep a spare top behind the bar, in case of emergencies,' she joked. 'Who knows what the Major would say if I had to work my shift in this state?'

I was feeling terrible.

'I'm sorry, Pauline. I really am.'

She ignored me and carried on.

'Leo was a good laugh, but we've needed someone like you for a while. I might even have a little treat for you one of these evenings if you're not up until all hours, drinking with the Major. I've been told it can get chilly out there at night, even at this time of year.'

After Teresa's elegant charm and my night of passion with the youthful Joanna, I was not even remotely interested in Pauline's earthy comforts.

'Pauline, you're an attractive woman, but I have come out of a long relationship and I'm not ready for anything like that.'

'Well, the offer's there if you want to take it up.' She laughed as we made our way back up the stairs.

*

John arrived through the front door as I took my place behind the bar.

'Good afternoon, Sir. It's good to see you again,' I greeted. 'What can I get you?'

'It's John, Simon. Call me John. I'm pleased to see you turned up. I had my doubts,' he replied. 'I'll have a pint of Nab's End. The brewery is only a few miles from here.'

I poured the pint and as I handed it to him, we were joined by the Major.

'John, dear boy, how did you get on? He was down at some car dealership in Kendal this morning, Simon. Looking at a new car.'

'What sort of car?' I asked, unable to hide my curiosity.

'A 2001 Jaguar XJR 100. It's a little older than I would like, but there are only 35,000 miles on the clock.'

'A fantastic vehicle,' I replied. 'The 100 series was a limited edition to commemorate the hundredth birthday of Sir William Lyons.'

'I never knew that,' said John.

'Yes, it got brilliant reviews when it came out. They only allowed one per dealer. It has 384 brake horsepower and will get you from nought to sixty in five seconds.'

'It's a beautiful car, but perhaps I should buy a sports model like the XKR.'

'As far as I'm concerned, John, the XJ has all the sports appeal anyone could want, but with a classic style that will be current for many years.'

'OK, you've convinced me. I'll give the garage a ring after this pint and tell them they've got a sale.'

The Major gave John a knowing look. 'You seem very well informed, Simon.'

'It's a passion of mine, even if I'll never be able to afford a decent car myself.'

'Never say never,' said John, with a self-satisfied look on his face. 'None of us knows what lies ahead.'

I didn't know why the Major and John were giving each other these odd looks, but they were being friendly enough and I didn't spare it another thought.

*

An hour later, the three of us were working flat out pouring drinks, passing food orders through to the kitchen and clearing away empty glasses.

'Where are they all coming from?' I asked the Major. 'I had imagined it would be quiet on a Tuesday.'

'You'd be surprised. There was a farm clearance sale up towards Grasmere this morning and a lot of them were over there. If you think this is busy, wait till tomorrow. There's the weekly market in Ambleside and that always brings them out.'

I was impressed with the Major's quiet efficiency, always

managing a brief word with the customers he served. At the same time, Shirley ran the kitchen with an air of calm organisation.

'I'll do you a bacon bap when it's a bit quieter,' she promised as she brought out another tray of lunches. 'Tell me when. I've got the bacon in the warmer.'

Eventually, it did start to calm down, and with a nod from the Major, I went through to the kitchen.

'Is it always this hectic, Shirley?' I asked before taking my first bite of the bap.

'Not all the time, but when it gets like this, it's not easy for Pauline and my husband to manage.'

'It must have been difficult after Leo passed away,' I suggested.

'To be honest, it wasn't a lot better when he was here – not for the last year or two. He wasn't in the best of health.'

I shook my head sympathetically.

'This pub has been my husband's life for the last ten years. It's everything to him, but it's been getting too much recently. That's why I'm so pleased you've turned up. It will be good for all of us.'

It felt good being needed for a change.

What Shirley had said made me realise I had spent years being taken for granted by Teresa and the boys. It was easy for Peter to say I had been a bad father, but how much better would I have been if I hadn't been able to give them all everything they wanted? The big house, the villa in France? What sort of father would I have been then?

Not once had any of them ever thanked me for anything.

I realised how much I was going to learn about myself over the coming months. When I did eventually leave, I wouldn't be the same person.

*

Back in the bar, it was almost three o'clock and there were only a couple of regulars left, talking to the Major.

'You look shattered. Why don't you go and have a lie-down for an hour or two and we'll see you back here at six?' he suggested.

'Thanks,' I replied. 'I could do with a rest. I'll see you later.'

I made my way back to my new home, where I pulled off my shoes and threw myself onto the bed, quickly drifting off into a deep and contented sleep. After the walk with Gunner, being traumatised in the cellars and the busy lunchtime service, I was exhausted.

An hour later, heavy rain woke me for the second time in the day and I reached for my book on Medieval Europe, which I still hadn't finished.

I managed one and a half pages before throwing it to the floor. That's enough, I said to myself. I am here to live my life, not to dwell on the past.

*

'You're back early,' greeted the Major as I arrived in the bar.

'I couldn't sleep.'

'Well, you're looking thirsty, so let's have a quick pint. We deserve it after our efforts earlier on.'

Pauline returned shortly before six and we started our evening service. This time, there was no food; it was only served at lunchtime.

John appeared about an hour later.

'I have to thank you, Simon. I've been back to the garage and signed the papers for the car. For the money, it's a great deal. Twenty-five thousand, I paid. Have you any idea what it would have cost new?'

'Seventy thousand on the road,' I replied.

'Exactly right. I'm only glad I'm not the person who's lost forty-five grand in four years.'

'Plus whatever profit the garage has made on it,' I added.

The evening dragged by, with only a few locals coming in for a quick drink before heading back out into the rain.

John left at about eight, having celebrated his purchase with a couple of pints, and the Major told me to go through to the kitchen for some supper.

An excellent hearty Irish stew: it was what I needed.

'That's how my mother used to make it,' said Shirley, taking away my empty plate. 'I hope you enjoyed it.'

'I certainly did; it was delicious.'

'In my day, we didn't eat it like that. My father worked on the docks and it was hard manual labour. Not like today, where it's all mechanised. He would take all the meat and the rest of us would make do with what was left; Stovies, we called it. It was the same for all the families where we lived.'

*

By eleven o'clock, the Major, Pauline and I were the only ones left in the bar.

'Time for a nightcap?' asked the Major, reaching for his bottle of Knockando, hidden under the bar.

'If you don't mind, I'll turn in for the night,' I replied.

Pauline caught my eye as I turned to leave, looking for a signal that I had changed my mind about her offer.

'Yes, I'll be straight off to sleep, Pauline,' I said with a polite smile. 'A good eight hours and I'll be ready for the lunchtime crowds tomorrow.'

FOUR

SETTLING IN

In the following weeks, I settled into my new life, and as the weather started to improve, I spent more and more time out walking with Gunner.

The walks were having a good effect on my health, both mental and physical. I missed them whenever the weather stopped me from getting out into the hills for a day or two.

When I was up there, I could spend time thinking about what had happened in the twelve days before I left the family home.

I was struggling to get over the shock of Teresa's death, especially after our last few days of closeness, and I needed to come to terms with what Mike had told me.

The initial shock had passed, but I often wondered how I would react when I finally discovered the truth. Mike may be his biological father, but Peter would still be my son and I was proud of him, despite what he thought about me.

Whatever happened on that night over twenty-five years ago, Mike had been my best friend since we were in our teens. As my accountant, I also owed him a lot for my success and financial wellbeing.

Then there was the money-laundering business to worry about.

It would be months before we heard back from Ken Roberts, but it was always in my mind, like a headache that refused to go away.

I knew Mike would keep me out of jail. The only way they could build a case would be if one of my clients said I had conspired with them, but they would have a lot more to lose than me.

Then there was Joanna. Even though I knew there could be no future in our relationship, I was vulnerable and I had allowed myself to fall in love with her.

She was to have been my reason to carry on, the one good thing left in my life. But when I needed her most, she dumped me.

How could I have carried on working at the garage when she would have been there, flirting with Darren? I asked myself. It would have poisoned everything.

Despite these challenges, or because of them, I started to rediscover myself in a way that had been impossible before I arrived at the Ferryman's. The garage had become my private kingdom, where I was the king, but it also became my prison. Now I was out on my own, finding out who I was.

Was I going to like who I found? I wondered.

I hoped so, but I wasn't looking forward to digging through all the shit of the last twenty-five years to get the answer.

Pauline eventually accepted there would be no late-night invitation back to my bedroom and we became good friends. She even gave me lessons on changing barrels and cleaning the lines, away from the watchful eye of the Major.

The pub's regulars were a friendly bunch and I was soon on good terms with most of them. There were quite a few farmers, the vicar from a nearby church, a couple of schoolteachers and a café owner from Grasmere. The pub was well known in the area and people would make the journey from Ambleside and even further afield.

I even became friendly with Paul and Linda during their regular Saturday visits. They made an attractive couple and I wondered what their married partners must have been like for them to seek comfort elsewhere.

The pub was welcoming and the Major was a perfect host. He was appreciated by all our customers, apart from those he took a dislike to, often for a reason only he knew.

'This is a local pub and we need to be careful who we let in,' he would say, much to Shirley's disapproval.

There was a piano in the bar. On Fridays, Shirley would play while the Major led us in an evening of singing that would often go on long after closing time.

He would start on his own with "Land of Hope and Glory" before getting everyone up on their feet to sing along with him.

'That's very patriotic,' I said to him the first time I heard it.

'They're all country yeomen up here. That song gets them all joining in and the more they sing, the thirstier they become,' he replied with a wink.

It was true that we got through gallons of beer on these evenings. It wasn't unusual for several of our guests, as the Major liked to call them, to end up staggering home in the early hours of Saturday morning.

John also became a good friend and insisted on giving me a ride in his new Jaguar a few days after buying it. It was in exceptional condition and the sort of car that I would have liked to have had in our showroom in West Kirby.

He would often join the Major and me for our late-night whiskies and I enjoyed our conversations when the three of us were alone in the bar.

'I've had an affectionate relationship with alcohol ever since my late teens,' the Major told us one evening. 'Unfortunately, I've started to spill more than I drink and we can no longer be as close as we were.'

We all laughed.

*

I was working behind the bar with Pauline one lunchtime when I first discovered that we had our problem customers, like any other pub.

'Good afternoon, Sir,' I greeted. 'What can I get you?'

'I don't want serving by you, mate. I'll wait until that young barmaid has finished with her order,' replied the customer, pointing towards Pauline with a hand as filthy as it was battered and bruised.

He must have only been in his mid-twenties, with unkempt curly red hair and a face that was unusually weathered for someone of his age.

'Hello, Ben. A pint of Badgers, is it?'

'Yes, and a pleasant smile, if you can be bothered, Pauline.'

'The smile's extra, I'm afraid. And watch who you're calling young. I'm almost old enough to be your mother.'

'Me mam was a lot older than you when she died. Anyway, who's this prat?' he asked, looking at me with disdain. 'Not from around here, is he?'

'I'm from Liverpool. I don't think we've met.'

'You should have stayed there. The last thing we need up here is foreigners like you.'

I was shocked by Ben's remark. In the short time since arriving at the Ferryman's, I had felt very much at home. Almost one of the locals.

'Now, look, Ben,' said Pauline before I had a chance to reply, handing him his pint. 'Simon's come to help us out. He's only been here a couple of weeks, so why don't you try to be pleasant for a change?'

'You must be kidding. I'll drink me beer outside. I'm not supping in here with the likes of him,' he replied, heading back through the front door with his glass.

'Who the hell's that?' I asked Pauline as soon as the door had closed behind him. 'What's his problem with people from Liverpool?'

'That's Ben Thorndyke. He's one of a kind, that's for sure. I do feel sorry for him, though.'

'His family had a sheep farm near Hawkshead. They'd been there for generations, but his father died when he was about seventeen,' said the Major, as he joined us. 'It was cancer, I think. Ben and his mother tried to run the place on their own, but it was a real struggle. They got a loan from the bank to help keep them going, but it wasn't enough.'

'Didn't the bank take the farm from them in the end?' asked Pauline.

'They did, I'm afraid, the bastards. Sold it to the National Trust. Ben and his mother asked to stay on as tenants, but they wouldn't hear of it,' replied the Major. 'They were thrown out onto the street without a penny. The disgrace killed the mother and Ben's never been the same. He was a good lad before all this happened.'

I gulped, remembering how I could end up if I were ever prosecuted for money laundering.

'And what's he doing now?' I asked.

'He's living in an old caravan somewhere up in the hills. The farmer lets him stay there in exchange for a bit of work from time to time.'

'It can get very bleak up there. Not like your luxury home,' added Pauline, shaking her head.

'Well, the poor guy won't get much sympathy if he carries on like that,' I said.

'If he even wants it,' said the Major. 'He's way past that point. It's a tragedy.'

At least my sons had careers, even if Peter did lose his job, I thought. Whatever happens to me, they'll be OK, even if they never want to speak to me again.

*

'Was there ever a ferry here?' I asked late one evening, as the Major, John and I enjoyed a whisky.

Heavy rain was lashing against the small window next to the front door. The darkness outside was relieved only by an occasional flash of lightning, illuminating the sky over Nab Scar.

'There was,' replied the Major. 'The locals say there used to be a small boat on a rope pulley to take people across the Rothay, just before Rydal Water.'

'That's where the river's at its deepest,' explained John. 'You can still see the remains of the wooden posts it was attached to on both sides. The ferryman lived in a wooden shack on the water's edge. Travellers could call him by ringing the bells that hung from the top of the posts.'

'It operated night and day, all year round,' added the Major, shaking his head. 'It must have been awful for him in the winter. It's said he disappeared the day the footbridge was opened. He was never seen or heard of again.'

Instinctively, the three of us turned towards the window to peer out into the rain and darkness.

'In Greek mythology, Charon, the Ferryman of Hades, carried the spirits of the deceased from the world of the living across the River Styx to the world of the dead,' I explained. 'If you couldn't pay the fee, you'd be left to wander the shore for a hundred years.'

'I suppose there must have been a few over the years who couldn't pay the Ferryman of Rydal because they'd spent all their money in here.' The Major laughed, reaching for the Knockando. 'Still, the only spirits in this pub come in bottles, so let's have another glass while we can.'

John had lived in the area all his life.

'That's not entirely true. Did you know this pub is haunted?' he asked me.

I shook my head as the Major nodded his agreement with John.

'It's the ghost of the previous owner, Eddy Thwaites. He appears late at night behind the bar, still wearing the angler's jacket and boots he had on the night he drowned.'

The lights flickered as another bolt of lightning flashed over the lake and I felt a shiver run down my spine as our eyes met over the bar.

'That's it,' I said, draining the last drop of whisky from my glass. 'I'm off to bed before the pair of you frighten me to death.'

Often when I lay in my bed at night, I thought I could hear the sound of the horses being taken into the stables before the coachmen went to join their passengers inside the inn. It felt as if everyone who had passed through the Ferryman's had left a shadow of their being.

The very fabric of the building had been steeped in centuries of history. I was now part of that history and I wondered if I would ever leave.

*

A few evenings later, after everyone had gone to bed, I came back inside to get a bottle of water from the kitchen.

As I was leaving, I was startled by a noise coming from the bar. Worried it might have been an intruder, I edged my way from the kitchen in the darkness.

I dropped the plastic bottle I was carrying when I saw an arm rising up above the bar, followed by a second one. John's ghost story had unsettled me and I was about to turn and run for my life when the Major's face emerged into the gloom.

'I was looking for my glasses,' he explained. 'I took them off to clean them earlier and they must have fallen on the floor. I only found out when I got upstairs and Shirley asked me why I wasn't wearing them.'

His age was starting to show and I wondered how long he'd carry on running the place.

'Life is like a holiday,' he told me late one evening. 'At the beginning, you think you have all the time in the world; in the middle, you're having too much fun to worry about how long you have left. Before you realise, you're at the end and your time is up.'

'There's a big difference, though,' added John, who had stayed for a nightcap.

'What's that?' I asked.

'At the end of a holiday, you know where you're going next.'

The Major looked at John thoughtfully before pouring us all another glass.

He was right, but was he talking about himself or about me in his metaphor? I wondered. Either way, I would need to start thinking about where I was heading before my working holiday in the Lakes came to an end.

*

Every day after the lunchtime session, I would check the mobile phone I kept in a drawer next to my bed, but it was rare that anyone had called.

I knew this meant I wasn't being missed, but, for the time being, at least, the isolation was doing me good.

There were occasional missed calls from Joanna, but even though I had been thinking about her a lot, I couldn't bring myself to call her back. I didn't know whether she wanted to tell me she wanted to "finish what she'd started" or that it had all been a terrible mistake.

Either way, I wasn't ready to face the truth. To give up my new life at the Ferryman's or to have her shatter my dream that one day I would be able to hold her in my arms again.

Peter would send text messages to tell me when he or Darren had made a sale and I would call him most Fridays to catch up. There was little warmth in our conversations, but he seemed to be managing and I hoped there would still be room for me when I went back.

One afternoon there was a message in my voicemail from Mike, asking me to contact him urgently. I closed the mobile home's outside door and settled into an armchair in the living room.

It had to be about the money-laundering case and my hands were shaking as I dialled the number of his office. 'I'm afraid he's in a meeting,' replied his secretary when she answered. 'Can I get him to call you back?'

'Yes, please, Julie. I'm only around until about four-thirty – otherwise, it will have to be tomorrow.'

In the space of a few minutes, it felt as if all the healing of the last few weeks had been undone and I had gone back to the dark place I had tried so hard to leave.

Although I had convinced myself there was nothing to worry about, the tone of Mike's message had set my nerves on edge. I sat back in the chair and looked around the room, trying to find something to keep my mind occupied until Mike called me. It was hopeless; I felt physically sick.

As the minutes passed, I became increasingly anxious and could feel small beads of sweat forming on my forehead.

If I had ever needed one of the Major's single malts, it was now, but I didn't want to go through to the bar and miss Mike's call.

It was a few minutes after four when the phone rang, just as my nerves were threatening to give in completely.

'Mike, thank God. I've been at my wits' end. What's been happening?' I asked.

'Simon, are you alright? It's me, Joanna,' came the reply.

I was lost for words and sat looking at the phone for a few seconds, wondering whether to hang up.

'What's going on?' she shouted, not sure if I was still there.

I took a deep breath before answering.

'Joanna, I'm sorry. I was expecting it to be Mike,' I stammered.

'For this money-laundering business?' she asked. 'It's been terrible, Simon. Mrs Davies has been off for a couple of days; it's the stress. I'm in her office.'

Despite what she was telling me, hearing her voice made me realise how much I had missed her.

'Have you not listened to any of my messages?' she asked.

I started to hate myself for not having called her back.

'I have, but I haven't had the time—' I lied.

'You haven't had the time to call me back. So what have you been doing that's so important?'

I didn't have an answer.

'Where are you, anyway?' she insisted.

'I'm somewhere peaceful. Away from you, Peter, Mike, the empty house. I needed to sort myself out.'

'And have you, Simon?'

'I'm starting to, but—'

'Then let me help you,' she interrupted. 'I want to hold you in my arms, to make love like we did that Sunday.'

The memory gave me an erection, but then I remembered what she had said at the funeral.

'So, why did you dump me, Joanna? After you told me you loved me,' I asked, confused by my own emotions.

'I do love you, but I needed to get my head straight. With everything that was going on, I was scared. I didn't know where it was all going.'

I could feel my head turning as I tried to get my own thoughts straight.

'Simon, are you still there?' she asked. I could hear the panic in her voice as if she thought I had gone.

'I am, Joanna, but I don't know what to say to you. You're one of the reasons I'm here, for Christ's sake.'

'Then why can't I be the reason for you to come back?' she asked.

'It's too early. I can't,' I replied, determined not to give in to her. Not to give up my new life, far away from her and all the other shit I had gone through.

'Well, I'll come and see you,' she suggested.

'I'm sorry. That's not going to be possible.'

Every muscle in my body tensed at the thought of how the Major and Shirley would react to Joanna turning up at the Ferryman's with a couple of suitcases.

'But I do love you. You know I do. Please let me come and stay with you. You want me to, don't you?' she pleaded.

I now knew she loved me and I wanted to see her more than anything else in the world. In my mind, I pictured us walking up in the hills, holding hands, and then coming back to the mobile home and making love together.

'I'm sorry, but I can't,' I managed to answer, despite every part of my being telling me to say yes. 'Look, thanks for phoning, but I have to get back to Mike.'

I could hear the distant sound of her starting to cry and then the line went dead.

I imagined her sitting in Mrs Davies' office, alone with her tears, and I didn't move from my chair as I took deep breaths, fighting to stop myself from calling her back.

I had almost forgotten about Mike's call when the phone rang again.

'How are you doing?' asked Mike, as I answered, checking this time that the call was from him. I couldn't face talking to anyone else.

'Quite well, considering, until I picked up your message,' I replied, still trying to catch my breath.

'Simon, you sound terrible. It's a good thing you haven't been over here; this investigation's been a nightmare.'

I could feel the blood draining from my face.

'We've had them poring through everything. They wanted details of every car you've ever bought or sold, going right back to the beginning.'

'But we've only got records for the last six years. Everything before then has been destroyed.'

'That point wasn't lost on them either. I reminded them of the six-year rule for keeping accounting records, but they felt you had been a little over-zealous.'

I remembered going through all the records with Mrs Davies before I left. I had put everything I could get rid of into empty cardboard boxes before getting Rob to take it all to the tip.

'And did they find anything?' I asked, trying to remember how many cars Nick French had sold us over the last couple of years. There had been at least half a dozen.

'They didn't say, but a small army of them turned up at the garage on Monday to impound the Bentley. The "proceeds of crime", they said. Peter had the good sense to call me before they had time to load it up on their truck.'

'They had a flat-bed to take it away? What the fuck did you do, Mike?'

I could imagine the scene at the garage. Mrs Davies cowering in her office with Joanna, while Peter desperately tried to get hold of Mike on the phone.

'I got Peter to put me on to the guy who was in charge and I asked him whether he had a court order.'

'And?' I could hear my heartbeat banging in my ears.

'He didn't. The problem with these people is that they're so fucking self-righteous that they forget that even they have rules to follow. Anyway, they left without the Bentley and I called that Ken Roberts shite who came to the garage.'

'What did he have to say?'

'He was quite unpleasant to begin with. Anyway, I told him we were getting an injunction preventing interference with the vehicle due to lack of evidence. The problem is that once they get their hands on something, it's a hell of a job to get it back. Even if you do, it will be trashed.'

I shuddered at the thought of the car arriving back at the garage. Careless scratch marks the length of its immaculate paintwork and cigarette burns deep in the soft leather interior.

'So, what's next?' I asked, even though I was afraid of the answer.

'He suggested I hold off for twenty-four hours; he'll come back to me once he's spoken with his director.'

There was a brief silence as I tried to take it all in.

'I can't see why you should have anything to worry about, but I had to let you know what's been going on,' said Mike, trying to reassure me.

My head told me that Mike was right; I had nothing to worry about, but that didn't stop my heart from saying the opposite.

'Mike, you were right to call me,' I replied. 'I only hope there weren't any clients there. Our reputation would be ruined.'

Not that it would be worth anything if this got to court, I thought.

'Peter would have told me,' said Mike. 'But he did say that, apart from Mrs Davies and Joanna, no one else knew what was going on.'

I breathed a sigh of relief. The last thing I needed was Darren talking about what had happened with his mates at the pub.

'Will you give me a call when you've heard back from Roberts, then?' I asked.

'I will, Simon. It should be tomorrow at the latest.'

I sat there for a while after the call ended, motionless. I had every confidence in Mike, but after my conversation with Joanna and then what he had told me, it would be some time before I would be ready to go back home.

*

I was not in the mood for working in the bar and, when I saw Ben waiting to be served, I had to resist the urge to go straight back outside.

'Hello, Ben. A pint of Badgers?' I forced myself to ask with a friendly smile.

'It's alright. I'll wait for Pauline.'

'You'll be waiting all night if that's the case,' shouted Pauline from the other end of the bar. 'It's Simon or nothing, I'm afraid, young man. You better get used to it or find another pub.'

He looked at me with an expression of bitter defiance but nodded as I went to pour him his pint.

'I should have got your job,' he whispered. 'Local jobs for local people. That's how it's done up here.'

'And did you apply? There was a note on the door,' I asked, forcing a smile and hoping that would be the end of the matter.

'Reading never was my thing,' he replied. 'Not something you need when you're rearing sheep from the day you're out of nappies. But someone could have told me they were looking.'

'The thing is, Ben, you don't have the experience. Not like Simon, with all the time he spent working on the Costa del Sol,' said Pauline, giving me a knowing look.

I couldn't help blushing and turned around, pretending to rearrange some glasses behind the bar.

'So why couldn't he have got a job in Liverpool? We don't need some "bay-window scouser" up here, dressed like a tailor's dummy and talking with his la-di-la accent.'

I was reminded of what Joanna had said about me being posh.

'Anyway, I'm having this pint and then I'll be off somewhere I'm welcome.'

*

Feeling drained, I was happy to let Shirley chat away while I ate my supper in the kitchen.

'My husband was one of twelve children and the only one to leave Liverpool. My dad didn't want me to marry him – he said he was common. But then he did his National Service as a steward in the mess at some army camp down south. That's where he learned his trade and how to behave like an officer.'

No one would call the Major common today, I thought.

'Our lives were far from easy. I couldn't tell you how many bars we worked in over the years; we even had a stint in a working men's club in Skelmersdale. You can imagine what that was like. If it hadn't been for my uncle leaving us the money we needed to buy the Ferryman's ten years ago, I don't know where we would have ended up.'

I shook my head.

'Do you have children?' I asked.

'No. We did hope for some time, but it wasn't to be. Probably for the best. There's not much time for youngsters when you're in this type of business.'

Listening to Shirley made me feel a lot better and thankfully, I had no idea of the news waiting for me later on.

*

'Simon, we're starting to get very busy. It was a nightmare last weekend with the May bank holiday and the garden's packed out the minute there's a bit of sunshine,' said the Major, as we cleared up at the end of the evening.

I knew he was right and wondered what was coming next.

'The thing is, even with Pauline, we're struggling to cope. I mean, look at you; you're exhausted. You can't tell me you've been yourself this evening,' he continued.

'Oh, don't worry about me. I'm coming down with a cold,' I lied, hoping I would never have to tell him the truth. If the investigation went further, it wouldn't only destroy everything I had built up on the Wirral. It would be the end of my new life at the Ferryman's.

'Well, try not to give it to me, but I've decided to take on someone else behind the bar.'

'Is that necessary?' I asked. 'We don't do badly most of the time.'

We needed help, but we were all getting on well and I didn't want anything to upset that.

'You may be right, but it's my niece, Alison, my brother's lass. She's a lovely girl, but she's been going through a rough patch. She's thirty-two and left her boyfriend a month or so ago. He's a footballer. Not one of the Premier League boys, but he does very well all the same. I think he plays for Tranmere Rovers.'

'Sounds like a good catch.'

'That's what she had hoped, but if I say he often played away, I'm not talking about football,' joked the Major, not a trace of a smile on his face.

'That's the problem with those guys. They never appreciate what they've got. When does she arrive?' I asked.

I might never have properly appreciated everything Teresa and I had worked to achieve, but at least I had never cheated on her.

'In a couple of days. But don't worry, you won't be disturbed in the mobile home. I'm giving her a room upstairs.'

It was the most challenging day I'd had since arriving at the Ferryman's, so I was pleased to take myself off to bed after a couple of large whiskies.

As I lay under the covers, allowing the alcohol to take its effect, I remembered my conversation with Mike. I instantly sobered up and reached over to pull open the top drawer of the cabinet next to my bed.

My phone was buried under everything else that had found its way in there, but I eventually managed to find it. I switched it on and as it came to life, I saw a missed call at about half-six.

I dialled the voicemail, holding the phone tightly against my ear.

"Hi, Simon, it's Mike. I've heard back from that Ken Roberts tosser. His director has told him to do whatever it takes to impound the car and he reckons they'll be back at the garage by the end of the week. I asked him for a meeting, but he says it would be premature."

FIVE

ALISON

The day of Alison's arrival, the Ferryman's was in a state of upheaval.

Mary was running up and down the stairs with buckets of hot, soapy water, a vacuum cleaner, and piles of sheets and towels, while Shirley was finishing off in the kitchen.

'After what she's been through with that bastard, I want everything to be ready when she gets here,' she explained, setting off to Alison's room with a bunch of flowers.

To prepare for this unwanted intrusion, I went off with Gunner for a brisk walk around Rydal Water. The sheep had been moved back up into the hills and I was able to let him off the lead for a run.

The fresh air did me good. I had enjoyed a few too many whiskies with the Major the previous evening, perhaps because it was the last one we would have alone. I needed to get my head sorted out before meeting his niece.

After all, we might even get on, I thought. It certainly wasn't fair to prejudge her, although Pauline wouldn't be happy having a younger, more attractive woman around.

*

By the time Gunner and I got back, Alison had arrived and was sitting in the bar chatting with her uncle.

She was attractive, with big blue eyes and shoulder-length blonde hair tied back in a ponytail. She was dressed in jeans and a polo shirt, but after years of weighing up our clients at the garage, I could see that her outfit came from designer boutiques.

'Come and meet my niece,' greeted the Major. 'I was telling her all about you.'

'Not everything, I hope,' I joked, shaking her hand bashfully.

'No, Simon. I've left the best bits for when we all have a drink later.'

This was what I had been afraid of, but I managed a weak smile.

'It's good to meet you, Alison. Can I give you a hand with your bags?'

'That would be kind. I've got half my wardrobe in the car and my uncle tells me that my room is right at the top.'

'Safest place for you,' said the Major, with a wink. 'Now, let's get those bags.'

*

When we got outside, I was not surprised to see she had a brand-new, full option Mini Cooper S.

'It's a miracle you've managed to pack so much into such a small boot,' I said as she opened up the car.

'Don't worry, there's plenty more on the back seat,' she replied. I was already wondering how many return trips it would take to get everything inside.

I had not been in the private quarters before and I was impressed by how well-appointed they were. There were oil paintings of Lakeland scenes running up the stairs and porcelain lamps on polished tables on the landings. Shirley's touch was everywhere.

Alison's room was furnished with a double bed, antique oak cabinets on either side and an old-fashioned wardrobe next to the door to an ensuite bathroom. A dressing table and upholstered chair stood in front of the window, looking out towards the woodland behind the building.

'It's beautiful,' she exclaimed as she followed me through the door.

'Yes, you should be comfortable in here,' I said as I put the last of the clothes on the bed. 'Even if it is a hike to get up all those stairs.'

'The exercise will do me good,' she replied. 'Would you mind telling my uncle I'm going to unpack and take a shower and then I'll be down to give you all a hand?'

As I made my way back downstairs, I realised my fears had been unjustified.

Alison was charming and I felt an instant attraction before reminding myself I was far from ready for a new relationship.

*

Pauline was alone behind the bar, serving the first guests of the day.

'How's the new arrival?' she asked. 'It will be nice to have an attractive young woman around, won't it, Simon?'

I had expected to have this discussion and wanted to get it over before there was a problem between us.

'She seems very pleasant, Pauline, but, as you know, the last thing I'm interested in at the moment is women, young or otherwise.'

'Tell me when that changes and I'll show you that experience is better than youth any day of the week,' she whispered, squeezing my bottom with her hand.

She seemed to have accepted we would never be lovers and I hoped she was only joking. Half an hour later, we were joined by Alison, looking refreshed from her shower.

'You must be Pauline,' she said. 'I expect my uncle told you I was coming here to help out.'

'He has. I hope you won't find it too dull up here after your celebrity life in Liverpool?'

'To be honest, Pauline,' she replied with a hint of a Liverpool accent slipping out, 'I wouldn't wish the life I've had over the last two years on anybody. Now, can you show me what I need to do? I've never worked in a pub before.'

'Another one,' muttered Pauline, looking at me before turning to serve a group of hikers.

'Don't worry,' I said, putting a hand on Alison's shoulder. 'She's got a heart of gold, but after me arriving and then you turning up, it's been a lot of change for her. She's been here for years.'

She gave me a grim smile.

'Anyway, let me show you the ropes while it's still quiet. You'll get the hang of it in no time.'

*

It stayed quiet for a Saturday in early June. At about one o'clock, Paul walked in and ordered a pint of lager.

'Would Linda like her usual cider?' I asked as I filled his glass.

'No, I'm on my own. Linda and I aren't seeing each other anymore.'

'That's a shame. You were so good together.'

'We were, but the wife's decided she wants me to teach her golf. She said she felt sorry for me, heading off on my own every Saturday.'

'So where is she now?'

'Doing a bit of shopping in Ambleside. I have to pick her up in half an hour and then it's off to Keswick Golf Course for the afternoon,' he answered.

'So I suppose poor Linda won't have to spend her Saturday

afternoons on all fours trying to find your balls in the long grass,' added the Major, smiling cruelly. When I saw the expression on his face, it was all I could do not to burst out laughing. Even Gunner seemed to be smiling.

*

The day went well. Despite my earlier doubts, I could see it would be good having Alison around.

She was confident but had a gentle way about her. Her infectious sense of humour had even brought Pauline on side by the end of the evening.

'I'm sorry I was rude to you this afternoon, but I'm not used to having another gorgeous young woman around. Now I've got to know you, I can see we'll make a great team.'

'Thanks, Pauline. I hope it will make things a bit easier for you. Simon tells me you've all been working flat out.'

'We have, love, so I hope it won't take as long to train you up as it did with this one,' she joked, giving me a playful shove.

Eventually, it was closing time and I wondered whether the Major would keep to his word and ask his niece to join us for a nightcap.

'Alison,' he started. 'Simon and I normally enjoy a glass of whisky at the end of the evening. It's the only chance we have for a chat. We'd both be delighted if you were to join us.'

I smiled at her encouragingly. I had not been looking forward to this, but now I had met her, I wanted her to agree.

'That would be lovely, thank you. Pauline told me about your late-night drinks and I was hoping I'd be invited.'

'Good, that's settled then,' said the Major, reaching for the Knockando.

'But none of your whisky. I'm a good girl. A glass of white wine would be lovely.'

Our conversation was limited to life at the pub and some of the more amusing regulars. I didn't want to be asked about my past and neither did Alison.

'Did you see the vicar was in again this evening?' asked the Major. 'With what he puts away on a Saturday night, I'm not surprised they have to ring the church bells to wake him up for the Sunday morning service.'

'Yes, he was a bit unsteady on his feet when he left,' said Alison.

'Wait until next Friday. You'll see a few in a far worse state,' I added.

Although Alison had told us she was tired and would only have a quick glass, at one point, it looked as if the Major and I would have to go to bed and leave her in the bar on her own.

'One more small one and then I'm off,' she repeated on at least three occasions, and there was nothing left in the bottle when she finally went up the stairs to bed.

Of course, as gentlemen, the Major and I were obliged to keep her company. After my third or fourth whisky, I knew I would pay for it the next morning.

*

When I came through to the kitchen after breakfast, I was surprised to see that Alison was up and dressed, already wearing walking boots and a waxed outdoor jacket.

'Shirley told me that you and Gunner like to go out for a walk in the morning. Any chance I can come along with you?'

Gunner appealed to me with his big brown eyes. She must have had a word with him before I arrived, I thought.

My solitary walks with Gunner were one reason I had been starting to feel much better about myself, but I agreed with all the grace I could muster.

Not feeling up to a hill walk, I decided to take the same route as the previous day. It was very scenic and there weren't too many steep slopes.

Alison was good company and my regrets about her accompanying me vanished. We were able to have a good chat as we walked, with Gunner happily running around on his own.

I learned that her father was a joiner. He had managed to drag their family up from its roots in Bootle to a respectable three-bed semi in leafy Aigburth when she was still young.

'That's where I was staying until my uncle persuaded my dad to send me up here for a while.'

For some reason, I had thought it would have been her father who had persuaded the Major to let her come and stay with us.

'What a beautiful island,' she said as we arrived where I had sat a few weeks earlier.

I resisted the temptation to tell her about the hairy, little Lakeland people who eat strangers and then write notes to their widows. Instead, I told her that it was called Heron Island and as the lake was privately owned, boating was not allowed and no one could visit it.

'What a pity,' she said. 'It looks as if it could be a delightful place to hide from the outside world. Can we sit down for a minute? My feet are killing me.'

We settled down into the grass and I felt happy to be sitting there next to her, taking in the scenery, as Gunner went off looking for rabbits.

After about ten minutes, she turned to me and put her hand on my knee.

'Simon, I've been through a terrible time. That bastard. He was so good and kind in the beginning, but once he got that transfer to Tranmere, he became a different person.'

I was surprised and embarrassed she was bringing this up with me, but I sensed she needed to talk to someone and I was the only person around.

'He was shagging every girl he could get his hands on. He couldn't help himself. One day, we were out in his Range Rover and I reached into the glove compartment to get the phone charger. Do you know what I found?'

I had a good idea but shook my head all the same.

'A pair of knickers. "*What the hell are these doing in here, Max?*" I asked him. Apparently, it was the only thing he could find to wipe the windscreen.

"'*I hope they're clean, then,*" I said to him, and then he had the nerve to laugh at me; fucking laugh at me.'

'How long did this go on for?' I asked.

'It would be on and off. He'd come home, all apologetic with flowers and chocolates, and it would be alright for a week or so, and then he'd be off again. Too much money and too much testost... I can't even say it properly.'

'Testosterone,' I prompted her.

'Yes, that's it, testosterone. The final straw was when another player's girlfriend told me her boyfriend and Max were seeing prostitutes in Manchester. Everyone at the club knew, apart from me. Can you imagine the shame?'

I shook my head again. I could well imagine how she must have felt.

'I couldn't carry on like that, and one evening, I told him I was leaving.'

'How did that go down?' I asked.

'Not well. His dinner ended up on the floor and I thought he was about to hit me before he got up and stormed out of the house. I called my dad and he came straight over with his van; we cleared out my belongings in one go.'

I struggled to imagine the scene. Teresa and I had our arguments, but there had never been any suggestion of violence.

'I haven't seen or heard from him since,' continued Alison. 'What a complete waste of two years.'

I put my arm around her shoulders and we sat there in silence until it was time to go back. Between me, Pauline and Alison, we were a hopeless little group of the abandoned and bereaved.

SIX

LIVERPOOL

Now Pauline had taught me everything I needed to know about running the bar, I was keen to pass on my knowledge to my new apprentice.

She was an enthusiastic student and I enjoyed showing her what she needed to do.

'Isn't changing the barrels more of a man's job?' she teased me one day after I had led her down to the cellar.

'That's a very sexist remark for a modern young lady,' I joked, reaching over to turn off the gas supply to the Heineken. 'How will you manage if the Major and I aren't here?'

She gave me a cheeky smile.

I grinned back as I undid the coupler, remembering how I had drenched Pauline on my first day. I beckoned to Alison to come closer to show her what I was doing and our eyes met as she knelt next to me.

I felt an urge to take her in my arms and kiss her. To feel the warmth of her body against mine.

'Aren't you going to connect a new barrel?' asked Alison, still looking into my eyes.

I felt myself blush, but she gave me a quick kiss on the cheek before standing up, ready to go back upstairs.

My heart sank as I reminded myself we could never be more than friends. Not for as long as she saw me as the person I had now become.

*

'You still haven't told me what you're doing in Liverpool,' complained Alison, as we set off on the seven-mile drive to Bowness a few days later.

She had been at the pub for almost a fortnight, but I hadn't said anything about Teresa.

'That's right,' I replied, smiling innocently.

'You're so annoying. I don't know anything about you. I've even asked my uncle and all he said was that you turned up one day for a drink and two days later you had moved in.'

I didn't reply.

'I mean, you could have come out of prison or something. It can't be that difficult to tell me what you were doing before you got here, Simon?'

She was right, but I was only beginning to come to terms with everything I had been through and I wasn't ready to open up to her.

'OK. I've never been to prison, but I've always loved the Lake District and this was my chance to move here.'

'So what sort of work were you doing?'

'Sales, but I'd had enough.'

'We are making progress. Can we talk about Liverpool?'

'I'm going because my wife was killed in an accident and there's a meeting to read her will.'

I looked sideways and I could see from Alison's expression that it was all starting to make sense.

'I'm sorry for being nosey. It must have been terrible,' she apologised.

'No, you were right to ask. No one else has been interested. Not even your uncle,' I said, realising he had never asked me anything about myself.

'That is strange. He's a terrible gossip. Can I ask how long you were married?'

'Twenty-six years. We married very young; there was a baby on the way,' I replied, starting to feel uneasy at Alison's questions.

'So you have children?' she continued.

'Yes, two boys. But I'm OK. My wife and I hadn't been close for years.'

I was relieved when our discussion was brought to an end by our arrival at the station.

'Will you be alright, Simon? I could always come with you?' she asked, touching my hand.

'No, honestly. I'll be fine and you'll be needed at the Ferryman's. But thanks for the lift.'

*

I sensed a change in my relationship with Alison that morning. In the time since she arrived at the Ferryman's, we had become good friends and I looked forward to our walks up in the hills. Even our late-night drinks with the Major.

I found her attractive and great fun to be with, but even though I could sense a spark between us, I didn't dare to dream of anything more than friendship.

She must have seen me as a middle-aged burnout, scraping a living in a pub, miles from anywhere. How could someone like her ever fall in love with someone like that? Especially after the life of luxury she must have enjoyed with Max.

I kept asking myself the same question over and over again as the train hurtled through the Cumbrian countryside.

But something in how she spoke to me as we drove to Bowness made me think there might be the hope of something more; the way she touched my hand and her offer to come to Liverpool with me.

Then there was Joanna to think about. I had been in love with her, but was this just because I was vulnerable? Gasping for air in the emotional vacuum left by Teresa's death? I still had feelings for her, but how could we ever have a proper relationship? She was two years younger than Peter.

*

The journey took almost three hours and it was just before midday when I stepped off the train under the Victorian glass roof at Lime Street Station.

Mike and I had arranged to meet at twelve-thirty at the San Carlo restaurant in Castle Street and I had the time for a stroll past some of my old haunts.

I wandered through the main entrance of Lewis's, at the top of Ranelagh Street, where the naked statue of "Nobby Lewis" had amused generations of giggling schoolgirls since the 1950s.

It was no longer the emporium of luxury where my mother used to take me to the Christmas Grotto as a small boy, wide-eyed with excitement. I didn't stay long, heading on towards Bold Street, where the fine ladies of Liverpool would do their shopping back in the 1960s.

Now it was a motley collection of discount and charity shops. I carried on down Church Street, past its big, modern fashion stores, loud music blaring out of their open doors.

There were people everywhere, and I felt uncomfortable after my self-imposed exile in the Lakes.

After my long journey and the depressing walk from the station, I wished I were back at the Ferryman's. As I walked through the glass door of the restaurant, however, I remembered how I had been looking forward to seeing Mike, despite what he had told me.

He was already sitting at the ultra-modern, white marble bar with a large gin and tonic. It was all glass and chrome, with only a large silver bowl of Sicilian lemons to add some colour.

'Simon, I've never seen you looking so good! What are you drinking?'

'I'll have the same as you. I guess I'm going to need it,' I answered. I wasn't expecting good news.

Mike ordered my drink before turning back towards me with a broad smile on his face.

'The good news is that Peter's doing well. I did have my doubts, but he's proved me wrong,' he told me. 'I was in the garage last week to see Mrs Davies and he looked as if he owned the place. You might need to find another business when you come back.'

Here we go again, I thought. All about Peter. How had Matt been getting on? Not a word about him.

'And the bad?' I asked, shifting my position in the chair.

'The bad news is that we're not getting anywhere with this money-laundering business. I tried to get a meeting for this morning with Ken Roberts, but he said they still haven't finished their investigations.'

My hand trembled as I raised my glass to my lips.

'There is one positive thing, though. When he applied for the court order to impound the Bentley, the judge told him he didn't have sufficient evidence.'

'So why is he carrying on with this pointless vendetta?' I asked. It was as I had thought: they didn't have anything concrete to go on.

'I've no idea, but he's getting stuck in. Peter called me a few days ago. He was in a right state. He told me Roberts had been to see Nick French and he won't be the only one he's contacted. Is there still nothing you want to tell me?'

I shrugged, shaking my head as I thought about the damage this was doing to my business. I had no idea how Peter must have been coping with it all, but I wouldn't have long to wait to find out.

'We need to get you back home, Simon,' started Mike before our conversation was cut short by a uniformed waiter who had come over to take us through to our table.

The restaurant was packed with the rich and famous of Liverpool. I was struck by the contrast between the bright and modern dining area and the Ferryman's cosy, rustic charm.

The décor was not the only contrast. I ordered linguini with lobster in a cream sauce to start and sea bass with grilled Mediterranean vegetables for my main course. I loved the home cooking at the pub, but I was ready for something a little more exotic, especially as Mike had offered to pay.

'Who said I'm coming back?' I replied after the waiter had left with our orders.

'You can't be serious? You'll be home before the summer, surely?' asked Mike, shaking his head in disbelief at what he had heard.

'Let's wait and see,' I replied, anxious to change the subject before our food arrived.

Mike realised it was pointless insisting and I started telling him about my adventures at the Ferryman's.

'The Major sounds like quite a character; I'd like to meet him, but I'm not sure about this Pauline. You'll need to watch yourself with her. And the Major's friend, John. He's a good guy,' said Mike. I couldn't remember having mentioned John, but we had been talking about so many different things. Perhaps he had slipped into the conversation.

'But seriously, you've got the money. Why do you need to work behind a bar? I told you before you left that you should be going off to your villa in the South of France. The weather's fantastic there and you could even buy yourself a dog if you're lonely.'

He smiled when he saw my expression.

'You've got the hots for this Alison girl, haven't you?' he asked.

I felt my cheeks flush. I didn't think it was that obvious.

'Look, I only met her ten days ago; I hardly know her. Anyway, nothing can come of it,' I tried to explain.

'But she sounds perfect. How old did you say she is?'

'She's thirty-two, Mike,' I replied, smiling.

'That's already an improvement on Joanna. She's what, twenty-four?' said Mike, giggling at his own comment.

'Yes, but I'm not getting drawn on that again, whatever you might want to think.'

'If you say so, but I'm sure I'm not the one who's been doing all the thinking. You know what my poor old Catholic mother used to say?'

I shook my head.

'The thought's as bad as the deed, so once you've had the thought...' he said, raising his eyebrows. 'Still, what's the problem with Alison?'

'Well, her ex is a footballer and as far as she's concerned, I'm a six-pounds-an-hour barman who's fifteen years her senior. Where's the future in that?'

'Tell her the truth. You're a wealthy garage owner on a sabbatical.'

'I can't; it would be too weird. And what about the Major? He'd boot me out.'

'I don't think he'd be bothered, so long as you're doing your job. Anyway, you're going to have to tell her the truth or get used to the idea of giving Pauline what she's after,' he joked, laughing as he saw me screwing up my face.

*

The solicitor's office was in the India Building on Water Street. It was built in a neoclassical style between the two World Wars and is one of the city's finest buildings.

Peter and Matt were waiting at the entrance to the shopping arcade that runs through the ground floor. From the way they looked at everyone who came through the door, I could see they were as uncomfortable as I was.

'Dad, it's good to see you. Will you have time to come for a drink later?' asked Peter, glancing at his brother.

It would have been nice if Peter did want to have a drink with me, but I wasn't convinced. I imagined Matt had told him to ask.

'Of course. Will you come along, Mike?' I asked.

'No, not this time. You and the boys have got a lot of catching up to do. I'll leave you to it.'

When we got upstairs, the receptionist took us straight through to a meeting room. Jonathan Harris, our family solicitor, was already sitting at the head of a long, polished wooden table.

I had met Mr Harris when I bought the garage and he had been the family's solicitor ever since.

Short, dark-haired and pale, he was dressed in a black suit, a white shirt and, as always, a dark tie as sober and humourless as he was.

'Thank you so much for coming to see me,' he greeted. 'I understand that Simon has had quite a journey, but it's best to get everyone together at times like this.'

The boys and I nodded.

He paused before continuing. 'Teresa came to see me last year and signed a new will. I have no reason to believe she has made another one since then?'

He gave us all a questioning look and we shook our heads. Mr Harris had prepared a joint will for us shortly after Matt was born, but I never imagined Teresa might have had one drawn up.

'Everything is left to you, Simon, apart from a bequest of cash and bonds that goes to Matthew.'

Peter and I turned to look at Matt, who had become bright red with embarrassment.

'I had no idea,' he protested. 'Honestly.'

'I can confirm that your mother told me she didn't want you to know about this while she was alive.'

'How much we're talking about?' asked Matt timidly.

'Yes, of course, I was coming to that. In total, we are looking at about £350,000.'

'Where did she get all that from?' I asked, surprised.

Again I was reminded how little I had known about my wife and how far apart we had become.

'A good question. You will appreciate that, as solicitors, we are obliged to keep an eye out for anything that might be irregular. Still, we have been through her financial records most carefully and all would appear to be in order.'

Mike looked at me to ask whether any of it might have come from my alleged money-laundering activities, but I shook my head and he seemed reassured.

'When her mother died, she left everything to Teresa. She had bought her council house years before and between that and Teresa's savings and investments, it all mounted up. Something you would do well to remember, young man,' he said, leaning over towards Matt, waving his pen at him.

'But why did she leave it all to me?' asked Matt.

From the way Peter was staring at Mr Harris, Matt wasn't the only one waiting for an explanation.

'I did ask your mother the same question and she explained that it was for your future. To buy a business, perhaps. I know your father will soon be giving Peter shares in his company.'

I looked at Peter and smiled, but he wasn't smiling back.

'If it hasn't been seized by the Serious Fraud Office in the meantime, along with everything else we've got,' he muttered, giving me a dark look across the table.

Peter was right. He could have ended up without a job and penniless, while Matt went off and spent his inheritance.

*

After we left the solicitors' office, the three of us piled into the New World, down towards the Pier Head.

This historic pub had survived on the edge of a Second World War bombsite for decades before escaping the redevelopment of the city centre. It was a reminder of how Liverpool had been a gateway for those leaving for new lives in the four corners of the world.

'I guess you're buying,' said Peter without humour, giving his brother a prod in the ribs.

'I'm sorry, it's the last thing I would have expected,' replied Matt.

Peter looked at him for a moment, before taking a deep breath.

'The decent thing to do would be to share it,' he suggested.

'Of course. That's a brilliant idea, Peter,' replied Matt, smiling and putting his arm around his brother's shoulders. 'And we can all have a chat about the shares in the garage. I'm fed up with driving round in a shitty van all day, fixing people's bogs.'

Peter shrugged off his brother's arm and moved away from him.

'It was quite a surprise,' I said, looking at both of them in turn. I hoped this wasn't going to be another reason for the destruction of the family I had once loved. 'And a lot more than I would have expected. Still, try not to spend any of it without talking to me first. I might have an idea or two for you.'

'Of course, Dad. Anyway, what are you both drinking?'

The conversation was strained. No one wanted to reopen wounds that were only starting to heal after the shock of Teresa's death.

'I can understand what mother was thinking, but what if they do close down the business?' asked Peter, shaking his head. 'The Bentley was only the start of it, I reckon.'

'Well, I hope you'll both come and visit me in prison if they do,' I tried to joke.

From Peter's expression, I could see that my comment had not helped.

'Sorry, that was stupid, but Mike and I had a long chat over lunch and he's got everything under control,' I lied. 'Give it a month or two and it will all have blown over.'

'I hope so,' continued Peter. 'I had a hell of a job explaining everything to Nick French. Thank God the Lamborghini deal's been done and the money's in the bank. I don't think we'll be seeing him again for a while.'

I wasn't so sure. Nick and I had known each other for far too long for something like this to keep him away.

I could see that Peter was worried sick by the thought of losing the garage, but what about me ending up behind bars? It was clear that I hadn't been missed at all. Peter had the garage to himself, for the time being at least, and Matt had the run of the house with Sarah. Who could blame them? Perhaps this was what I deserved for being such a dreadful father.

I looked around the pub as we stood drinking our beers. The smoke-stained walls were covered with nautical memorabilia: old photos of ocean liners, dinner plates from the RMS *Mauretania* and the porthole of a ship, long since scrapped.

I imagined the travellers drinking their last pint of ale on British soil before departing on some long sea voyage. It made me think how the three of us were also on a journey.

A journey to where? I asked myself. We didn't have tickets with our destinations printed for all to see. Our ship had sunk beneath the waves and we were waiting in the lifeboats to be rescued.

'How's Sarah getting on?' I asked, trying to end a long silence that was becoming quite awkward.

'She's fine.' Matt grinned. 'I don't know how we'd manage without her.'

'And Joanna?' I continued, pretending not to be particularly interested.

'She hasn't been herself since the funeral, although she and Darren seem to be getting on OK,' replied Peter.

'A bit too well, from what Pete's been telling me,' added Matt. 'It won't be long before he gets his leg over.'

'If he hasn't already,' muttered Peter, thoughtfully.

I felt a sharp pang of grief as I remembered our last telephone conversation, with Joanna sobbing at the other end of the line.

'I almost forgot. Brian came to the garage yesterday,' said Peter, taking a mouthful of beer.

'Brian Arkwright? What did he want?'

'He's made a load of money from a record deal. Apparently, the revival tour was a great success. He wanted to know if the Bentley was still available and when I said it was, he made me an offer I couldn't refuse.'

'How much?' I asked.

'£95,000. It's a bit below the £110,000 we were asking, but we'll still make a decent turn.'

'You'll need to speak to Mike before you hand over the keys, but there shouldn't be a problem. Anyway, well done; I'll be pleased to see that car gone. The only good thing to come out of it was the day after the funeral when I drove up to...'

I stopped myself mid-sentence. Apart from Mike, no one had any idea where I was staying and I wasn't ready to give my secret away.

'Up to where?' asked Peter, raising an eyebrow. 'Is that where you're hiding from us all?'

I ignored the question. 'Tell Brian and Anne that I'm very pleased for them both.'

We didn't stay at the pub for a second drink; I was facing another three-hour journey. Although it felt strange to be heading off without the boys, I looked forward to getting home to the Ferryman's.

SEVEN

A BIT OF BOTHER

We were kept busy in the pub over the next few days, and I looked forward to my morning outings with Alison.

Now that I was getting to know her better, I could sense a fragility that I had not seen before and she would often take my arm in hers as we walked.

The way her relationship with Max had ended must have dented her confidence. I reckoned it would take some time for her to get back to how she had been before they met.

As her feet were now used to our walks, we became more adventurous and often climbed Nab Scar to take in the views.

Gunner would have been happy to have stayed out all day but work always called us back before we could go too far.

'Does he never tire?' Alison asked me one day as we struggled to keep up with him.

'He's making up for lost time. He hadn't been out much before I arrived.'

I desperately wanted our relationship to be more. However, I was still afraid of rejection and how her uncle would react.

I often wondered whether I should take Mike's advice and tell her who I was, but would this shatter the innocence of our idyllic rustic life?

I was caught in the horns of a dilemma and I couldn't see any way forward. My greatest worry was that if something didn't happen soon, we would become such good friends that there could never be any question of romance.

*

Spring soon became summer and visitors flocked to the Ferryman's to enjoy cold beers in the pub gardens. It was now over a month since Alison had arrived and I sensed that, while she wanted to find out more about me, she was afraid of what she would discover.

'Your two sons,' she started during one of our walks.

'Peter and Matt,' I replied.

'How old are they?'

'Peter's twenty-six and Matt's twenty-four. They were at the solicitors' the other day; they seem to be getting on OK.'

'I'm pleased.' She smiled, happy to have managed to get another scrap of information.

Another time, we were clearing up after lunch and she asked me if I planned to invite them up to stay at the Ferryman's.

'They could stay with you in the mobile home.'

'I have invited them a couple of times, but they don't have much free time,' I lied.

Alison was trying to build a picture of the real Simon. However, it was still too early for me to abandon the anonymity I had grown to value.

*

The following Wednesday, it had been busy at lunchtime, after the Ambleside market, and Alison and I were left to clear up.

'Simon, it's a lovely day outside. Why don't you pour us a couple of lagers? We can drink them in the garden,' she said, touching my hand.

Something in her eyes told me I had no choice.

'I'll go and pick a table,' she continued. 'And mine's a pint.'

I did as I was told. When I got outside, I found Alison at the far end of the garden, sitting in the shade of a large monkey tree.

'Thank you,' she said as she took a first mouthful of beer. 'I needed this. I've never worked so hard in my life.'

We sat for a few minutes, drinking our beer and watching the traffic drive past on the main road.

After a while, Alison turned to look me in the eye and placed her hand on mine.

'Have you travelled much?' she asked. 'Max used to take me all over the place. We had some good trips before he lost the plot.'

I could imagine the exotic destinations and the luxury hotels, Max splashing his cash.

'Not as much as you have,' I answered, truthfully for once. 'France mainly.'

After Teresa and I bought the villa, we rarely went anywhere else. My work routine made it hard to get away.

'Doesn't watching these cars going past make you think there's a whole world out there, waiting to be explored?' she asked.

'Well, you're young enough,' I said, with no idea where she was heading with this.

She squeezed my hand before carrying on.

'So are you, Simon. Why don't we try to go away somewhere for a few days? We could go to London, for example, and see a show.'

'And eat something Shirley hasn't cooked,' I joked, thinking back to my lunch with Mike.

Alison looked at me, waiting for a proper answer.

'Of course, Alison. That could be great fun. There's a hotel I know in Marylebone that's close to everything,' I suggested.

She smiled and turned back to face the road, still holding my hand.

I was confused. Was she suggesting we went away as a couple or as friends? Yes, she was holding my hand, but she had been very tactile from the day we met.

I would have to wait and see, I told myself. Or else I would have to pluck up the courage to take the first step.

*

In contrast to lunchtime, the evening was quiet.

John came in for a quick pint at about six and then left. After that, the only custom we had was a few regulars drifting in and out.

At about eight, I was polishing some glasses when two uniformed police officers came through the door and took a pair of stools at the bar.

It reminded me of the fateful morning at the garage and I felt a shiver run down my spine. PC Wainwright and WPC Carter's visit was something I would never forget and never wanted to go through again.

'Good evening, officers. How can we help you?' greeted the Major.

'We'll take two of pints Nab's End, please,' said the older of the two.

'Not on duty then?' asked the Major, catching my eye.

'We've finished, but I'd have given anything not to have been working this evening,' said the other. 'We've been helping to scrape up what was left of some poor sod up the road towards Grasmere.'

He paused as he remembered the scene before carrying on, shaking his head. 'I've never seen anything like that, thank God; run over by one of those livestock trucks. He didn't stand a chance.'

I instinctively moved closer to join the conversation.

'The head was pretty much all that was left. A young lad in his mid-twenties. Curly red hair. I don't envy whoever has to tell his parents,' he continued. 'Anyway, how are we doing with those drinks?'

'Here you are, gents; these are on me. If it's who I think it was, you don't need to worry about his parents – they died years ago,' said the Major, looking at me sadly. 'He was a tortured soul. Still, it's all over for him now.'

As much as I had disliked Ben, I would not have wished his fate on anyone, but the Major was right. His life of misery was over.

*

I felt relieved when the police officers left after a second pint. By about nine o'clock, we were on the point of having a drink ourselves when the door opened and in walked three men in their early thirties.

They were typical of the flash footballer crowd and I didn't like the look of them at all.

Dressed in coloured shell-suits, they had more jewellery on display than a counter at H. Samuel. From their expressions, they looked as if they owned the place.

'Oh, shit, it's my ex,' whispered Alison, grabbing my arm before disappearing off into the kitchen.

'What can I get you guys?' I asked, glancing towards the Major, who was at the end of the bar.

'I'd like to see Alison,' replied the taller one in the middle, who I took to be Max.

'I'm afraid she's off duty. Was she expecting you?' I asked, trying to remain polite.

'Don't give me that shit, mate. Just go and get her for me,' shouted Max, looking me straight in the eye.

'Now, look. I'm happy to serve you some drinks, but I'm telling you she's not available,' I insisted, now not so politely.

Before he could reply, Alison had slipped back into the room.

She was standing next to me behind the bar, expressionless.

'It's alright. I'll deal with this dickhead. What do you want, Max? You've got some nerve coming here.'

'Your dad told me where you were. He wanted us to give it another try,' attempted Max, now speaking quietly and trying to sound conciliatory.

I bet he did, I said to myself, thinking of Max's money. He can't have been happy to have his precious daughter stuck in the middle of nowhere, working all hours for nothing.

Alison looked at Max and then at each of the others, with an expression of contempt before continuing.

'If you want to give it a try with my dad, go ahead, but I don't think you're his type. As far as I'm concerned, you and your mates can piss off.'

The two remaining guests drained their glasses and left, and the Major looked over at me with raised eyebrows as if asking me what we should do.

Alison was sticking up for herself admirably and I left her behind the bar to start clearing the tables.

'Where are you off to?' demanded one of Max's friends.

'I'm tidying up; it's almost closing time,' I replied calmly, forcing a smile.

'I suggest you get back behind that bar,' he continued, raising his voice.

They might have been younger and fitter than me, but I wasn't used to being intimidated.

'I'm sorry, but I have work to do.'

He leant over towards me until his face was a few inches from mine.

'Don't you understand English, mate? Get back behind that fucking bar!'

Alison looked disappointed as I did as I was told but, back next to her, I turned to face the three of them.

'This has gone far enough. Max, I'm closing the pub now and I must ask you and your mates to piss off like Alison asked a few minutes ago.'

'You haven't heard the end of this,' shouted Max. From what Alison had told me, he was used to getting his own way and his face was red with frustration.

'I think we have. You see that camera up there in the corner? It was put there because of idiots like you. If you try to contact any of us again, one copy of this evening's recording will go off to the police, one to the press and one to your club.'

The three of them stared up at the camera and Max started to reach up as if he were going to try to rip it down.

'Don't waste your time. Everything is already on a computer server in Manchester.'

He stopped himself and turned to face me, unsure whether I was telling the truth.

For a few seconds, nobody spoke or moved.

The silence was finally broken when Max turned to Alison, shouted, 'Fuck,' shook his head and led his friends out to the car park.

As soon as we were sure they had gone, the Major reached for a bottle of whisky and poured two large measures.

'Simon, come and have a drink. You deserve it,' he said, sounding embarrassed. 'I'm sorry I didn't do more to help, but the pair of you were doing pretty well on your own.'

Without a word, Alison grabbed the bottle out of the Major's hand, poured herself a glass and took a big gulp.

'Yes, Simon. Thank you for helping me. If you hadn't been there, I don't know how it might have ended.'

A chapter of Alison's life had been closed that evening. Although none of us was in the mood for conversation, we were happy to be there together, sharing each other's company.

*

I was woken at about two by the sound of the outside door opening and someone stumbling through in the darkness.

I felt every muscle in my body tense up. It had to be Max coming back to sort me out. Lying there under the duvet, I was defenceless.

I rolled over and sat up, grabbing a pillow to protect myself from the blows I expected to feel raining down on me.

'Go back to sleep,' whispered Alison, letting her dressing gown fall to the floor and climbing into the bed beside me.

She settled close to me, lying on her side with an arm across my chest. Her head was on my shoulder and I could feel her warm breath on my neck.

After a while, I finally managed to doze off, but my sleep was light and interrupted. I was in love with the woman lying naked next to me, but I would have to wait until the morning to show her how much.

*

The sun rose shortly before five and I felt the hand that had been on my chest move inside my boxer shorts.

'He's ready,' she whispered, pulling me on top of her.

As I entered her, our lips joined in a full embrace and we made love as I had imagined more times than I could remember.

We finally climaxed and fell back onto the bed, exhausted.

'Oh my God, I didn't think; I stopped taking the pill after I left Max,' she whispered once she got her breath back.

'It's alright. I had a vasectomy years ago.'

'Thank God for that. I hate children.'

'You said you came from a big family?'

'I did. My grandmother gave birth to twelve children. By the time she finished breastfeeding that lot, she had nipples like walnuts.'

I looked sideways to see her small but pert breasts crowned by two small raisins.

'And we wouldn't want that, would we now?' she whispered, kissing me on the cheek.

Within seconds, her eyes were closed and she was asleep, but I forced myself to stay awake to make the moment last as long as possible.

Eventually, I couldn't keep my eyes open any longer and slipped into a contented sleep. When I woke again, I was upset to see she had slipped away, back inside the Ferryman's.

I followed, fed, washed and dressed, and I was relieved that everything was as it was every morning. The Major in his armchair with his tea, Shirley and Mary busying themselves with breakfasts for the overnight guests, and Alison and Gunner waiting to go out on our daily walk.

The fine weather made the day perfect and as soon as we were out of sight of the pub, I allowed myself to put an arm around Alison's waist.

I was full of self-doubt. What if last night had been a reaction to what happened in the bar? Would she still feel the same in the clear light of day?

I was put at ease when she turned her face towards me and gave me a kiss.

'Well, one of us had to make the first move, Simon,' she said, her beautiful eyes bright and smiling. 'And if I had waited for you, I would have been waiting forever.'

I pulled her closer to me and we carried on walking in silence until we drew level with Heron Island.

'Why didn't you try to kiss me that day we were down in the cellar, Simon?' she asked. 'I knew you wanted to; it was obvious.'

I thought for a second before replying.

'I have wanted to kiss you since the day you arrived, Alison,' I said.

'And?' she asked.

'I was afraid of rejection. Of losing you. That you wouldn't be interested in a middle-aged barman, with tons of baggage.'

She looked at me, questioningly.

'How can you lose something you don't have? *Carpe diem*, Simon. You're caring, fun to be with, fit, handsome... What more could a girl want?'

Her comment made me guiltily think back to what Joanna had said over lunch at her parents'.

'A future?' I asked.

She laughed before replying.

'There's plenty of time for that. Let's enjoy the present first. The past hasn't been kind to either of us.'

I wrapped my arms around her.

'And there I was, thinking you hadn't had much experience recently,' she teased me.

'It's true, but I do practise a lot on my own.'

She kissed me again, but this time on the mouth.

'We'll have to make sure you don't need to do that anymore, won't we?' she joked.

*

Back at the Ferryman's, we hardly saw each other all day. It was Pauline's day off and, every time we had the chance of a couple of minutes alone, someone would want serving, or Alison would be called away to the kitchen.

At the end of the evening, the last few stragglers finally

wandered off into the night and, as usual, the Major reached down for his bottle of Knockando.

'You know what?' said Alison. 'I'm exhausted. I'll leave you boys to it.'

'Alright,' replied the Major. 'Have a good sleep.'

'Thank you, Uncle. Simon, you look tired. You shouldn't stay up too late either,' she added, giving me a meaningful stare.

'Don't worry, I won't. I'll have one drink and then I'll be off to bed.'

The Major cleared his throat as though he was wondering what to say. It was not a problem he often had to struggle with.

'A good girl, my niece. I wish she'd never met that piece of shit. From what I was told by my brother, he was still a nice guy when they first met two years ago; treated her like a princess.'

'It's always the same, I'm afraid,' I said, shaking my head. 'As soon as these footballers start to earn a bit of cash and get their pictures in the papers, they think they can do whatever they like.'

I finished my glass before getting up to leave.

'You're a good lad, Simon. I knew it the day we met. Sleep well.'

*

When I opened the door to the mobile home, I was hit by the smell of soap and perfume.

The lights were off, but there were candles everywhere and Alison was lying on the bed under the duvet, her blonde hair spread out on the pillow like a halo.

'I thought you were going to be forever. I've put a clean towel in the shower room. Why don't you go and freshen up? I'll still be here when you've finished.'

It was the quickest shave and shower I have ever had in my life and within minutes, I was at the side of the bed, trying to hide my arousal behind my hands.

'Do we need this duvet?' she asked. 'It's hot in here.'

It was on the floor in less than a second, and I stood there, admiring every inch of her.

'Come here; there's no need to be shy,' she joked, pulling me onto the bed and kissing me.

I ran my hands over her body, finally settling on her stomach. There was not a single blemish and I moved my mouth to her breasts, lingering for a moment before working my way down to her navel. She parted her legs as an invitation to continue my explorations. Moments later her body arched with pleasure.

'Get on top of me,' she whispered. 'I can't wait any longer.'

We had reached such a point of excitement that neither of us could last as long as we had at five that morning, but it was as enjoyable as it was brief.

'How about a repeat performance tomorrow morning?' she asked as she curled up next to me.

'Wake me up whenever you like. I've got a lot of catching up to do.'

*

I did a lot of catching up the following morning until we finally snuggled up together, our bodies intertwined, dozing motionless on the bed.

'Oh, shit; it's nine o'clock!' I blurted when I finally noticed the time.

'You're joking,' replied Alison, pulling the duvet up to her chin, as though she were a naughty teenager caught in bed with her boyfriend. 'What are we going to do?'

'We'll take a shower, get dressed and go through to the kitchen as though it were the most natural thing in the world.'

'But my uncle; he'll throw us both out.'

'Why would he do that? Don't worry. It will be fine.'

I was worried, though. It was one thing being a good lad, but how happy was he going to be now that his underpaid and overworked barman was sleeping with his precious niece?

*

My heart was pounding when we arrived in the kitchen.

Alison and I held hands for mutual support. Still, the scene was no different to the previous day: the Major sitting in his armchair, reading his paper and Shirley smiling as she offered us mugs of tea.

Alison glanced at me as she released her grip on my hand and I smiled back at her, feeling the tension in my body melt away.

We both accepted Shirley's offer and sat there, wondering whether there was still time to take a walk with a miserable-looking Gunner.

The decision was taken away from us by the Major.

'Simon. As soon as you have finished your tea, I'd like you to join me in my office downstairs if you don't mind.'

'I'll be right down,' I answered, feeling the tension working its way back into my body.

Nothing in his expression gave any hint of what he was thinking, but Shirley looked at him knowingly as he rose and left the room.

Alison gave me a nervous glance and I gulped down the rest of my tea before going to learn my fate.

*

As I made my way through the cellar, I could see the Major's face illuminated by the light on his desk. I was reminded of the days when, as a teenager, I would be called to the headmaster's office.

I was a serious student and it was generally to talk about a school project or my plans for an academic career.

That morning, I wasn't expecting such a friendly chat and I took deep breaths as I prepared myself for the worst.

'Come in and take a seat. It's a bit early for a drink, but we'll make an exception.'

He poured two generous glasses of his precious Highland Park before looking at me across the desk in the same magisterial way as he had on the day after Teresa's funeral.

'I love my niece as though she were my own daughter,' he began.

I went to speak, but he raised his hand to silence me.

'And I'm old enough to be your father.'

I took a big sip of the whisky, bracing myself for whatever was coming next.

'Why do you think I persuaded my brother to send Alison up here to stay with us? You both needed someone and I knew you would be right for each other.'

'You mean that you set this up?' I started, as relieved as I was surprised.

'An inconsequential detail, Simon.'

'But how do you think I could support her on what I earn here?' I asked.

'I trust you and I know everything will work out in the end,' he replied. We both stood up and he came round the desk to shake my hand.

'Look after her. She's special. You both are.'

EIGHT

A DOCTOR CALLS

The next few days were amongst the happiest of my life.

As I went back upstairs to break the news to Alison, I worried she might have felt it was all happening too quickly, but she was overjoyed.

'Oh, Simon,' she cried, pulling me close. 'I'm so excited. We can move my things this morning and this afternoon, we'll drive into Ambleside to do some shopping.'

Gunner knew there would be no morning walk and wandered off to the bar while Alison headed upstairs to start getting her things together.

By the evening, my sparse home of the last two months had been transformed. There were flowers in the living room, a fully stocked fridge and a couple of wildlife figurines that had caught Alison's eye as we wandered around the shops.

I had enjoyed the brief period of being a carefree bachelor, but now I was looking forward to building a new life with someone I loved.

Over the next few days, our lovemaking became even more confident. Our walks with Gunner also became more rewarding as we ventured further and higher than ever before.

'Aren't you two ever miserable?' asked the Major one lunchtime in the bar. 'People will be coming here just to see the pair of you giggling away.'

Our happiness was infecting everyone around us, with one exception.

'Here I am again,' sighed Pauline one day when we were alone. 'Passed over for a newer model with fewer miles on the clock.'

'Don't you worry, Pauline,' I replied. 'A lot of men prefer a car that's run in and has got over all its teething problems.'

'Yes, Simon. The thing is that no one's been under my bonnet for a very long time; the next service is long overdue.'

'I tell you what. Leave it to me and I'll find you the man of your dreams, but you'll need to give me a week or two.'

She was reassured; I had no idea how I would deliver on my promise, but I had some time to come up with a plan.

*

The only cloud in my blue sky was that I was living a lie and, the more time we spent together, the closer I was to being exposed.

We had both run away from comfortable lives and were living in a mobile home on less than fifty pounds a day. Like a dream, it couldn't last forever, but I wondered whether I could ever take Alison back to Caldy without upsetting our relationship.

Was she in love with me or enjoying a stress-free life with no responsibilities and no real commitments?

'When will you tell me who you are, Simon?' she asked me one afternoon as we lay in bed.

'When I find out who you are, my love,' I replied, rolling over and lifting my head up to look at her. She knew what I wanted and giggled as I raised myself up on one elbow and she slid her body underneath mine.

*

A few days later, the well-constructed walls of my secrecy started to crack.

It was about five in the evening and Alison and I were alone in the bar. That morning, she had persuaded me that we needed a painting to brighten up our living room. So after lunch, we took Gunner along with us on the three-mile walk up to the art galleries in Grasmere village.

The route took us along the shores of Rydal Water and its neighbour, Grasmere. In the June sunshine, it was difficult to imagine anywhere more beautiful.

We returned empty-handed, but it had been a happy afternoon and I was sorry we had to spend our evening back behind the bar, serving pints.

'Do you love me?' asked Alison as she arranged a tray of glasses.

'You know I do. I have loved you from the moment we met, even if I didn't dare hope we'd be together one day.'

'Then come here and give me a kiss.'

We were alone and I took her in my arms and kissed her as though my life depended on it. My hands were around her waist, pulling her pelvis towards mine, and she was gripping my shoulders. Neither of us wanted to let go, even though a customer could have walked through the door any minute.

As our tongues touched playfully, I suddenly sensed we were no longer alone.

'Dad? What are you doing here?'

'Peter,' I exclaimed, pulling myself free.

We were both lost for words as Alison's gaze flicked between the two of us.

'I work here. And you?'

'I've booked a room for the night. I had to get away, what with all the stress over this—'

'Are you on your own?' I interrupted.

Before he could reply, we were joined at the bar by a tall, handsome man in his late thirties.

'Dad, this is Doctor Myers.'

'Lovely to meet you,' he said, shaking my hand.

'My God, Peter. You're not ill, are you?'

'Don't be silly. Richard is a Doctor of Psychology. He was one of my lecturers when I was at university.'

'That's a relief.'

'Yes, but do you remember how we used to come here when Matt and I were kids? I wanted to come back. We've booked the Rydal Suite right at the top.'

Shirley called it the bridal suite because it was the most luxurious room we had, with a large, four-poster double bed.

The silence that followed was broken by Alison.

'Since we're doing introductions, I'm Alison. Richard, why don't I give you a quick tour while Peter catches up with his father?'

*

'So, you and Richard are…?' I asked Peter as soon as the others had left. I was looking directly into his eyes, awaiting his response.

'Partners, Dad. Ever since we met at university – it was love at first sight,' he replied, smiling at the memory.

'I see,' I said as I gathered my thoughts together. 'Did your mother know?'

'Of course she did. Why do you think she was embarrassed when you tried to pair me off with Joanna or whoever else you liked the look of?' he asked, folding his arms defensively.

'So why didn't you tell me?' I asked. Peter's revelation had come as quite a shock and I was upset he hadn't been as open with me as he had been with his mother.

'Because you're homophobic,' he said, almost shouting but still trying not to be overheard.

Now it was my turn to fold my arms.

'That's rubbish! Whatever gave you that idea?' I said, trying to remember what I had said that could have been misinterpreted.

'For a start, what about when Matthew Cartwright came out at school?' he asked. 'You were always joking about him.'

'I don't remember,' I lied, trying not to smile. 'What did I say?'

'You laughed, saying you'd known for some time and that you'd heard he was going to put it behind him.' Peter wasn't smiling either.

'At least we've got to the bottom of how you've been spending your time over in Liverpool,' I joked tactlessly. I immediately regretted my remark. It had just slipped out.

'There you go again. You're disgusting!' replied Peter, uncrossing his arms and looking around the room, trying to find something other than me to look at.

*

Our conversation was saved from degenerating further by Alison and Richard's return.

'Simon, Richard's been asking if there's somewhere to eat nearby. He didn't know the kitchen's closed in the evenings,' said Alison.

From the way Peter was sitting, she could see we'd been arguing and she gave me a questioning look.

'There's that smart place up the road on the left. The Wordsworth. I've heard it's excellent. Otherwise, you'll need to drive into Ambleside,' I replied, ignoring her unspoken question.

It was the Major's turn to make an entrance, but he stopped in the doorway as soon as he saw the four of us together.

'Major, may I introduce my son?' I started when I saw his raised eyebrow.

'You must be Peter,' he replied. 'I recognise you from the photos your father's been showing me.'

Peter looked at me, but I remained expressionless.

'Yes, he's very proud of you, young man. He's always telling me how well you're doing.'

I wasn't prepared for Peter's tears as he touched my hand.

'I'm so sorry for what I said. Matt and I have really missed having you around and this evening… It's been such a shock, finding you here, seeing you with Alison. I wasn't prepared for any of it.'

It was too much for me and I could feel the tears starting to run down my face.

'That does it,' announced the Major. 'I was about to have a quick half, but it's going to have to be a large whisky. Who else wants a drink? It's on me!'

*

The bar soon began to fill up. Alison and the Major left me to talk with Peter and Richard, and I managed to warn them not to mention the house in Caldy or Hallmark Cars.

'Can you tell me what you're doing here, Dad?' asked Peter. 'Everyone thought you'd gone off to France or somewhere hot and sunny.'

'You know how much I love the Lakes and this place in particular,' I replied. 'Do you remember when I told you and Matt the story about the little cannibals on Heron Island?'

He smiled. 'I do, along with the other stupid stories you used to tell us. But why take a job in a pub? You've got enough money to do whatever you like.'

'Like what?' I asked. 'Wander around all day looking at the countryside? At least here, I am part of a family and we have a good time in the bar.'

Peter frowned. 'But you have a family back home.'

That hadn't been his attitude in the kitchen the day his mother died, I thought. Perhaps we would be able to avoid the chat I had promised him, after all.

'What's that I heard about families?' asked Alison as she came back to join us. 'Your dad promised that when we get married, I'll be able to adopt you and Matt. Then we'll be a lovely big family. I've always wanted boys.'

We all laughed at the joke, especially Richard, who I reckoned was at least five years older than Alison.

After the initial surprise, I was happy that Peter was in a relationship and not sad and alone, as I had imagined.

'So how long have you and Alison been together?' asked Richard, trying to find a way to get into the conversation.

'A couple of weeks,' I replied, not thinking.

'A couple of days, more like, but it's like we've been together forever, isn't it?' added Alison, kissing me on the cheek.

'No kissing behind the bar,' joked the Major. 'It puts our guests off their beer.'

*

I was disappointed when the boys left for dinner, but we agreed to meet up the following morning for a walk.

'Peter's nice,' said Alison, having checked no one was waiting to be served. 'You did a good job bringing him up. Is Matt like him?'

'No, they're complete opposites, although Sarah, his girlfriend, has quietened him down. He met her the day after his mother died and they've been inseparable ever since,' I explained. I grinned at the memory of the bed-hopping the evening of Nicola's lunch.

'Well, I hope I'll be able to meet them both soon,' she replied, smiling. 'It looks like I'm starting to get to know you and your family after all, Simon.'

A group of customers came in and I left Alison to serve them, returning a few minutes later.

She was looking thoughtful and I guessed she was going to say something about Peter and Richard.

'Richard's alright; very handsome,' she started as soon as I was back beside her. 'A bit older than Peter.'

She had a mischievous expression on her face and I knew what was going through her mind.

'We're not best placed to talk about age differences, are we, darling?' I replied grimacing.

Before she could reply, the front door opened and I was in for another surprise.

'What are you doing here?' I was asked for the second time that evening.

It was the taxi driver who had brought me back to the Bentley and drove me up to the pub from Windermere two days later.

'I guess I couldn't leave,' I replied.

'And what about the…?'

I knew he would ask about the car and I raised a finger to my lips.

He didn't understand for a second but then smiled and nodded his head.

Out of his taxi, I could see he was good-looking and self-assured. About my age.

'Aren't you going to serve this gentleman a drink?' asked Pauline, who had just arrived. 'I'm sorry I'm late. My car wouldn't start and I had to wait for the bus.'

'You did tell me a service was long overdue,' I replied, smiling.

Pauline pretended to ignore me.

'I'll have a pint of lager, please, and could I see the food menu? I've come straight from dropping off a fare and I'm ready for something hot.'

'I'm sorry, love, but we don't do food in the evenings,' answered Pauline, miserably. 'I could get you a couple of packets of crisps if you like?'

The taxi driver sighed. 'I suppose that will have to do. I've been on the road all day and I haven't had a chance to do any shopping since I threw my girlfriend out last week.'

From the broad smile on her face, I could see it was all getting too much for Pauline. It was as if her dream had come true.

'Oh, you poor thing!' she cried. 'Let me look at what I can do for you – we can't have our customers starving to death, can we?'

She disappeared off to the kitchen and returned a few minutes later with a plate of hot stew.

'Here you are, get this down you. It's Simon's supper, but he won't mind helping out a mate,' she said, giving me a stare.

He took the plate, thanking her, and started to eat hungrily.

'Simon, you haven't introduced me to your friend,' asked Pauline, with a big grin on her face.

'Oh, of course…' I started, trying to remember the name on the card he had given me.

Thankfully it came back to me. 'This is Derek – Derek Bradshaw,' I said.

'Hello, Derek, I'm Pauline. We haven't seen you here before, have we? I would have remembered.'

'No, I normally go to the Golden Rule in Ambleside.'

'A very nice pub. I used to go there with my ex from time to time. Do you live in Ambleside, then?' asked Pauline, smiling.

He nodded. 'Born and bred.'

'I don't suppose you could give me a lift home later? The last bus has already gone.'

'After this lovely supper, it would be my pleasure. I can have a quick look under your bonnet if you like. I can be pretty handy when I want to be.'

'I can imagine,' replied Pauline, kicking me in the shins when she saw the look on my face.

NINE

FRANCE

It had been a long day and Alison and I excused ourselves as soon as the last of the guests had left.

'How did the Major know it was Peter?' I asked as we climbed into bed.

'From the photos, I suppose.'

'But I don't have any photos with me. I've never spoken to him about the boys.'

Alison looked puzzled.

'I suppose he must have overheard me talking to Richard when I was giving him the tour. It was funny, though, him saying how proud you were. Perhaps he could tell Peter was upset?'

'And what about Pauline and that Derek guy? He seems nice enough,' she continued. 'Pauline certainly seemed interested.'

I'd had enough surprises for one day and only hoped he wouldn't say anything to Pauline about the Bentley.

'He does. She won't have wasted much time getting him down under her bonnet. Talking of which...'

*

The sun was out again when I joined Peter and Richard in the front garden with Gunner the following morning.

Alison was finishing her make-up, giving me a chance to brief Peter on what I needed him to do for me.

When she finally arrived, she looked stunning and the boys were as impressed as I was.

'I didn't want you thinking I always look the way I did behind the bar last night.'

'I love you however you're looking,' I replied. 'But you've put the rest of us in your shadow this morning.'

We set off up the road and were soon over the wooden bridge and down onto the shores of Rydal Water.

Peter looked at me as we approached Heron Island and we had a little chuckle. Those days when the boys were young were my happiest, but the past is another country.

Peter's visit was a turning point. Despite what Alison had said, as much as I was enjoying the present, I knew I could no longer ignore the future.

'This is beautiful,' said Richard. 'If it weren't so far from the university, I think Peter and I would be moving up here.'

'Not when I've got to run the—' started Peter before I cut across him.

'How was the restaurant last night? I've heard some good reports.'

'It was perfect,' replied Richard. 'Not cheap, especially the wine list, but delicious food. Classic, upmarket French cuisine; they even had foie gras.'

'We should go one day when we've got a bit of spare cash,' I said to Alison, who smiled in agreement.

'Talking about French food, Dad, I had a call from Uncle Gordon last week. He asked if any of us would like to stay at his villa in the South of France. He's still recovering from his hip operation and can't travel for the time being.'

His eyebrow was raised and I was pleased he seemed to have accepted my relationship with Alison.

'You know, that could be worth thinking about. What do you reckon, Alison? It's beautiful, right on the water's edge.'

'If we could get the time off, why not? We could go before the summer rush. My uncle won't miss us for a few days mid-week.'

I could feel my heart pumping with excitement. This would be a chance for us to be alone, far away from the artificial bubble we had created at the Ferryman's.

'Will the flights be expensive?' she asked as an afterthought.

'No, we'll take EasyJet from Liverpool to Nice and hire a car at the airport. Once we've got the dates sorted, I'll get it all booked.'

*

The walk gave us all a chance to get to know each other and we made an interesting group. Peter was the youngest, I was the oldest, and Richard and Alison were somewhere in between. It felt more as if we were a group of friends than father, son and the in-laws.

It was late morning when we finally got back to the pub.

'Dad, it's been good to see you again. Let's not leave it so long until next time,' he said, wiping tears from his cheeks. 'And Alison, I'm so pleased you're with my father. Do look after him for me.'

'I promise,' she replied, putting an arm around me.

'Richard,' I said. 'I can see why Peter has been spending so much time in Liverpool. I'm looking forward to getting to know you a lot better.'

'It's been great, Simon. You're not how I expected after what Peter has told me.' Richard's smile made me wonder what might have been said, but I knew it would be better if I never found out.

I thought again about the chat that Peter and I were still due to have and struggled to hold back my own tears as they left to get their bags.

*

The Major was waiting for me inside.

'Can you give me a hand? I've looked at the weather forecast and I want to get some extra parasols out at the front. It always brings in the tourists when they see the garden properly decked out in the sunshine.'

I followed him through the kitchen and back out behind the building, where he had opened a big pair of double doors. Inside, the space was full of outdoor furniture, garden equipment and packing cases that looked like they'd been there forever.

'I didn't know this was here. It must be at least double the size of the lounge.'

'It used to be the stables in the days when the Ferryman's was a coaching inn for travellers heading up to Keswick. Those who couldn't afford a room in the inn would bed down in here with the horses.'

'But why didn't you break through and give yourself more space?' I asked. 'That door at the far end looks like it was connected through at one time.'

'I did think about it, but the lounge never gets full,' explained the Major. 'In the summer, our guests want to be in the garden and sometimes, when it's quiet, there's no one in there. All the regulars stay in the bar.'

'You're right, but it's a pity not to put the space to good use,' I replied before going to give him a hand with the chairs.

The Major was right about the lounge, but there had to be something he could do with the extra space. A games room, perhaps, or a weekend carvery. I decided to give it some thought and come up with a plan; it would be good to have something to keep my mind active.

*

We carried the parasols round to the front and met Pauline, who was waving goodbye to a smiling Derek, as he headed back towards Ambleside in his taxi.

'The car still off the road?' I asked.

'Yes. Derek will have a proper look at it later. He's coming back to pick me up after lunch.'

'A ride for a ride?' I joked.

'He'll be running me around until the car's fixed and so I guess I'll have to find some way of thanking him.'

We both laughed.

'But thank you for introducing us. I knew you'd keep your promise to find me the man of my dreams.'

'And is he?' I asked casually.

'I think so. He's kind and gentle. No children to worry about and he works in the evenings and at weekends. I won't need to worry about what he's getting up to when I'm up here.'

'Be careful, Pauline. Few of us are who we seem to be.'

'I remember the last time you said that. I was driving you down to Ambleside and we had passed that beautiful car parked at the side of the road. Was it a Bentley? I haven't seen it around here since.'

She looked me straight in the eyes as she spoke and I hoped my secret would be safe with her.

*

The drive from Nice airport took an hour and a half and it was about four on a Monday afternoon when I parked in front of the villa.

Built out of the local stone, it had once been a fisherman's cottage. Years later, it had been extended to create a comfortable home, with a pool running to the edge of a cliff, high above the sea.

We left the car and went to stand at the far end of the garden, waves lapping on the beach below.

'It's beautiful, Simon. Look at the view; I've never seen water so clear,' said Alison, smiling and taking my hand.

'We're lucky today,' I replied. 'It's often windy on this part of the coast, but look at those yachts with their empty sails.'

I let go of her hand and pulled her close to me. I was as happy as I had ever been.

'What's that town over there called?' asked Alison, pointing to the other side of the bay.

'It's Bandol,' I explained. 'We can go there this evening if you like. It's half an hour's walk along the shoreline, but we can get a taxi to bring us back.'

'Can't we go over in a boat? It would be fun,' she suggested, grinning.

I could see I was going to enjoy our trip. I had been right about us needing to get away from the Ferryman's.

'There used to be a dinghy in the boathouse, but I'd be a bit worried about coming back in the dark after a few drinks. Who knows where we'd end up?' I joked.

She laughed and kissed me on the cheek. 'Thanks for this; it will be good for us. I'm sorry it's only for three days.'

'And three nights,' I continued.

'Yes, Simon. We're going to have to make the most of our time here,' she said, winking at me.

'We are, but shouldn't we unpack first?' I teased. 'And then we can go for a swim. It will freshen us up after the journey.'

I panicked when I realised that my swimming trunks were tucked away in a drawer in Caldy.

'Don't worry,' replied Alison, reading my mind. 'We won't need our costumes. Who can see us up here, apart from the seagulls?'

I was becoming aroused at the thought of our naked swim and quickly went to dig the house keys out from under a plant pot in the garden.

Once I had got our bags, I unlocked the front door and led Alison through to the living room.

It was decorated in the rustic style of a Mediterranean beachside home. There was a bleached pine floor and the white walls were covered in nautical memorabilia we had bought on our trips along the coast.

Above the fireplace, there were shark jaws the boys had found on a market stall years earlier. Despite Teresa's protests, they had begged me to buy them and she wasn't at all pleased when she saw where they ended up.

'That's a lovely photo of you and the boys out sailing,' said Alison, looking around the room. 'You don't look old enough to be their father.'

I followed her gaze.

'I still don't,' I joked, trying to remember what else she might find that would undo my web of deceit.

'We were in the boat with Uncle Gordon. He gets on very well with the boys; he never married and doesn't have children of his own. We can take it out, if it's still there.'

She smiled and followed me up the stairs and through to the main bedroom.

'Why don't you relax on the terrace while I unpack?' I suggested, thinking about what she might find when she started to put our clothes away.

'Don't be silly. You've done more than enough today and I need to be able to find my things afterwards.'

She was not persuaded and I sat on the bed, trying to work out how I would explain my way out of the mess that was about to unfold.

'This wardrobe should do,' she continued, opening the doors to reveal men's clothes on one side but nothing on the other. Peter must have cleared away Teresa's things when he was last over.

'Are you alright?' asked Alison, seeing I had started to sweat. 'You look terrible.'

'I'm fine, but I'm very hot. I'll go and get some water.'

When I arrived back upstairs, Alison was holding up one of Teresa's bikini tops. 'At least we know that Uncle Gordon isn't gay. I found this at the bottom of the wardrobe.'

'He could be a cross-dresser, I suppose,' I replied, handing her a glass. If that was all she found, I was safe for the time being.

*

Our naked swim in the pool led to the bedroom and it was seven o'clock before we set off to Bandol, happy and relaxed.

The walk was all downhill and Alison loved the early evening views over the bay.

'Where are those ships heading?' she asked, pointing to the distant shadows on the horizon.

'The one on the left is a ferry; it will be going to Corsica. The other one is a container ship heading towards Fos on the other side of Marseille.'

'You know a lot about this area. Did you used to come here often?'

'When the boys were young, we'd visit when we could, but we haven't been for a while,' I replied, this time truthfully.

That evening, my honesty was going to be put to the test.

'This place looks nice,' said Alison as we passed a bar on the promenade. 'Shall we stop for a drink?'

'I'll take you to another one. It's a bit further but worth the extra distance.'

The Tchin Tchin was not as busy as the bar we had passed, mainly because of the prices, but it had a more upmarket feel to it and Alison was pleased with my choice.

'Good evening, Monsieur Duggan,' greeted the owner as we took a table on the terrace. 'A vodka and tonic for you as usual? And what can I get for the lady?'

'I'll have a glass of dry white wine, please,' Alison answered for herself.

'Of course, Madame. Bandol or Côtes de Provence?'

'Which would you recommend?'

'The Bandol, of course. I'll bring the bottle over to show you.'

'He must have a good memory. When was the last time you were here?'

'Sometime last year, I suppose,' I replied, wanting to change the subject. 'What do you feel like eating?'

'It would be a shame not to have fish when we're so close to the sea. Did you see all the fresh seafood on display in front of that restaurant we walked past?'

'The Auberge du Port? It's decided then. We'll go there once we've finished this drink.'

'Have I told you how much I love you?' she asked, taking my hand in hers. 'You make me very happy.'

*

We lost all sense of time sitting there, watching the world pass by. It was only after the third drink that we left to go to the restaurant.

We treated ourselves, sharing fresh crab and lobster as a starter and a whole sea bream, baked in a salt crust, for our main course.

'A wise choice, as always, Monsieur Duggan,' said the waiter as he took our menus. 'I will send over the sommelier to take your wine order straight away.'

'They all know you down here,' teased Alison.

'It's because of Uncle Gordon. He's a larger-than-life character who leaves a lasting impression wherever he goes.'

I was starting to believe my own invention. I had to remind myself that if Uncle Gordon was larger than life, it was because he had only ever lived in my imagination.

At the end of the meal, we were each given a generous glass of Poire Williams, a popular digestif in the South of France.

'I suppose the free drinks were to prepare us for the bill,' whispered Alison when it arrived on the table. 'Let me look after it. You've already been so generous.'

I could see she was dividing the cost of the meal by the six pounds an hour I earned at the Ferryman's.

'You'd have to work for a couple of days to pay that.'

'Don't worry,' I replied. 'I have a secret piggy bank for special occasions. This is my treat.'

After I'd paid, the waiter called a taxi and we were soon back at the villa, lit up against the dark night sky.

'Come on, time for bed,' I said, opening the front door, and we steadied each other as we climbed the stairs.

We had left the French doors open to let in the cool evening air. It was rich with the scent of rosemary, thyme and lavender, mixed with the spice of the pine trees, bent over after years of the Mistral blowing across the bay.

'Goodnight, Alison. I love you,' I whispered, giving her a gentle kiss on the cheek, but she didn't reply. She was already asleep.

*

We made the most of our three days away. When we were not out on the boat, we would go into one of the local towns, picking up fresh food from the market to enjoy with a few glasses of wine back at the villa. Everything was so colourful compared with what we were used to back home.

It was good to be away from the claustrophobic environment of the Lakes and the long shifts behind the bar. Our greatest pleasure was sitting with a bottle of Rosé, watching the sun go down behind Bandol, making way for the lights of its many bars and restaurants.

After seeing the shark jaws, it had been difficult to persuade Alison there were no man-eaters in that part of the Mediterranean. On our last day, however, I managed to get her to go for a swim.

I pretended to be a Great White looking for its next meal and we splashed around and laughed for what seemed like hours, until we finally collapsed together on the beach.

It was a magical time and it made me happy to see Alison enjoying herself away from the Ferryman's.

After letting me pay for dinner on the first night, she made a big point of paying for everything. I could see she was in her element: how she must have been when she was with Max and all his money.

Any fragility was now gone and she had a determination and self-assurance that had been kept hidden until now.

I was pleased to be discovering the real Alison, but I wondered how she would settle back into the simple life we had been enjoying in the Lake District.

'That's beautiful,' she said, pointing to a large oil painting hanging in a gallery in Le Castellet, a medieval village up in the hills behind Bandol.

'That was Bandol market before the tourists came,' offered the elderly gallery owner. 'Let me check – yes, it's dated 1855. A local artist, Joseph Castelli. We have handled several of his works.'

Alison looked at him encouragingly.

'Of course, Madame, the price. We are asking €2,850, but I could let you have it for €2,500 if you pay cash.'

'We'd never get it home, I'm afraid, and it's too big for our living room. Still, thanks for your help, Monsieur.'

'We can always ship it for you, Madame,' he replied. 'Here, take my card, in case you change your mind.'

I knew she would have bought it, had she been on her own, but she didn't want to embarrass me.

I also wanted to buy it, but how would I have explained where I had got the money? She would never have believed it had come from my secret piggy bank.

TEN

TIME FOR THE TRUTH

Before we knew it, we were off the plane and driving up to Rydal in the pouring rain.

Our trip was over far too quickly; as I watched the windscreen wipers moving backwards and forwards in front of me, all I could think about was going away together again.

The summer season was already in full swing and, as we struggled back into our routine at the Ferryman's, I was pleased to have the memories of our short holiday.

'Do you think we could go back to France again in the autumn?' asked Alison one evening as we were locking up.

'Of course we will,' I replied, hugging her. 'I'll get Peter to have a word with Uncle Gordon.'

It wasn't all work, though. The weather was generally fine and we made the most of our walks with Gunner up on Nab Scar.

We would also take Alison's car and go shopping in Ambleside or Bowness, although we looked forward to September when there would be fewer tourists.

'They're a bloody nuisance, but they're our lifeblood,' muttered the Major, one day after he served a group of Germans who had taken over the garden. 'At least we can look forward to a quiet whisky this evening when they've all gone.'

One day we left the car in Ambleside and took the lake steamer down to Bowness, getting Derek to drive us back so we could be at the Ferryman's in time for lunch.

As we stood on the deck, leaning against the handrail and watching the shore passing by, I wouldn't have wanted to be anywhere else in the world.

It was a good time for me, but Alison was finding things difficult. I knew the trip to France had reminded her of the life she had enjoyed before meeting me.

'Do you ever worry about the future?' she asked me one evening, lying in bed. 'I've enjoyed every day I've been here with you but, sooner or later, we'll need to do something else.'

I wasn't sure where this was leading and I let her carry on.

'I mean, this mobile home. It's very cosy, but we can't live here forever, can we?' she continued.

'We can't, my love, but don't worry, it will be alright. I promise you,' I said, trying to sound reassuring.

'And I believe you. I've no idea why, but that's why I love you so much,' she replied, kissing me on the cheek before turning over to go to sleep.

I had meant what I said, but I had no idea how I was going to make good on my promise. Take her back to Caldy and the garage? Move to France and start a motor business there?

I didn't have the answer, but I knew I would have to find one soon.

*

A few days later, a door opened to the new life I had promised Alison.

After breakfast, the Major drove us to the Rydal Country Show that was taking place down the road towards Ambleside.

'We'll do the rounds and see who we know,' he said, climbing out of his ageing Land Rover. In his tweed suit, yellow waistcoat and brown trilby, he looked every bit the country gent. He had come a long way since his childhood in Bootle.

Alison and I followed him as he took us past the Coniston Foxhounds. The judges were dressed in white coats and black bowler hats, carefully looking over each of the dogs lined up in front of them.

There were nods of acknowledgement wherever we went. Almost everyone there must have been to the Ferryman's at one time or another.

'That's George Hutchins,' he said under his breath, stopping to point out a tall man in a red huntsman's jacket, standing with two beagles.

He had an air of authority and looked very much in charge of what was going on around him.

'He owns a farm on the other side of Grasmere. The family's stinking rich, but he's an arrogant, two-faced piece of shit,' he whispered, before calling out to him. 'Morning, George. Good luck with the show.'

'Thank you, Malcolm – do you have an entry?' he asked, hardly raising his head to acknowledge him.

'No, we wouldn't have much of a chance, would we?' he muttered, looking down at Gunner, who ignored him.

'Come on, let's go and see how they're doing with the sheepdog trials,' suggested the Major, striding off across the field.

We followed him to the bottom of the hillside behind the showground and got a good position next to a rope fence separating us from the competitors.

There was a red-faced farmer up on the hill, waving his arms and desperately whistling instructions to his dog, who had lost control of his sheep.

'For God's sake, Harry. You should have left Charlie at home and rounded them up yourself,' shouted the Major, to the amusement of everyone apart from poor Harry.

'I'll buy you a pint later if you come up to the Ferryman's,' he shouted before turning towards Alison and me.

'A bit of free advertising. It can't do any harm, can it?' He laughed.

*

There was no need for advertising that day. The bar was packed all afternoon and evening, exhibitors and visitors alike stopping off for a drink on their way home.

'We've got enough dogs in the garden to organise our own show,' joked Pauline.

'We should get one of the border collies to round up all these lovely children,' replied Alison, with an evil-looking smile. 'They're everywhere, the little buggers.'

I hadn't noticed any children at the show, but now it seemed as if we were in the middle of a school outing.

One small boy had managed to get himself stuck up a tree, his anxious father standing below, and there was a group of girls playing hide and seek in the car park.

Alison had helped Shirley out in the kitchen at lunchtime and she came into the bar in the afternoon, but her heart wasn't in it. She still smiled for the customers, but it was forced and I knew her mind was elsewhere.

'I'm sorry, Simon,' she said, as soon as the last of the drinkers had left. 'I've never been so tired. You stay up and have a whisky with John and my uncle – I'm off to bed.'

*

'How are you and my niece getting on?' asked the Major after she left us. John looked on with an air of conspiratorial interest. 'She hasn't been her normal, happy self since you came back from France. Is everything alright?'

'We're fine. The break did us both a world of good but, now we're back, she's finding the work quite hard.'

'We all are, but it will quieten down again in a few weeks. Isn't that what she's worried about, though? When she came here, it was to get over that bastard, Max. Now she's found love with you, she's ready for a new challenge,' continued the Major.

'It's the same with you, isn't it?' asked John as the two of them eyed me searchingly.

I wasn't sure where the conversation was heading, but I could see it had been planned between the two of them.

'The thing is, I need to move on as well,' continued the Major. 'And before it's too late. I'm sixty-nine, for God's sake, and I don't want to end up like poor Leo.'

John shook his head in agreement.

'But where will you go?' I asked him, worried about how I would manage after they left. The Major and Shirley had become family for me and I couldn't imagine what the Ferryman's would be like with a new landlord.

'Oh, that's no problem. Shirley and I have a place in Tossa del Mar.'

'It's beautiful,' added John. 'The Major and I spent a week over there last year.'

I smiled as I imagined the two of them on the Costa Brava, far away from Shirley's sobering influence.

'And what about this place, Major? You've invested ten years of your life here; it is your life.'

'That's why John and I want to talk to you.'

The Major poured us all another drink.

'You'll need this when you hear what I'm about to say, young man. You see, I've had the pub valued. What with the freehold, the goodwill and the stock, we're looking at about £850,000.'

'That's a lot of money,' I replied, looking thoughtfully at the two of them.

'It is and I could get a bit more if I wanted to.'

'Well, if there's anything I can do to help,' I chirped.

'There is, as a matter of fact. I would like you to buy it.'

'But Major,' I stammered.

'Don't you "but Major" me. I know you can access that kind of money and I also know how much you love the place.'

As long as I wasn't prosecuted for money laundering, I thought. In any event, I would need to speak to Matt and see if he wanted to invest his inheritance. He had said he was fed up with driving his shitty van.

Before I had a chance to reply, it was John's turn.

'I saw the way you looked at me that first day when you came here for a drink. You knew you'd seen me before, but you couldn't remember where.'

He looked me straight in the eyes and I smiled my agreement, racking my brains, as I tried to place him.

'I thought the same thing about you. It was only after Pauline told us about the Bentley after dropping you in Ambleside that it all fell into place.'

'You mean you've known about me all along?'

'We all have, apart from Pauline. You see, I came to your garage about three years ago to look at a Mercedes G-Wagon. I bought a Range Rover in the end, but that was when we first met.'

I did remember him now. He had been keen on the car but never got back to us.

'But we had to be certain you were who we thought you were,' continued the Major. 'That's why I asked John to get in touch with your accountant, Mike O'Mara. It wasn't difficult to find him. His name is on the annual accounts at Companies House.'

'And what did he tell you?' I asked John, taking a mouthful of whisky.

'Everything. The accident, the boys; Peter running the garage, Matt the wild one. He was very helpful.'

'But I saw him in Liverpool three or four weeks after I came to stay here. He didn't say anything to me.'

'He wouldn't have. We agreed to keep it between us. You have a good friend there,' continued John.

'I can't believe you managed not to say anything until now,' I said, shaking my head.

It all started to make sense. John's surprise that I turned up to work on the Monday, his probing when we were discussing the Jaguar and the Major pairing me off with his niece. Even what he said to Peter.

And then there was Mike's comment about John when we had lunch at the San Carlo.

'And what about Alison?' I asked, suddenly panicked.

'I haven't said anything, but you'll need to deal with that situation as soon as possible.'

'But—'

'There are no buts,' continued the Major. 'The price is right, you want to buy it and I want you to have it. We only need to sort out the details.'

'Such as?' I asked.

He smiled broadly. He knew that if I was asking about the details, I was ready to do the deal.

'You must agree not to change the character of the place. It may be the tourists who give us most of our income, but it's the locals who give us our capital.'

I thought back to when I had first discovered the old stables. If I became the owner of the Ferryman's, finding a use for them would be the first thing I did. 'And if I wanted to put a restaurant in that storeroom behind the lounge?' I suggested.

'That wouldn't be a problem. It's more the bar I'm worried about,' said the Major, giving me a stern look.

'It's the bar that made me want to come and live here,' I said, looking around at the wood-panelled walls, the timber beams and all the other reminders of the generations of drinkers who had passed through its doors. 'I wouldn't want to change any part of it. Is there anything else?'

'Yes. Gunner's included in the sale. He loves you and I can't imagine him wanting to come and live with us in Spain.'

*

The following morning, I was woken again by the sound of heavy rain on the roof.

The three of us had finished off a bottle of Knockando as we talked about my ideas for the Ferryman's and the Major's new life in Spain.

'You stink of whisky. What time did you come to bed?' asked Alison as I turned to look at her without daring to lift my head off the pillow.

'I've no idea, but it was very late,' I answered. 'Did you get a good night's sleep?'

'Until you came back and started snoring. Don't you remember me kicking you?'

I couldn't remember leaving the bar, let alone anything that happened afterwards.

'And what were the three of you talking about half the night?'

'Oh, the usual rubbish. You know how the Major gets when he's had a few.'

She sat up and eyed me suspiciously.

'I'm sorry, darling,' I mumbled, pulling the duvet up to my chin. 'I need another hour. Do you mind?'

She kissed me on the cheek, grinning. 'Of course not. I'll go and see Shirley in the kitchen. She'll do me a mug of tea and a bacon sandwich.'

I waited until I heard her close the front door and rolled over to go back to sleep.

It was hopeless. Even I wasn't too sure what the three of us had been talking about. I could vaguely remember buying Gunner and then it struck me: I had agreed to buy the pub as well.

Before I had time to remember anything else, my phone started ringing in the drawer next to the bed.

It was Matt.

'How are you doing?' I asked.

'Dad, you sound awful!' replied Matt, giggling.

'No, I'm fine. A bit of a party last night, that's all,' I explained.

'That makes a change. Normally, it's me suffering in bed. Anyway, I'm calling because Sarah and I have found this flat in West Kirby. Two big bedrooms and views right across the estuary.'

He sounded excited and I imagined the two of them sitting together, planning their future. Just like I used to do with Teresa before Peter was born.

'It sounds brilliant. How much is the rent?' I asked.

'No, it's for sale, but I said I'd speak to you before I spent Mum's money,' he said hesitantly. I was sure Sarah would have been next to him, waiting for my response.

I started to remember my discussion with the Major and John, and was struck by the timing of Matt's call.

'It's a good thing you have. I've got something far more interesting for you to look at. No sea views, I'm afraid, but you and Sarah will love it,' I said, trying to sound enthusiastic, despite my head pounding with my hangover.

I could hear whispering at the other end of the phone as he explained to Sarah what I had said.

'So, what is it then?' he asked.

'I can't tell you over the phone; it's too complicated. When can you both get up here?'

There was more whispering before he replied.

'We're finishing a job in Ellesmere Port tomorrow, but we could come up the day after, if that's soon enough?'

That would give me enough time to explain everything to Alison and go through the details with the Major, I said to myself before replying.

'Friday then? OK, that's great and, if you don't like my idea, I'm sure the flat will still be there on Monday.'

*

I quickly got washed and dressed before going through to join Alison in the kitchen.

'Here you are, Simon. Have half of this bacon sandwich I made for Alison. I'll make another one,' said Shirley. 'You look as if you need something to soak up all the whisky my husband forced you to drink last night.'

I was sure that she was in on the plan with her husband and knew exactly what had been discussed the previous evening. After all, it was her uncle's money that had allowed them to buy the Ferryman's ten years earlier.

The Major was in his usual armchair and looked up with a smile from his morning paper.

I poured myself a mug of tea from the pot sitting on the table.

'Alison, I could do with a good walk in the fresh air. Are you up for it?'

'We haven't got the time,' she replied. 'It's ten o'clock already.'

'Don't worry about that,' said the Major, giving me a knowing look as he continued. 'Pauline and I will cover in the bar until you get back. I can see that Gunner's ready to get out.'

*

Ten minutes later, we were down on the shore of Rydal Water.

After the rain, the moss covering the mounds of rocks along our route had turned a bright green colour and stood out against the mist hanging over the lake.

We were alone and the only sound was our own footsteps as we walked.

'Let's stop here a minute,' I said to Alison. 'I need to get my breath back.'

My head was still pounding, but I could no longer put off what I had to do.

'You poor thing.' She laughed. 'That will teach you not to stay up drinking all night.'

As we stood there, I turned towards her and took her hands in mine.

'Alison, I've got something important to tell you.'

Her face turned white as she looked at me, almost in horror, waiting to hear what I had to say.

'I've agreed to buy the Ferryman's from your uncle.'

The colour immediately came back to her face as she smiled. 'That's wonderful news, but how are you planning on paying for it? I don't think your secret piggy bank is big enough and no one will lend you the money if you don't have a good deposit.'

'That's what I wanted to talk to you about. You know I said I worked in sales before I came here? It's true – luxury motor sales. I own a garage in West Kirby.'

'What, the Hallmark Carriage Company? Max used to show me the adverts in *Cheshire Life*. He had a thing about Ferraris. So where were you living?' she asked. 'Not in a mobile home, I imagine!'

She pulled her hands back and glared at me as though she hated me. For a moment, I thought she was about to slap my face.

'I've got a house in Caldy,' I continued, not understanding her reaction. 'You'd love it, sea views, a big garden for Gunner.'

I saw his ears prick up when he heard his name and he looked over before continuing his search for rabbits.

I had to wait for Alison's reply as she tried to deal with what I had told her.

'And the house in France. It's yours, isn't it?' she eventually asked, almost shouting at me.

I nodded, now expressionless.

'So there's no Uncle Gordon. You made him up, didn't you? And that bikini top. It belonged to your wife?'

All I could do was nod again, hopelessly.

She burst into tears and started wringing her hands as her anger gave way to distress.

'Simon, you've been lying to me. Ever since we met, it's been a pack of lies!' she stammered.

'But I never deliberately lied to you, Alison,' I tried to explain. 'I just wasn't ready to share all the baggage I had tried to leave behind when I came to the Ferryman's.'

'But why did you leave it so long?' she demanded. 'Instead of letting your lies get bigger and bigger until they were out of control? If you hadn't agreed to buy the pub, when were you going to tell me?'

'I'm telling you now,' I replied, becoming desperate. 'I'm telling you because I'm in love with you and I want us to spend the rest of our lives together.'

I tried to step closer to her, to take her in my arms, but she stepped back from me, making it clear she didn't want me to touch her.

'I don't know,' she shouted through her tears. 'How could I ever trust you again? I left Max because he was always lying to me. Now I've found out you're no better than he was.'

Her comment struck me like a body blow and I reeled as it sunk in.

Before I could reply, she turned to go and, as she made her lonely way back along the shore, I knew there was nothing I could say or do that would stop her.

*

I carried on walking around the lake with Gunner, replaying my discussion with Alison in my head.

Her reaction to what I had told her had completely surprised me and I was worried she was back in the mobile home packing her things.

The only lies I had told had been about the non-existent Uncle Gordon and the villa in France. If that was the worst thing I had done, she was overreacting. Everything should fall back in place before Matt arrived with Sarah, I thought, more in hope than expectation.

I managed to compose myself by the time I got back to the Ferryman's.

'She's gone up to her old room,' whispered the Major. 'Best to leave her for the time being. She'll come around.'

My heart wanted me to run upstairs to be with her, but my pounding head told me it would only make matters worse. She needed time to deal with what I had told her.

In the meantime, I would have to go about my work pretending everything was normal.

The hangover wasn't helping matters, but I did manage a smile when I told the Major that Matt and Sarah were visiting in a few days.

'Let's hope Alison will be speaking to you again before they arrive. Otherwise, we'll have to put them up in the mobile home with you.' He chuckled.

*

I couldn't face moping around inside all afternoon, so I took Gunner out again after lunch.

I almost forgot my problems when I was up on Nab Scar, but as soon as I was back at work, my dark mood returned.

Every time the door through to the kitchen opened, I looked to see if it was Alison, but there was no sign of her all evening.

'Have you seen her at all since she came back this morning?' I asked Shirley as she served me my supper.

'She hasn't been down here, I'm afraid, but I did take a sandwich and a glass of wine up to her half an hour ago.'

'How was she?' I asked.

Shirley's expression told me all I needed to know.

'She looked like she'd been crying a lot. She'd changed into her pyjamas. I'm sorry, Simon, but she'll be fine in a day or so. It's been a big shock for her and she needs to get it all sorted out in her head.'

'I'm beginning to wonder whether I should ever have agreed to buy the Ferryman's, to be honest, Shirley.'

She shook her head. 'You know it's the right thing to do. It all had to come out in the end and at least you've got it over with.'

As usual, Shirley was right. Her quiet, common-sense approach to life was what had made the Major the man he was today and I valued her support.

Eventually, it was closing time and I helped Pauline clear away the last few glasses from the tables.

'I'd really like you to have a drink with me,' said the Major, touching my arm, 'but you're not in the mood for conversation. Have an early night. It will all sort itself out tomorrow.'

I nodded my agreement and shuffled off out into the darkness. It was going to be a long night.

*

I hardly slept, and the following morning I dragged myself from my bed, got ready and managed a bowl of cereal before wandering through to the kitchen.

Any hope I had that Alison would be there was lost the minute I saw the look on Shirley's face.

'She's left,' she said. 'We didn't even see her go; she went before we were up. I think…'

I didn't wait for her to finish and rushed out to the car park, looking everywhere for her Mini.

It was nowhere to be seen. As I headed back inside, I was met by the Major, who was waiting for me in the doorway.

'I hate to say this, but you're behaving like an adolescent schoolboy. I want you to have the day off and sort yourself out. When Alison does come back, and she will, I don't want her to find you in the state you're getting yourself into.'

'You're right and I'm sorry. If you don't mind, I'll take Gunner up to Grasmere and have a wander around. I need to get away from here, even if it's only for a few hours.'

The weather was fine and it took me less than forty minutes to get to the village. The walk did me good. I managed to forget about Alison for a while, as I visited a couple of art galleries and browsed through the history section in a second-hand book shop.

At lunchtime, I made the mistake of popping into Ted's Tea Rooms, one of Alison's favourite places, for soup and a sandwich.

'Out on your own today?' asked the owner, a regular at the Ferryman's.

'I am, I'm afraid, Ted. Alison's gone to spend a few days with her father in Liverpool,' I replied, imagining that was where she had gone.

'Give her my love when you see her. She's a great girl – you were lucky to find her.'

He was right, but this wasn't what I needed to hear.

'I will, thanks,' I replied, fighting hard to keep a smile on my face. 'We'll be back next week if we don't see you at the pub before then.'

'I'm sure you will. The wife wants me to take her to the music evening on Friday.'

Having got into a positive frame of mind, everything in the café now reminded me of Alison and I was pleased to finish my lunch and head back to Rydal.

*

The walk back gave me time to reflect on my predicament and by the time I was back in the bar, I was in survival mode.

I had been happy before Alison arrived, and there was no reason I couldn't be happy again without her. I could even invite Joanna up for a few days. Away from the pressure of family and friends, we would be able to finish what she had started.

Anyway, why should I have to suffer because of Max's lies?

The Major could see I was back on form and we managed to have a good evening.

'A pity you introduced me to Derek, isn't it?' whispered Pauline as she passed behind me to serve a customer. 'I told you you'd be better off with a more mature woman rather than a flighty young thing.'

I could tell from her smile that she was teasing me and I gave her a look of mock disappointment.

After last orders, I stayed up for a nightcap and went to bed later than usual, making up for the time I had lost the previous evening.

'The funny thing is, I don't even have her mobile phone number. It's not as if I've ever needed it,' I said to the Major, as he poured me another generous measure of Knockando.

'It's for the best; she'll call you when she's ready. Anyway, when are you taking her to Caldy to show her that big house of yours?' he asked. 'Most women are nest-makers and I'm sure Alison is no exception.'

'I'll have to get her back here first. Hopefully before Matt and Sarah arrive.'

*

I went to bed feeling surprisingly happy and I slept well, waking up in a very different frame of mind to the day before.

The morning was spent up in the hills with Gunner and a busy service at lunchtime kept me occupied and positive.

The Major was right. Everything would sort itself out if and when the time was right. In the meantime, I still had my future to think about, with or without Alison.

After lunch, I was feeling tired and I went back to my room for a nap. I hadn't checked my mobile since speaking to Matt, and I took it out of the drawer and switched it on.

There was a missed call from Joanna and this time she had left a message.

I felt butterflies in my stomach as I dialled 121.

"Simon, it's Joanna. I need to speak to you as soon as possible. Can you please call me when you get this message?"

I lay down on the bed, still holding the phone in my hand. Although she hadn't said what she wanted, I could tell from her tone that it wasn't to say it had all been a big mistake.

I couldn't decide what to do. I loved Alison and what we had was deeper than my relationship with Joanna had ever been. But then Alison had left and I was about to find myself single again for the third time in less than six months.

I sat up and took a deep breath before starting to dial Joanna's number. As I keyed in the final digit, I had a sudden change of heart and I hung up before the phone had a chance to ring.

My life was already complicated enough without bringing Joanna back into the picture.

*

I pulled the duvet over my shoulders and I was in a deep sleep within minutes, dreaming that Alison and I were making love in the sand dunes on Caldy beach. It was only when I dreamt we were driving back to the house in the open-top Bentley that I started to wake up.

I slowly opened my eyes and saw Alison lying under the duvet beside me with what looked like teardrops painted on her cheeks with red lipstick. Was this still the dream?

'I love you, Simon. I'm sorry I walked off like that, but it was such a shock to me. At least it means we won't have to live in a mobile home forever.' She giggled.

'I love you too, Alison,' I said, kissing her lightly on the lips. 'I'm sorry I lied to you. It was for all the best reasons, but it all got out of control.'

Her eyes were shining as she looked deep into mine for a few seconds before replying.

'I know,' she said quietly. 'I spoke to my dad about it and he said if you weren't pretending to have something you didn't, he couldn't see the harm in it.'

After the episode with Max, I imagined that her father would have said anything if it kept her from moving back home again.

'For me, it was the opposite, really. I was pretending not to have anything. That's why I thought you were going to be pleased when I told you,' I said, kissing her on the lips again.

'Of course I'm pleased,' she replied. 'It was just too much for me to take in all at once.'

I took her in my arms and held her against my body.

'Let me make it up to you. I'll give you anything you want.'

'Then make love to me,' she whispered. 'Make love to me like you did that first morning.'

*

'What is it, darling?' I asked Alison, seeing the look on her face as she stepped out of the shower.

'What's what?'

'You're thinking about something and it's worrying me,' I explained.

'OK. If I ask you a question, do you promise to tell me the truth?'

After all the lies I'd been telling since Teresa's death, this was a big promise to make, I thought, before answering.

'You can ask me any question you like and I'll try my best to answer as honestly as I can.'

Her face broke into a big smile. She knew it was the best answer she was going to get.

'Simon, I'm trying to be serious,' she continued. 'Are there any other secrets you need to share with me, now we're getting everything out into the open?'

'Like a large, second family in Liverpool, for example?' I suggested.

'Exactly!'

'Then no, I swear. There's nothing else,' I answered, trying to manage a serious expression.

I did briefly wonder about telling her about the money-laundering investigation, but it would be too difficult to explain. Anyway, I had every confidence that Mike would sort it out for me.

'OK, I believe you, but now there's something I need to tell you,' she said.

She wasn't smiling anymore and I could feel my heart pounding.

'Simon, it's nothing to worry about, but I know you've always thought of me as a footballer's WAG. Someone who struck lucky and is now back where she belongs.'

'Alison,' I protested. 'I never thought anything of the sort.'

She could tell from my grin I was lying.

'Don't try to deny it. It's true,' she said, smiling again and putting her hands on her hips.

'Anyway,' she continued, now trying to look serious. 'Before coming here, I was working in Winslow as an interior designer. I built up a good network of footballer clients with lots of money but no taste. That's how I met Max.'

'But will they have you back after all the time you've been away?' I asked. 'It's been about two months.'

'They will if it's what I want. I've been keeping in touch. You're not the only one with a phone.'

My brain started to stir.

'You know, people with expensive homes drive expensive cars,' I suggested, thinking about the footballers who came to the garage.

'And all my clients have expensive homes,' replied Alison.

I wondered how many clients we already had in common.

'This could be quite an opportunity for us,' I continued. 'Think about how much money we could make if we work together.'

'What. More than six pounds an hour?' she joked, laughing.

I pulled her close to me and looked her straight in the eye.

'Yes, a lot more, but we're going to need to get away from this mobile home first.'

ELEVEN

THE BIG PLAN

When I arrived in the kitchen the next morning, the Major was waiting and asked me to follow him down to the cellar.

'I want to show you the books,' he said. 'You need to know what you're taking on.'

We spent the next two hours looking through the suppliers' files, the takings records and the accounts for the previous year.

Everything had been kept in meticulous order.

'There's an accountant who comes in for the VAT and he does the accounts and tax return once a year. I'll introduce you next time he's here.'

'It all seems pretty straightforward,' I said, helping the Major put everything back in the cupboard behind his desk.

'Just remember to keep up to date with the suppliers. The last thing you want is to run out of beer,' he told me, chuckling as if it had happened before.

Although the accounts only showed a small profit, I was reassured to see that the Major and Shirley had been earning a decent income as well as being housed and fed for free.

*

The Major remained in his office as I went upstairs into the kitchen. Matt and Sarah were already seated, drinking tea with Alison.

'Matt, Sarah, how are you both? I wasn't expecting you until lunchtime; you must have set off early?' I greeted them, giving my son a hug.

'We're fine. We were so excited about coming to see you that we hardly slept last night,' replied Matt.

'That's a better excuse than usual,' I whispered to Alison, much to Sarah's amusement.

'Simon!' said Alison, giving me a light smack on the bottom. 'Pour yourself some tea and try to behave.'

They smiled and I was relieved to see them hit it off with Alison.

It would have been difficult planning our future if my sons had not accepted her into our new family.

'This is an awesome kitchen,' said Sarah. 'May I see your menu?'

'We don't have one. Shirley, who you'll meet later, does pies, baps and a ploughman's at lunchtime, but there's nothing in the evening,' I replied.

'That's a pity,' said Matt. 'Food would do well here. You're on a main road, a couple of miles from Ambleside and Grasmere, and opposite a beautiful lake.'

'You're right, but the Major is happy with what he takes at the bar and on the bed and breakfasts,' I explained.

From Matt's expression, I could see he wasn't convinced.

'Anyway, as soon as you've finished the tea, I'll give you both a tour,' I continued, watching Alison go to help Shirley get ready for lunchtime.

'This is all great, Dad,' replied Matt, looking puzzled. 'But why were you in such a hurry to get us to come up here? You said you had something for us to look at.'

I was expecting Matt's question, but I wanted him and Sarah to get a feel for the place before I set out my proposition.

'I do, Matt. Let me show you around first, though. That way, it will all make more sense,' I explained, smiling at the two of them.

Their bags were already in their room and I started at the residential end of the building, where Shirley and Mary were preparing for new guests.

'It's like stepping back in history,' said Matt when I took them through to the bar and lounge. 'I can see why you were in no rush to come home.'

'We have a good time in the bar. You'll see what it's like this evening. Friday is our music night.'

We went outside and past the mobile home to stand in front of the old storeroom.

'This is a bit of a waste of space,' said Matt after I opened the doors. 'Aren't we at the back of the lounge?'

'We are indeed. You see that door at the far end? It goes straight through.'

'Interesting,' he replied, looking at me thoughtfully.

*

Back in the kitchen, we were greeted by the Major, who was sitting with Shirley and Alison.

'So, you're Matt, Simon's youngest son, and you must be Sarah. It's lovely to finally meet you both.'

'It's good to meet you too,' replied Matt. 'This is a beautiful place you've got here.'

'Thank you. It will be a shame to leave, but life has to go on, I suppose.'

'You're leaving?' asked Sarah. 'But you seem so comfortable here.'

'We are. Very comfortable. Still, I'll let Simon explain everything to you. I'm going through to open the bar.'

Shirley went off to carry on with lunch and I got everyone to sit back down at the table.

I got straight to the point. 'The Major and Shirley want to retire and I have agreed to buy the pub.'

'And Gunner, the dog,' added Alison.

'What sort of price are they talking about?' asked Matt, suddenly interested.

'We're looking at £850,000 plus about £50,000 of legal costs and stamp duty.'

'Have you got that sort of money, Dad?' asked Matt.

'I don't, unfortunately,' I replied, shaking my head. 'That's why I wanted you both to come up here. You see, I have a plan.'

From the way Matt and Sarah were sitting upright in their chairs, I could see I had their full attention.

'Right,' I started, taking a deep breath. 'The idea is that I'll put in some of the money I've put aside. Matt, you'll put in the £350,000 that your mother left you and we'll get a bank loan for the rest. You and Sarah will then run the place, and Alison and I will come back as often as we can to help out.'

'And you'll go back to run the garage?' asked Matt.

'I don't think Peter will let me. I'll give him his shares in the business and we'll run it together. What I want to do, though, is to split my time between here and Caldy.'

I waited while they all took in my proposal.

Sarah was the first to speak. 'There is one thing, Simon.'

I desperately hoped she wasn't about to say she still wanted to buy the flat in West Kirby.

'My dad has been putting money aside in a trust fund for years,' she continued. 'He'll be delighted when he hears I want to invest in a new restaurant business. Before you speak to the bank, let me see what I can come up with.'

'You said he had to sell some of his paintings to pay for your cookery course,' said Matt.

'That's what he told me, but he was making a point. It didn't take him long to replace them,' replied Sarah.

'That sounds like a good idea, Sarah, but we don't have a restaurant,' I pointed out.

'We do if we convert the storeroom,' said Matt, raising his hands above the table and looking very excited.

I was pleased Matt was saying "we". It meant he had already accepted my proposal.

'And whatever you borrow to buy the freehold, you could get a bit more for the renovation,' added Alison. From her faraway expression, I could see she was already thinking about the décor of the new dining room.

'It shouldn't cost too much,' said Matt. 'I could get some of my builder mates to come up for a week or two. They could stay in the mobile home.'

'So long as they don't drink the bar dry,' I joked.

'No, that's what we want them to do. They'll spend everything they earn on beer and we'll get all our money back,' explained Matt, with a big grin.

As we all laughed, Shirley left her work and came over to us, wiping her hands on her apron.

'Simon, I'm so pleased for you and your family. I've been telling my husband for years that this place needs a good restaurant.'

Shirley was not the only one who was pleased. The discussion with Matt and Sarah had gone better than I'd hoped and I was ready for a celebratory pint as we went through to the bar.

'I tell you what,' said Sarah, before I could take orders for drinks. 'Why don't Alison and I go into Ambleside and buy some provisions, and I'll make us all lunch? You and Shirley will join us, won't you, Major?' she quickly added.

'A very kind invitation, my dear. We'd be delighted. Shall we say three o'clock? If anyone's hungry before, Shirley can give them a quick sandwich.'

It was all agreed and Sarah went off with Alison while I led Matt round behind the bar.

'Pauline, this is my other son, Matt. Matt, this is Pauline. She keeps the place running smoothly, despite having to put up with the Major and me.'

'And a good thing too. When I remember what you were like when you started here, I can't believe I've turned you into a highly skilled barman,' replied Pauline.

I blushed when I remembered her beer-soaked breasts pressed against me as she raced to stop me flooding the cellar.

'So, Matt, have you worked in a pub before?' she continued.

'Never. I'm a plumber by trade.'

'That's good news. You'll come in pretty handy when we need to change a barrel,' she replied, giving me a knowing look. 'Anyway, don't worry, I'll show you what needs doing – after your dad and Alison, you'll be my third apprentice this year. I should start charging for tuition.'

I left Pauline to run through the basics with Matt and went to give the Major a hand.

It was a usual Friday lunchtime, not too busy, but we had a couple of regulars in for a pint and a bite to eat.

'Is that your son, Matt?' asked John as I poured him a pint of Nab's End.

'It is, John. He's going to be running the Ferryman's with his partner, Sarah. She's gone down to Ambleside with Alison to pick up some supplies.'

'Good in the kitchen, then?'

'She's a trained chef.'

'Won't she find it a bit dull, serving up pork pies and baps every lunchtime?'

'She would, but Matt and I plan to convert the store at the back of the lounge into a restaurant.'

'Just remember you agreed not to change the character of the place, Simon.'

'We won't,' I explained. 'The bar will stay as it is but the lounge is never busy and the store is full of rubbish. We need to put the space to good use. With the right approach, people will come from far and wide.'

John smiled. 'It sounds like a great idea and I will be delighted to be one of the first customers. There are only so many ploughman's a man can eat,' he joked.

*

When the Major, Matt and I arrived in the kitchen a few minutes before three, we were greeted by Alison, who handed us typed menus.

'Shirley helped us print these and I've been doing some peeling and chopping.'

'I wanted to keep it local,' explained Sarah, lightly stirring the contents of a large cast-iron pot she had taken out of the oven. 'But you know me, Simon. I like to add an extra touch. A fusion of old and new, of different cultures.'

We were given Morecambe Bay potted shrimps with thick slices of freshly baked bread for the first course. Instead of cold shrimps, with a solid crust of butter, it was served warm and the butter was soft.

'What's the herb in there?' asked the Major, cleaning his plate with what was left of his bread.

'Coriander and there's a bit of chilli,' replied Sarah. 'Not too much. I didn't want to overpower the shrimps.'

The main dish was Irish stew.

It was exquisite, with tiny, trimmed spring lamb chops and thick-cut pieces of bacon, braised in the oven with baby root vegetables. It was topped with fresh parsley and there were individual bowls of mashed potatoes made with lots of butter and cream.

'This is delicious, Sarah,' said Shirley, between mouthfuls.

'Thank you so much,' replied Sarah. 'I'm glad you're enjoying it.'

'I am, but if my mother had given Irish stew like this to my father, he wouldn't have been at all happy. It's so light and fresh.'

'That's what I'm trying to achieve,' explained Sarah. 'Traditional dishes brought up to date.'

'You've convinced me,' added the Major. 'With food like this, you'll be booked up months in advance.'

*

By six o'clock, after the beers at lunchtime, wine with the meal and a whisky with Matt and the Major, I wasn't ready for an evening working in the bar.

'Come on, Dad,' said Matt, prodding me as I sat dozing in the armchair in the kitchen. 'It's wakie-wakie time!'

I managed to get up on my feet and followed him through to where the Major and Pauline were serving a growing crowd.

Matt was as happy behind the bar as I imagined he used to be in front of one and he was soon chatting to our customers as if he had known them for years.

'Derek, I'm not used to seeing you here on a Friday evening,' I said when I saw him at the far end of the bar.

'Pauline called me earlier to tell me you had family here and I wanted to come and meet them,' he explained.

'That Matt's a good laugh and I do like Sarah,' continued Derek. 'I bet she keeps him under control.'

'Someone has to,' I replied. 'I gave up years ago.'

I could imagine Matt and Derek getting on well. Matt had an easy way about him that his brother would never have.

*

At about eight, the Major took up his position next to the piano and prepared to get the evening going with another rendition of "Land of Hope and Glory".

This was followed, as tradition required, by several other British anthems that would have gone down well on Last Night at the Proms.

The bar was heaving, the beer was flowing and everyone was having a good time. I watched as Matt went over to Shirley and whispered something into her ear.

'I'll need a different music book for that one,' she said as she got up off her piano stool and lifted the lid. 'Let me have a look.'

She soon found what she was looking for and Matt turned to face us all, clearing his throat.

'Ladies and gentlemen. I would like to sing something this evening that means a lot to me and I hope it will mean a lot to all of you.'

Shirley started with the introduction and then Matt took a deep breath and began his delivery.

The room fell silent as he worked through the verses of "Unchained Melody". Even people who had been waiting to be served at the bar gave up their places to watch.

Every note was perfect and the whole time he was singing, he was looking at Sarah, as though she were the only person in the room.

'I bet she's never kept him hungry for long,' I whispered to Alison, who had come over and put an arm around me. 'Where did he learn to sing like that?'

'Karaoke night at the Punch Bowl, I guess.'

I had never heard such applause at the Ferryman's and there was soon a crowd of people offering to buy him a drink and asking him to sing another song.

'I'm sorry, ladies and gentlemen, but my doctor has said I can only sing like that once a week. Otherwise, the strain on my system could be fatal,' he joked.

I didn't know about the strain on his system, but I was happy when eleven o'clock arrived and it was almost time for bed.

'Matt, Sarah,' I said, as Alison and I were about to head off. 'Thanks so much for coming up to Rydal. We've had a wonderful day and we're going to have a lot more like it.'

'No, Dad. It's Sarah and I who have to thank you. This is going to be great,' replied Matt.

I slept well that night.

Alison and I had a future to look forward to, Peter was back on side and our new project at the Ferryman's would bring Matt and me together.

A lot had happened in the space of a few months, but it finally looked as if we would be a family again.

*

Matt and Sarah stayed until Sunday. As well as walks up in the hills and another good evening in the bar on Saturday, we had the time to talk about how we would turn our plans into reality.

I agreed to call Jonathan Harris, our family solicitor, on Monday to make an appointment to discuss buying the Ferryman's.

Matt would give notice to leave his job, and he and Sarah would return the following weekend with his builder friends to draw up a quote for the works.

'I'm so excited about what you're planning that we might have to stay,' joked the Major when we were having a cup of tea on Sunday afternoon.

'No we're not,' replied Shirley, giving him a stern look.

'But you'll be welcome to come back and see us whenever you like,' I added with a broad smile.

'I'm looking forward to getting home and researching our new menu,' added Sarah. 'There's so much potential, I don't know where to start.'

'If you want to bounce any ideas around, give me a call,' said Alison. 'And Matt, don't go agreeing to anything with the builders until we've spoken about the décor.'

'I hope you won't be touching my bar,' protested the Major. 'Simon promised me—'

'He did, but don't worry. The bar will stay as it is, but I do want to tie in the lounge with the new dining room,' Alison said, her voice drifting off.

The Major looked at me for reassurance and he could see from my expression that we were all on the same side.

*

After the previous days' excitement, I felt deflated after Matt and Sarah left.

'Don't worry,' whispered Alison, sensing my mood. 'They'll be back next weekend. Anyway, when are you going to show me around that house of yours in Caldy?'

I thought back to my late-night conversation with the Major earlier in the week.

'Why don't we go there after we've seen the solicitor? Your uncle won't mind if we spend the night and come back the next morning.'

*

I had arranged for us to meet at the solicitor's office on Thursday morning, and Matt and Sarah were already there when Alison and I arrived.

We were shown through to the meeting room where Mr Harris had gone through Teresa's will a few months earlier.

'I understand that you intend to buy a public house in the Lake

District and that Matt and Sarah will run it,' he started after the introductions.

'Yes, Matt and Sarah will live there, but Alison and I will give them a hand, especially as we plan to develop a new restaurant,' I explained.

'I see. It should be straightforward, but we need to ensure you are all protected if things don't work out as you intended. No one can see what the future holds,' he continued.

There was a moment's awkward silence as we all tried not to look at each other.

'So, we will set up one company to buy the freehold property. The shareholdings will be in the same proportion as the investment made by each of you. Then a second company will operate the business. Since you are all bringing your own skills to the venture, you should each hold twenty-five per cent of the shares. Afterwards, you can agree on salaries and other remuneration between yourselves.'

'Do we need to have two companies?' I asked.

'It will be more expensive, but the ownership of the property and the operation of the business are different things,' said Mr Harris. 'This way, you will always be able to sell the business but keep the property. Also, if the business fails, your investment will still be protected.'

'I can't imagine our regulars ever giving up their beer,' I joked. 'But I see what you mean. Is everyone else happy with this?'

There was a general nodding of heads.

'There is one other matter that I need to raise at this point,' said Mr Harris. 'I have assumed that I will be acting for all of you. If anyone would like to have their own solicitor, now is the time to tell me.'

I looked around at the others, but this time, there was no reaction.

'Good. Simon, you've already given me the details of Malcolm

Flint's solicitors. All I need from you is a copy of everyone's passport and a utility bill or bank statement to prove where you all live.'

He had mentioned this on the phone and I gave him an envelope with everything he needed.

'I have another question, Mr Harris. How long will this take?' I asked.

'Where are we now? Early September. With a bit of luck, we should be done by the end of October.'

Everything was falling into place so quickly, I thought, before my excitement was dampened with a feeling of apprehension.

What if Mike didn't get the money-laundering investigation out of the way? All of this would be for nothing.

*

After the meeting, Matt and Sarah stayed to have lunch in Liverpool and Alison and I set off to visit the family home in Caldy.

Earlier in the week, I had called Mrs Williams and asked her to make up the bed in the main bedroom. Sarah had already said she would leave something for us to eat at lunchtime.

'You'll need to give me directions. I haven't been this side of the Mersey since my parents used to take me to New Brighton for a day on the beach,' said Alison, as we emerged from the Queensway Tunnel.

We kept to the motorway until Upton and then took the country lanes, heading up Black Horse Hill to arrive at the garage.

'Pull over onto the forecourt, here on the left,' I said as we arrived at the top of the hill. 'It's only half twelve. We can pop in to say hello.'

I had been hoping that Joanna would have gone out for lunch and thankfully, Peter was alone, eating a sandwich at his desk.

'Hello, Dad, Alison,' he said, standing up to greet us. 'I'd hoped to see you both today. Everyone's gone out, I'm afraid. Still, how did it go in Liverpool?'

Matt and Sarah had told him about our plans when they arrived back home on Sunday evening.

He was smiling and seemed as excited as the rest of us. I had no doubt this was because he realised this would give him free rein at the garage.

'Fine, Peter, although these solicitors can make everything very complicated. How are you getting on?'

'Oh, the usual. A couple of deals on the go and Darren's doing well. You were right; the clients love him.'

I could see Alison looking at each of the cars on display as though she were making a choice.

'It looks as if you might have another sale, Peter,' I joked.

'That one would do me,' she said, pointing at a pearly white Range Rover Sport parked next to my old desk.

'Very low mileage, Madam, and fully loaded. There isn't an option that hasn't been put on that car.'

'And the price, young man?' she asked, continuing the charade.

'I'm afraid you'll have to speak to the owner of the garage. He insists on dealing personally with our more important clients,' said Peter, gesturing towards me.

We laughed and I gave Alison a kiss on the cheek.

I felt a strange mixture of pleasure and apprehension to be back in a place where I had spent all my adult life until escaping four months earlier.

'Come on,' I said. 'Let's leave Peter to do his deals – I'm getting hungry.'

*

'Oh my God, it's beautiful,' cried Alison as we pulled into the driveway. 'And the view. Is that Wales over there?'

'It is, darling. You can see Snowdonia in the distance. I don't suppose you get much of a sea view in Wilmslow?' I teased as I carried our bags inside. 'Come on, I'll show you around.'

'There's so much space. How do you manage to use it all?'

'For years, we haven't, but I want this house to be alive again like it used to be when the boys were in their teens. Full of friends and family.'

She kissed me on the cheek. 'We'll make sure it is, Simon.'

We worked our way through the ground floor, up to the first floor and eventually arrived in what had been Teresa's and my bedroom suite. It took up all the top floor and I watched as Alison discovered the dressing room, the Victorian-style bathroom and the views over the Dee Estuary.

'This is palatial! You'll have to buy me lots of new clothes to fill all those wardrobes.'

For a brief but uncomfortable moment, my mind went back to the two rows of black bin bags filled with Teresa's clothes lined up in the hallway. One row for the charity shops and the other for the tip.

As happy as Alison seemed, I sensed a tension as she sat on the edge of the bed and picked up a small bouquet of flowers that Mrs Williams had placed on the pillow.

'I'm sorry, but I'm not going to be able to move up here straight away,' she said, eyeing the empty wardrobes again with an unreadable expression on her face. 'Is there another room where we could sleep tonight?'

'But Alison—'

'Don't worry, Simon. I'll be fine,' she said, forcing a smile. 'I just need some time to get settled into the house before I move into…?'

She didn't need to finish her sentence. We could both feel Teresa's presence in the room.

'It's no problem. There's a guest suite behind the kitchen. We can stay there until you're ready. It's very comfortable.'

I immediately regretted my suggestion, as I remembered my night of passion with Joanna. Perhaps we could sleep in Sarah's old room.

*

When we got back downstairs, there was a note from Sarah on the kitchen table.

"There's a salmon salad in the fridge and a bottle of chilled Sancerre. If you're still hungry, I've left a baguette on the side and you'll find cheese in the chiller drawer. Matt and I will eat out this evening with Peter. Sarah."

'We're being left on our own so let's make the most of it,' I said to Alison, who was still taking everything in. 'Do you realise, other than our trip to France, this is the first time we've been able to enjoy a proper meal on our own?'

'I do, Simon. Now I've seen the house, I don't know how you could have lived in that mobile home for months on end.'

'My days in the Lakes have been some of the happiest in my life. It's not about the space or the comfort. It's about what you're doing and who you're with.'

'Talking of which,' she replied, 'what should we do this afternoon?'

'The sun's out, so we should go for a walk down to the beach. It's only ten minutes away.'

My mind flashed back to my dream. As teenagers, Teresa and I would make love wherever we could, hidden in the gorse bushes up on Caldy Common, in a car down a country lane. But I could imagine the headlines in the *Liverpool Echo* if Alison and I were caught naked in the sand dunes.

'That sounds lovely. Can we stay here for supper?' asked Alison.

'I was going to take you to an Italian restaurant in Hoylake,' I suggested. 'We can get a taxi.'

'Let's do that next time. I want to be here with you. To feel at home.'

When we got to the shore, the sun was going down and spread its waning light over the estuary.

The tide was on the ebb and the water left on the beach had formed little streams as it rushed to join the retreating sea.

We were alone, apart from flocks of seagulls, white against the darkness of the newly uncovered sand, probing in search of tasty morsels.

I pulled Alison close to me and we stood wrapped in each other's arms, admiring the view.

'This is beautiful, Simon,' whispered Alison. 'Thank you for bringing me here. I don't think I'll ever want to leave.'

*

I threw together spaghetti, prawns from the freezer, olive oil and some fresh garlic for supper.

It was simple but delicious and, washed down with a bottle or two of red wine, we were both fast asleep in the living room by nine o'clock.

'Where are we?' whispered Alison, waking me as rays of sunlight started to find their way through gaps in the curtains. 'The last thing I remember is you opening that bottle of… whatever it was we were drinking.'

'You're a very bad girl,' I said. 'I was planning a quiet evening in and a cuddle on the sofa. You can't even blame the Major this time – he wasn't here.'

'He was in spirit. You know he was. Still, I had one of the best evenings I can't remember,' she joked.

I laughed. It had been a wonderful evening.

'And I'm already starting to feel at home. When we come back next time, we'll be upstairs where we belong.'

'I don't want to rush you,' I said. 'Take all the time you want.'

'You're not. This is going to be our home and nothing is going to stop that happening.'

I could feel the determination in her voice and I knew she would keep her promise.

*

Back at the Ferryman's, the next few weeks flew by.

Matt and Sarah arrived late the following evening, in time for the last couple of songs on music night.

'I can see they'll be no more Night at the Proms once we're gone,' sighed the Major, after Matt had finished belting out "Holding Back the Years" by Simply Red. 'I hope it won't put the regulars off.'

Judging by the applause, I doubted it.

On Saturday, we were joined by Matt's friends and Alison was able to discuss her ideas for the lounge and dining room.

'We have to get a balance between light and shade; plaster, oak and natural stone. It's all about lighting,' she said. 'If we can get the lighting right, we're ninety per cent there.'

'That's great, but I'm worried about the noise on Friday evenings,' said Matt. 'The singing brings in the drinkers, but it will upset the diners.'

'You're right, Matt,' I replied. 'But hang on, isn't there an old doorway on the other side of the lounge? It's hidden by a dresser, but we could make a separate entrance.'

'I'll take a look at it for you,' said one of the builders. 'We can also improve the sound insulation. These thick stone walls are fine, but we'll need to do something with the doors.'

On the legal side, Mr Harris kept me advised of progress. At the beginning of the first week of October, I got a message that he was ready for us to sign the papers.

The only dark cloud was the money-laundering investigation. With everything going on, I didn't have time to think about it, but it was always there, like a dull pain at the back of my mind.

I called Mike to see if he could get a meeting arranged with Ken Roberts when we were in Liverpool.

He rang me straight back. 'He'll see us in my office at eleven. He wanted us to go to Manchester, but they have cells over there for people who've been naughty. We can't be too careful, can we?' he joked.

'Eleven will be fine,' I replied, ignoring my friend's attempt at humour. 'Let's hope he doesn't bring that shrew-like creature with him this time.'

*

On the day of our trip, Alison could sense that I was anxious.

'Are you alright?' she asked. 'You should be happy. It's all coming together.'

'I'm fine, but I have an important meeting before lunch.'

'Anything you want to share?'

'It's nothing. An old legal dispute that's been dragging on, but we've got it sorted,' I explained. I hoped I was right, but there would be plenty of time to explain things later if I wasn't.

'Do you want me to come along?'

'No, I'll be OK. Why don't you do a bit of shopping? We can meet at San Carlo's for lunch before we see the solicitors. We're only due there at two-thirty.'

If I haven't been dragged off and locked up, I thought to myself, struggling with a growing feeling of hopelessness.

*

As I hurried towards Mike's office, my spirits were lifted by the Royal Liver Building, standing imperious over the Pier Head, bathed in the sunshine.

I still had a smile on my face when I walked into his reception, but this was wiped off by the glacial atmosphere inside.

'Good morning,' I greeted Ken Roberts and his pet rodent, but they carried on muttering between themselves.

By the time Mike came out and took us through to his meeting room, I was ready to leap out of the window.

Before anyone could speak, Ken Roberts took a thick file out of his briefcase and threw it down onto the table.

'Mr Duggan, for the last twenty-five years, you have been a habitual and shameless money launderer,' he started, staring me straight in the eyes.

Mike and I exchanged glances, and it was all I could do not to piss myself.

I imagined Alison sitting alone in the restaurant, patiently waiting and wondering why I hadn't turned up.

'Yes, twenty-five years. James Hennessey, Nick French, I could go on and on, but you don't need me to give you their names, do you?'

He paused for a second, but I didn't offer a reply.

'Every fucking rotten apple in the North West buzzing around your garage like flies on a turd.'

'Be careful, Mr Roberts. You're mixing your metaphors,' interrupted Mike, with a raised eyebrow.

'This is no time for humour, Mr O'Mara. Money laundering is not a victimless crime. Do you realise how many youngsters die of drugs overdoses in the North West every year? Prostitution, stolen goods, terrorism. It's all controlled by the sort of people that your client counts amongst his customers.'

Mike could see that I was starting to lose control of my faculties and launched his attack.

'You'll have to produce some concrete evidence if you're hoping to get anywhere with this case. Everyone knows that luxury motor cars often attract the less desirable members of society, but having dodgy clients isn't a crime, is it?'

Roberts stared at him with a look of total contempt.

'I'm sorry, but we've cooperated with you for long enough, Mr Roberts. It's time to shit or get off the pot.'

I braced myself for what I was sure was coming next.

It was the rodent who spoke first.

'Mr Duggan, we know what you have been doing and with whom, and you haven't even tried to hide what you've earned out of it. Your big house in Caldy, the place in France – not bad for someone who started out as a car salesman.'

'Get on with it,' said Mike, now raising his voice. 'We're getting bored with this pointless innuendo and conjecture.'

Now he's blown it, I thought, as Roberts stood up and took over with renewed vigour, shaking his finger at me.

'But despite everything we have against you, our director has told us to drop the case. Insufficient evidence, apparently. If it were up to me, I'd lock you up and throw away the keys. I hope you're proud of yourself.'

I couldn't believe my ears and looked at Mike to see his reaction.

'I suggest you sit down and try to calm yourself, Mr Roberts. My client is prouder of his successful garage, his staff and the service he gives his loyal clients than you will ever be,' replied Mike. 'So why don't the pair of you take your file and leave my client to get on with his life?'

Mike had won and he wasn't going to let them off.

'How much taxpayers' money do you think you have wasted on this ridiculous crusade? One thing's for sure. If the rest of your cases are like this one, there's no way the pair of you will be getting a Christmas bonus this year!'

They had the decency to look embarrassed and Mike and I stayed seated as they shuffled off out of the meeting room.

As soon as they left, Mike went over to a drinks cabinet in the corner of the room and pulled out a bottle of whisky and two tumblers.

'You're a lucky fucker, Simon Duggan. You always have been. Don't tell me what you've been up to or who got you off, but promise me you won't do it again, or you will be in the shit.'

'You got me off, Mike. You told me right from the start they didn't have anything concrete to go on.'

Mike looked at me suspiciously as he poured the drinks, his hand shaking slightly, and pushed a glass across the table towards me.

'And I suppose they won't have anything to go on next time or the time after that, will they?' he asked, still struggling to get over the stress of the meeting.

I didn't reply, staring into my glass as I waited for him to carry on.

'And what are you going to say to Peter?' he continued. 'He's been worried shitless. After what these bastards have put us through, do you think he'll want to deal with the likes of Hennessey and French? He's a good lad, Simon. You need to be careful what you're dragging him into.'

He looked at me searchingly, but I knew he didn't expect me to answer.

We sat in silence for a couple of minutes until I swirled the whisky around in my glass, took a first sip and cleared my throat.

It was time for me to deal with the question that had been gnawing a hole in my stomach ever since the lunch at Nicola's.

'Mike, I can't thank you enough for sorting out this misunderstanding,' I said carefully.

He smiled and knocked back a good mouthful of the whisky. I understood how difficult the investigation had been for him, protecting a good friend rather than a client who had walked in off the street.

'It's just there's something else I need your help with before I can get my life back on track.'

He laughed, hitting the table with the palm of his hand.

'You're a cold fish, Simon. I wondered when you would bring this up, but you wanted to get this fucking investigation out of the way first, didn't you?'

I tried very hard not to react.

'You couldn't risk losing my friendship until you were either in the clear or locked up in prison.'

'How do you know what I'm talking about?' I asked.

'I may have been pissed, but I could never forget what I told you that afternoon, out on the terrace. It's been torturing me night and day, but it never seemed the right time to bring it up.'

'So how can I be certain Peter isn't your son? The dates match.'

'Because I never shagged Teresa.'

'But…'

I was staggered and couldn't finish my sentence. Either my friend who had saved me from prison was lying to me, or I had suffered months of mental turmoil for nothing.

'Look, she was upset,' continued Mike, trying to smile. 'I was pissed and horny. We went up to the bedroom, had a quick snog—'

'And…' I interrupted, desperate to get to the point.

'And then she started throwing up all over the place: on the walls, the carpet, even on me. I still don't know where she got it all from – it was disgusting. I was down on my knees next to her, gagging.'

I felt sick, imagining the scene with Mike covered in Teresa's vomit.

'But why did you tell me you'd been to bed with her?' I asked, looking for signs of dishonesty in his expression.

'It was a joke, Simon. A bad joke that didn't come out how it was meant to, but I never said I'd shagged her,' explained Mike, shaking his head. 'I was in a state after my shitty birthday and, although you heard what you did, it wasn't what I meant.'

'But why are you always making such a fuss of Peter?' I asked. 'You couldn't care less about Matt, for God's sake.'

Mike smiled and raised his hands as though he were about to make an important point.

'Because I'm a good Irish Catholic and I take my responsibilities as a godfather seriously,' he replied. 'We're not like you Proddies. A couple of glasses of champagne after the christening and a birthday present once a year.'

I became lightheaded as the stress started to lift. Having struggled for months to keep my emotions under control, I finally broke down in tears.

'Simon, you're in a good place now,' said Mike, coming around to my side of the table. 'And you don't even need to look for a new best friend.'

'Or a new accountant,' I stammered, trying to catch my breath.

He was right. Teresa was dead, but I had found Alison, my relationship with the boys was the best it had been and I wasn't going to be locked up.

For the first time in months, I had a future I could look forward to without anything standing in my way.

*

Matt and Sarah came to the Ferryman's whenever they could, preparing for when their move was permanent.

The Major was a generous and patient mentor for Matt, but he looked increasingly tired as we progressed with our plans. He knew there would soon be nothing left to keep him occupied and he was finally starting to feel his age.

When Sarah wasn't with Shirley and Mary, looking after the residential side of the business, she was trying out recipes in the kitchen.

'You'll make me fat if you carry on using me as your chief taster,' said John one evening as he finished off her latest creation.

'But John, I need a sophisticated palate like yours to tell me if I'm getting it right.' He smiled appreciatively.

A few days later, I received another call from Mr Harris.

'We're ready to complete the purchase. Could you speak to the vendors and agree on a date? I'd normally call their solicitor, but since you're living under the same roof…'

*

'Friday 28th October,' I told him when I called back later that day.

'And have you discussed vacant possession?'

'They're planning to move out the following week. I don't see it as a problem, after all the help they've been giving us.'

I immediately told Alison and called Matt to give him the news.

'Dad, that's brilliant. Sarah can't wait. One thing, though. We were chatting with Peter this morning and he wants to throw a party to celebrate you coming home. It would be a good way for Alison to meet your friends.'

I could sense the excitement in Matt's voice and I didn't want to disappoint him.

'It sounds like a great idea,' I said. 'But who'll look after the pub?'

'Pauline and Mary should be able to manage for one night. Derek could even give a hand behind the bar,' he suggested.

'Did you have a date in mind?' I asked.

'Saturday 29th October, the day after completion. Peter will organise everything while we're finishing things up at the pub,' said Matt. He had already planned everything.

'Yes, he won't want us interfering. OK, let's do it; it will be good to have the whole family together.'

*

While Alison, Sarah, Matt and I were getting ready to take over the Ferryman's, Peter was pulling in as many favours as he could for the party.

'We need to get the invitations out straight away. It's already later than I would have liked,' he told us.

We each had to give him a list of guests and no one could see the other lists.

'That way, the evening will be full of surprises,' he explained.

Alison and I agreed that we'd invite the Major and Shirley.

'What about John?' I asked.

'Of course John should come, after everything he's done for you,' replied Alison. 'The three of them can drive down together.'

A couple of days later, Peter called in a state of panic. 'We've got a hundred and fifty invitations and we could easily end up with a hundred and twenty guests.'

'And…?'

'Where will we put them all?'

'We'll hire a marquee. There's that company we used for the Porsche promotion last year; Mrs Davies will have the details. They can lay on heating, lighting, toilets and everything.'

'That would be great, Dad. I'll get on to it straight away.'

*

After a glorious summer, autumn had arrived, and it was a wet and miserable morning when Alison and I cleared out the mobile home.

By midday, our bags were in the kitchen, waiting to be loaded into the Discovery when Matt and Sarah arrived later.

'I'll miss this place: our own little love nest." Alison laughed.

'It has been special, but if someone had told me a year ago that I was going to spend six months in a mobile home, I wouldn't have believed them. Still, we'll be more comfortable in your old room when we come back.'

Mr Harris called after lunch to confirm that the sale had gone through at two o'clock and that the Ferryman's was ours.

'Congratulations,' said the Major when I gave him the news. 'I hope the four of you will be as happy as Shirley and I have been over the last ten years.'

'I know we will, and remember, you must both come back to visit.'

'That is kind of you. Now that it's all done, we'll need to sort out our travel arrangements. We'll have to fly down and buy a car when we get there. The overnight crossing from Portsmouth can be very rough at this time of year.'

Given how organised he was usually, I was surprised the Major hadn't got everything booked.

*

As it was Matt's last day at work, he finished at midday and he and Sarah arrived at the Ferryman's by five.

'It was good to get through Liverpool before rush hour for a change, although it was wet and windy on the motorway,' he said as he joined us in the kitchen. 'It's too early for a celebratory drink, I suppose?'

'I'm having some tea. It will be a long night and we'll need to be fresh for the party tomorrow.'

Matt nodded, a look of resignation on his face, before grabbing an empty mug.

'I hope the weather improves. They were struggling to put the marquee up at the house when I was leaving this morning.'

'Don't worry, I've had a look at the forecast and we should be alright. Either way, it'll be a great party. Peter's put a lot of effort into it.'

*

The evening got off to a good start and most of the regulars braved the bad weather to come and say goodbye to the Major and Shirley.

'"Unchained Melody",' someone cried out as Matt finished a moving performance of "The Air That I Breathe", by The Hollies.

'Alright,' he replied. 'But is there a doctor in the house?'

Everyone looked around and eventually, a hand went up at the back of the room.

'That's good because this is going to be so moving that some of you may need medical assistance,' he joked.

He had a natural way about him that drew people to him. I knew he would be a great asset to our new business.

TWELVE

THE PARTY

As forecast, Saturday morning was bright and sunny, and at half-nine, we set off in a three-car convoy, with Matt and Sarah leading. The Major and Shirley were tucked safely in John's Jaguar behind them, while Alison and I brought up the rear.

'Will you be OK?' I asked Pauline as we got ready to leave. 'It's only for one night.'

'Don't you worry. Mary's helping with the lunches and I've got Derek giving me a hand later. We'll sleep in the mobile home if that's alright. We've got a few guests staying overnight and someone needs to be here.'

'Of course. That would be brilliant, Pauline.'

'Thank you. It also means that Derek can have a few without having to worry about driving.'

It felt a little strange having another couple staying in what had been my home with Alison, but it was time to move on.

*

When we arrived at the house, Matt and Sarah took the others up to their rooms and I went with Alison to take a look at the marquee.

Peter was there, helping place the tables around the wooden dance floor, and Richard was off talking to the caterers, who were busy stocking the bar.

'This is all very grand,' I said, giving him a hug. 'Please don't tell me what it's going to cost.'

'It will be worth every penny. There's the pub, you and Alison, me and Richard, Matt and Sarah, and even Joanna and Darren to celebrate.'

'Who's Joanna?' asked Alison, touching my arm.

'Oh, she's the receptionist at the garage. She's seeing Darren, who used to work for us as a mechanic. Now he's with Peter in the showroom.'

'She's not seeing him. They're renting a flat together in West Kirby. It's somewhere off Bank's Road,' added Peter. I thought back to the message Joanna had left on my mobile two months earlier. Not for the first time, I felt sick at the idea of her being with someone else.

Matt took our bags up to our room and I was pleased when Alison suggested unpacking. This would give us a moment alone before lunch.

'I'm so happy we're finally here,' said Alison, as we finished emptying our cases. 'It will take me a day or two to sort out what goes where but at least we've got everything we need.'

'We can come back up later,' I replied. 'It's been a hectic twenty-four hours and we should try to have a lie-down before the party.'

'As long as you don't go wearing yourself out, Mr Duggan. I expect you up on the dance floor later,' joked Alison with a smile.

*

Sarah had laid out plates of ham, cheese, pork pies and salads she had bought the previous morning and we all sat comfortably around the kitchen table.

'This is kind of you, dear,' said Shirley. 'It's just like what we serve at the Ferryman's.'

'I didn't want you to feel homesick.' Sarah laughed. 'There'll be something more exotic this evening.'

'There's an Italian theme,' said Richard. 'The starters will come through while we're still standing, but the main course and dessert will be served at the tables.'

'How many are we expecting?' I asked nervously.

'About a hundred and thirty, including us, but don't worry, Dad – you've been living for free for the last six months.'

The Major wasn't looking at all well. We had been up late the previous evening for our last nightcap together and he would have found the drive quite tiring.

'Major, what are you and Shirley planning for this afternoon? You could go into West Kirby. It's beautiful on the promenade when the weather's like this.'

'We'll stay here with John. When you've got a wonderful home like this, it's hard to imagine why you'd want to go anywhere else.'

Sitting there with my new family and friends, I couldn't disagree with him, but six months earlier, it was the last place I wanted to be.

It was left to Alison to break the awkward silence.

'Well, you're back here now, aren't you, Simon?'

*

Alison and I spent the afternoon upstairs and, having slept for a couple of hours in each other's arms, it was soon time to shower and dress for the party.

'I know the earth is meant to move when you make love, but that doesn't mean the floor and the walls.' Alison giggled. 'I used to worry we were going to bounce the mobile home off its supports.'

I laughed with her, but she was right. It was going to take us some time to get used to being back in a proper house.

A few minutes after seven, there was a knock on the bedroom door. It was Peter telling us the guests were starting to arrive and we needed to go downstairs.

'There's no need to panic. We're on our way,' I replied, stepping out onto the landing.

Alison was wearing a long black dress that shimmered in the light of the stairway and a simple, understated pearl necklace.

'You're looking wonderful,' said Peter.

'You're going to see a lot more of me like this. There was no reason to dress up in the Lakes, but now we're back in civilisation, I plan to make full use of my wardrobe.'

'I'm sorry I won't be around to see it. I wanted to tell you both earlier, but I'm moving in with Richard tomorrow. With Matt and Sarah leaving, you'll have the house to yourselves.'

Peter had promised an evening of surprises and I wondered how many more we would have before the night was over.

'I hope it has nothing to do with me arriving?' asked Alison.

'Don't be silly. I've been planning this for months and now seems to be the right time.'

'Well, I hope it all goes well for you but remember, if you ever need to come home, even for a short break, you don't need to ask,' I added. 'It can be tough when you first move in with someone, especially when you've been used to a lot of freedom.'

Alison pretended to give me a nasty look.

'Thanks, Dad,' replied Peter. 'Hopefully, it will never come to that, but it would be good if Richard and I could spend a weekend over here from time to time.'

'And don't forget, Peter, we still need to have our chat,' I said.

My son gave me a broad smile. 'That terrible evening seems such a long time ago, Dad. I don't think there's anything we need to chat about anymore.'

I felt my emotions welling up inside me as I took hold of Alison's hand and we set off down the stairs.

*

When we arrived in the marquee, a small band was playing and Matt was with Sarah, talking to a group of guests next to the bar.

'What would you like to drink, darling?' I asked as we went over to join them.

'A white wine would be nice. If all the stories you've told me are true, I'm going to need some alcohol before meeting your friends.'

I handed Alison her wine and was getting a glass of red for myself when Mike arrived, followed by Martine.

'Simon, it's good to see you back here at last. You must be Alison. I'm Mike and this is my wife, Martine.'

He had a broad smile on his face and looked ready for a party. I hoped he wouldn't get carried away again and end up telling me that Matt wasn't my son or some other nonsense.

'I'm pleased to finally meet you both,' replied Alison. 'Simon has told me so much about you, especially how important you've been to his business, Mike.'

Mike gave me a questioning glance, but my look told him I hadn't said anything to her about the investigation.

'Well, never mix business with pleasure,' I said, topping up Alison's glass. 'But I must introduce you to John later on. I gather that you already know each other.'

Mike looked very embarrassed.

'But Simon…'

I put my hand up to stop him. 'Mike, you telling John what I was doing in the Lakes was one of the kindest things you could have done for me.'

Alison smiled and pulled me closer to her.

I had been waiting for Martine to have something to say and, as always, she didn't disappoint me.

'You're a lucky man, Mr Duggan,' she started, looking over at her husband. 'We all know a man is as young as the woman he feels.'

It wasn't what she said, but how she said it, and Alison seemed quite shocked.

'Darling,' I exclaimed, imagining her reply. 'Let me introduce you to Lawrence and Nicola. They've just arrived.'

*

'Alison, this is Nicola and Lawrence. We have been friends since Lawrence and I were at school together,' I said, smiling at them both.

Nicola didn't immediately reply. Her smile was forced as she turned to look at her husband, imagining him with his young lover in Liverpool.

I didn't want another difficult introduction and leapt back in with a compliment.

'I'm pleased to see you're looking ravishing as always, Nicola. I hope Lawrence has been treating you well?'

It worked, as it always did with Nicola.

'Very well,' she replied. 'I'm so pleased you didn't have this party last week. We were away on a cruise in the Caribbean; it was wonderful. You can imagine the food. Either I'm back on a diet tomorrow, or I'm going to need a lot more exercise!'

'We're getting more than our fair share already,' said Lawrence, laughing when he saw his wife's expression.

'Lawrence, you are terrible,' she replied. 'But Simon, we must have you and Alison over for lunch with Mike and Martine. It would be great fun; Joanna usually comes to the house with Darren on a Sunday.'

'Yes, that would be lovely, Nicola. Thank you,' I replied, but I was horrified by the thought of sitting between Alison and Joanna, with Mike getting pickled on the other side of the table.

'Are your friends all obsessed with sex?' asked Alison, as we went to talk to Mrs Davies, who was standing with Rob and Alan.

'It's the sea air. It has the same effect on everyone us in this part of the world.'

'I can't wait,' she replied giggling.

I was introducing Alison to the team from the garage when I caught sight of Joanna coming towards us, holding hands with Darren. Although I had tried to prepare myself for this, I felt my heart miss a beat and tightened my arm around Alison's waist.

'Are you alright?' she asked, seeing my expression.

'I'm fine. It's just a bit of indigestion from that pork pie at lunch,' I replied before turning to Joanna.

'Joanna, how are you? And Darren, Peter's been telling me how well you're doing. Joanna is Lawrence and Nicola's daughter,' I explained to Alison.

Apart from her phone call when I was at the Ferryman's, I hadn't spoken to Joanna since she dumped me and I felt uneasy about seeing her again.

'It's nice to meet you, Alison,' she said, turning back to face me with a strange, almost challenging look.

'Darren and I moved into our own place at the beginning of the month. Free from parents at last,' she continued, with a nervous laugh. 'It seems everyone's moving at the moment – Peter told me he's going over to Liverpool to be with Richard. How will the pair of you manage, alone in this big, empty house?'

'We'll get lodgers in if we're lonely,' joked Alison a little abruptly. 'Come on, darling, Sarah's calling us.'

The introductions had not gone well, but there would be time later in the evening to build some friendships.

*

'Alison, this is my father, Angus. He drove up from London this afternoon,' said Sarah, after she led him over to us through the growing crowd of guests.

'It's good to meet you, Angus. Sarah's told me about your art gallery; I'd love to hear more about it. I'm always looking out for different ideas for my clients.'

'It would be a pleasure. We could have a chat tomorrow. And Simon, how are you getting on, now you're back with your family?'

'It's only for a day or two. They're all deserting me, I'm afraid.'

We were interrupted by Peter tapping a microphone to attract everyone's attention.

'Ladies, gentlemen,' he announced. 'We'll be serving the starters in a few minutes and this would be a good time for a couple of short speeches.'

'You mean you want to get them over with before we all get stuck into the booze,' shouted Mike from the back of the marquee.

Peter ignored him, as usual.

'As many of you already know, my father has spent the last six months living at the Ferryman's Inn, a few miles north of Ambleside. During that time, he was adopted by the owner of the pub, who everyone calls the Major, and his wife Shirley, both of whom we're proud to have here with us today. Major, may I ask you to say a few words about life with my father up in the Lakes?'

'It would be my honour,' said the Major, after Peter passed him a microphone. 'Although I'm afraid I'm not used to public speaking.'

'Unless you're behind the bar,' shouted John, to the delight of Shirley, who was standing next to him.

'Thank you, John. Now let's talk about life with Simon. I thought he was different when he turned up in our pub one Saturday lunchtime in early May. I didn't realise how different until I discovered the man I'd employed on six pounds an hour had come to his interview in a Bentley convertible.'

'That's my car you're talking about,' came a voice I recognised as belonging to Brian Arkwright.

'And that, having said he had lots of experience, he soaked Pauline, our barmaid, with beer when he tried to change a barrel for the first time in his life.'

'She said she'd keep that story to herself,' I muttered to myself, grinning.

'But he became part of our family, seducing my lovely niece, Alison, and eventually buying the Ferryman's along with its loyal dog, Gunner. To sum up, Simon has become the son Shirley and I never had and we are both delighted to be here today with his family and friends.'

'I thought you seduced me,' I whispered to Alison, unheard behind the heavy applause.

An army of black-aproned servers was now making its way amongst the guests with trays of antipasti.

'Thank you, Major,' said Peter, taking back the microphone. 'I know you all hate long speeches, but I would like to say one last thing before handing over to my father. Six months ago, many of you were here to support us because we had lost a wife and mother. Today, my friends, we are together again, but this time it's because we've found our father. Dad, it's great to have you back. If you do go away again, please tell us where you're off to.'

I waited for the applause to die down.

'Thank you, Peter. I'm also going to be brief. Those of you who were here six months ago will have heard me say that the loss of my wife made me appreciate the value of my family. That has never been as true as it is today. My sons, Peter and Matt, who will be at the bar, have become my business partners, but we have become a family again with Richard, Sarah and Alison. A family ready to take on new challenges as we build our future together. When I arrived at the Ferryman's, the day after my wife's funeral, I was a lost soul. The person who had been part of me for over a quarter of a century had gone and I had nothing left to live for. But Malcolm and Shirley showed me that life carries on. I want to thank them for their trust and support, and to wish them all the best for their new life in Spain. Alison and I will be splitting our time between our home and the Ferryman's, and I hope that some of you will make the journey up to the Lakes to see us. We'll even give you a discount if any of you would like to stay over,' I joked.

'How much?' cried Mike. 'Tell us how much.'

There was a ripple of laughter before I carried on.

'I know you all thought highly of Teresa, and I would like to assure you that she is still in our hearts and will always be there for us. At the same time, I hope you'll want to join me in welcoming Alison to Caldy. She is looking forward to meeting everyone this evening. Anyway, you must all be hungry and I will finish by saying how happy we are to have you with us on this special occasion.'

*

Peter had arranged a table overlooking the dance floor for our family, the Major, Shirley, John and Angus. As we sat waiting for the main course, there were three loud taps on the microphone.

I realised I was about to have my second surprise when I looked across the table and saw the smile on Peter's face.

'I hope you're all having a good time!'

'Oh my God,' cried Joanna on the far side of the dance floor. 'It's Brian Arkwright from The Mac.'

'Thank you for the introduction, Joanna. She's my greatest fan, you know,' replied Brian. 'Now, when I heard my friend Simon was having a party, I had to make sure Anne and I were invited...'

Everyone turned to look at the wispy Anne, standing next to him in front of the band.

'And to pay for our supper and to thank him for bringing my Bentley back from the Lakes in one piece, we wanted to sing a number I've written about his odyssey. It's called "On the Road".'

The band played a few chords and he started to sing, with Anne providing the backing vocals.

"I'm on the road once more,
There's nothing I've not seen,
I dunno where I'm going,
But I do l know where I've been.
I need to find someone,
To help take away my pain,
I hope I'll find you soon,
I want to feel alive again..."

It was quite catchy and, after a couple of verses, we were all singing along.

There was a great round of applause when he finished and I leapt to my feet to go over and thank him.

'Welcome back, Simon,' he said as I approached him. 'We've all missed you, haven't we?'

Another round of applause.

I leant over to take the microphone.

'Brian, I'm so pleased to have you and Anne here with us this evening. When you first came to our showroom, I had no idea we would become good friends, sharing a love of beautiful motor cars.'

'And beautiful women,' he added, pointing over to Alison, who turned bright red with embarrassment.

*

'I didn't realise you had such famous friends,' said Alison, when I got back to the table.

'Don't you worry; there'll be plenty more for you to discover,' I replied, wondering what other surprises the evening still had to offer. The rest of the meal was excellent. After his afternoon rest and a few glasses of wine, the Major had recovered his usual form and kept the conversation at our table bubbling along.

'Who'll bet me ten pounds I can't get this cork out of the bottle without breaking it?' he asked, holding up an empty wine bottle with the cork pushed right inside.

It was a crazy bet and we all put our hands up.

'I've made myself eighty quid,' he whispered loudly to Shirley as he pushed a cotton napkin into the bottle, folded to look like the lower half of a duck's beak.

Within seconds, he had the cork cradled in the napkin and, to everyone's amazement, pulled both cork and napkin out onto the table.

*

'Dad, you and Alison should lead the dancing. I've asked the band to start with "Hello", by Lionel Richie,' said Peter, leaning across the table.

I took Alison's hand and led her to the centre of the dance floor. Deborah Gibbons, who had sung at Teresa's funeral, joined the band and I listened to the words as we moved in time with the music, our bodies together as one.

Our guests waited until the end of the dance before joining us and it wasn't long before almost everyone was up on their feet.

'Thank you for everything, Simon. I love you so much,' said Alison, kissing me before going over to sit with the Major and Shirley.

I wanted to mix with our guests and I was about to join Mike over by the bar when I felt a tap on my shoulder.

The voice that whispered in my ear sent a shiver down my spine. 'I need to speak with you. Go and wait for me in the folly. I'll join you in a couple of minutes.'

This was the moment I had been dreading. I couldn't refuse. Perhaps she wanted to clear the air before we met at work the following week. Still, I suspected whatever she had to say would only put a dampener on the evening.

*

With most of our guests dancing and Alison chatting away at our table, it was easy to leave without being seen.

Outside, I allowed my feet to slowly take me towards the folly, remembering what had happened the last time I had been there.

The wait seemed endless, and after all the food and wine I had consumed, the butterflies in my stomach were making me feel quite nauseous.

Joanna finally appeared. She stopped for a second in the doorway and my eyes were drawn to her perfect body, lit up by the moonlight shining through the light fabric of her dress.

'Do you remember the last time we were here?' she asked as she came inside.

'When you dumped me,' I replied, trying to force a smile.

'I didn't dump you, Simon. I asked you to give me some time to sort myself out.'

I didn't reply.

'And then you went away. I didn't even know where you were.'

'No one did. Even I wasn't too sure.'

'Why didn't you return any of my calls? You only spoke to me that one time because you thought I was Mike.'

Her remark wounded me and I shook my head, embarrassed.

'You have no idea how much I love you,' she continued. 'I can't stop thinking about what might have happened if I hadn't said what I did at the funeral. We'd be together today. Not you with Alison and me with Darren.'

'But I love Alison and you love Darren,' I added, hopefully.

'I don't love him. He's kind to me and great fun to be with, but I don't love him.'

'At least you get on,' I said, forcing another smile. 'That's more than most couples ever have.'

She put her arms around me, pulling me close, a look of satisfaction in her eyes as she felt my erection pressing against her stomach.

'Simon, I need more. I want to be with you; to make love with you.'

I tried to push her away, but this only made her pull me closer, more determined than ever.

'I have to finish what we started, Simon,' she continued. 'Make love to me now. No one will miss us.'

I remembered how we had kissed that first evening in the doorway and every part of me was longing to do what she asked.

Suddenly, all I could think about was holding her, naked in my arms, without a care for Alison and the plans for our future together.

Seconds later, reason took control back from my emotions and I managed to pull myself away from her.

'Joanna, you have to stop this,' I said, trying to sound annoyed. 'I care for you and I would do anything for you apart from this. It can't happen. I'm sorry, but I won't let it happen. I've been through too much.'

'Then tell me you don't love me. Go on, Simon. Tell me to my face you don't love me.'

We both knew I couldn't.

'I'm sorry,' I said, kissing her on the forehead. 'I really am. Go back to Darren. He's a good man and he'll make you happy if you let him.'

After my six-month journey from despair to happiness, I was finally going to have to listen to my head and not my heart.

*

The last of our guests left at about two o'clock and Alison and I made our way up to our bedroom, tired but happy.

'That went well. Peter did a fantastic job organising everything. We'll have to use him for the wedding,' joked Alison, as she undressed for bed.

'It was wonderful. Everyone had a good time. The food, the wine, the music, and having Brian and Anne was an unexpected bonus.'

'And we were great together. I loved our first dance. Everyone was thinking how lucky we are.'

Not quite everyone, I thought, kissing her on the cheek. 'They were, darling. We're very lucky; it's been a long journey, but I've finally arrived.'

'Or perhaps the journey's only beginning, Simon.'